Fade into the Bright

JESSICA KOOSED ETTING
ALYSSA EMBREE SCHWARTZ

DELACORTE PRESS

Text copyright © 2021 by Jessica Koosed Etting and Alyssa Embree Schwartz
Jacket art and design by Casey Moses
Title page art by Shutterstock.com/vectormann
Chapter opener art by Shutterstock.com/aniana

All rights reserved. Published in the United States by Delacorte Press, an imprint of Random House Children's Books, a division of Penguin Random House LLC, New York.

Delacorte Press is a registered trademark and the colophon is a trademark of Penguin Random House LLC.

Visit us on the Web! GetUnderlined.com

Educators and librarians, for a variety of teaching tools, visit us at RHTeachersLibrarians.com

Library of Congress Cataloging-in-Publication Data
Names: Etting, Jessica Koosed, author. | Schwartz, Alyssa Embree, author.
Title: Fade into the bright / Jessica Etting and Alyssa Schwartz.
Description: First edition. | New York : Delacorte Press, [2021] | Audience: Ages 12 and up. | Summary: Abby spends the summer after her senior year of high school—and a life-changing diagnosis—with her aunt on Catalina Island, reconnecting with family, forging a new path, and finding love.
Identifiers: LCCN 2020002682 (print) | LCCN 2020002683 (ebook) | ISBN 978-0-593-17491-3 (hardcover) | ISBN 978-0-593-17492-0 (library binding) | ISBN 978-0-593-17493-7 (ebook)
Subjects: CYAC: Genetic disorders—Fiction. | Dating (Social customs)—Fiction. | Aunts—Fiction. | Sisters—Fiction. | Santa Catalina Island (Calif.)—Fiction.
Classification: LCC PZ7.1.E8564 Fad 2021 (print) | LCC PZ7.1.E8564 (ebook) | DDC [Fic]—dc23

The text of this book is set in 11.75-point Bembo MT Pro.
Interior design by Andrea Lau

Printed in the United States of America
10 9 8 7 6 5 4 3 2 1
First Edition

For our families

Fade into the Bright

1

can finally breathe.

The fog hovering over the ferry clears, and like an illusion, this island I've been hurtling toward all morning materializes.

It doesn't matter that my only connection to this place is a woman I barely know. That I have no clue what really awaits me once I step off this ferry. All those fears bounce off me, as if I'm a human tennis racket. Because, on this boat, I can finally take these deep, lung-filling breaths that were impossible at home.

That has to be a good sign.

Around me, the ferry buzzes with activity, families keeping track of children and tote bags and inflatable rafts, couples holding hands, groups of friends taking photos together. I twist around in my seat and get my first real glimpse of Catalina, a place I'd never heard of until yesterday. It's plopped down in the middle of the ocean, twenty-two miles off the coast of Southern California, looking like both a desert and deserted island. Bone-dry mountains meet the clear aquamarine ocean, a few palm trees swaying on the crescent beach that greets us. As far as places to escape to go, I seem to have nailed it.

"Welcome to Two Harbors!" the captain squawks from the speaker.

Before we even fully dock, I scramble down to the luggage hold and grab my fancy new wheely suitcase. It's a gift from Will, Mom's boyfriend—he gave it to me the day Colorado recruited me to their volleyball team for this fall.

You'll need it for your travel games, he'd said with his trademark shy smile.

And to drag all your laundry back home, Mom had added with a laugh.

The memory slices through me like a paper cut.

Enough. Don't think about it. Keep going.

I beeline for the exit, like I'm like one of those sharks that has to keep moving in order to survive . . . but then I step onto the wooden dock, and it dawns on me that I have no idea what my aunt Cynthia looks like. I haven't seen her since I was five.

When she emailed me yesterday, offering me a place for the summer to "get myself centered again," I jumped on it so quickly, we never even had time to plan where we'd meet.

I deftly navigate around a few groups on the dock, the cool ocean air hitting my skin, when a spirited woman rushes toward me, arms outstretched. This must be Cynthia. Her outfit is farmer meets Coachella, and her hair is fully gray, like she's announcing to the world she has better things to do than think about hair dye.

"Abby!" She hugs me tight, her cheek squished against mine.

"Hi, Cynthia," I mumble into her hair. It smells like fresh lavender and espresso beans.

When she pulls away she gives me one of those long-lost relative, head-to-toe appraisals. "Look how tall you are! You're a stunning woman now."

I scuff my Converse on the wooden planks. She means well, but it's a blatant sympathy compliment. My first one. I should get used to them.

She beams at me and adds, "I'm so glad you decided to come."

My muscles tense. Here we go. I can feel her searching for the right words. But we both know a simple "sorry" isn't going to cut it, and I'm nowhere near ready to hear anything else. The Pit of Doom swells in my stomach.

"Let's get going so you can relax," she says to my relief. Thankfully, she seems to be sticking to the promise in her email about "giving me space" this summer.

I exhale and hobble after her, my suitcase click-clacking behind me. Even though I was on a plane most of the morning, my muscles ache like I sprinted here. I guess in a way I did.

Cynthia sweeps her arms in the air as we reach the end of the pier, motioning around us. "This is where all the action is. I guess you could call it our Two Harbors version of a downtown."

The breeze catches my hair, and I untangle it from my face so I can give downtown Two Harbors a once-over. It takes all of three seconds. Small beach, pint-sized store, and a no-frills indoor/outdoor restaurant and bar that spills out to the sand. I'm the first to admit that my brain feels like it's stuffed with cotton candy, but if this is where the action is—I don't think there's a lot of it.

She gestures toward the kayaks and paddleboards piled on the sand next to us. "Most of the water activities start out of here: snorkeling, scuba diving, sailing. We have the best marine life on the island, if you're interested."

I nod, as if I'm considering it. Maybe I am. Who knows? When I booked my ticket here, I hadn't thought much beyond getting the eff out of Colorado, but now that I'm here, on this beach, I realize there's a whole summer stretching before me.

"Avalon is the main city of the island," she explains. "That's where most of the tourists go. Two Harbors is more like the shy, unassuming little sister, but I think you'll see the charm here, too."

She strolls down a dirt path and it's unclear where we're headed. I don't see anything resembling a parking lot. Just sunbaked mountains, winding trails, and an ATV wedged between a stubby palm tree and some overgrown wildflowers.

She stops short in front of the ATV. "Here we are!"

"This is yours?"

"What were you expecting?" She squints at me, genuinely perplexed.

"Um . . . I guess a car."

"A car?" She tilts her head with a half smile. "Only a small number of cars are allowed on the island. The waiting list is twenty-five years to bring one here. A few of us have ATVs, though we try not to use them much. They're so noisy."

"How does everybody else get around?"

"Legs."

I nod like this is completely normal. Maybe I should've read that Catalina visitors' guide on the ferry.

She grips my suitcase and straps it to the back of the ATV. She's long, lean, and deceptively strong, reminding me of those unassuming older women in a yoga class who do perfect headstands while you fall on your ass. At least that was my experience in the one yoga class Brooke forced me to go to, per Dr. Gold's suggestion, of course.

"Hop on." She gestures to the passenger seat and hands me a warm foil-wrapped package. "A breakfast burrito I made this morning. It's one of my specialties. I provide most of the food for the tours across the backcountry, and a few of the other guided excursions, too. I figured you'd be hungry."

"Thank you, I'm starving." I haven't had a real meal in twenty-four hours. I gobble it down in about three bites.

When Cynthia revs up the engine, I jump a few inches off the seat, startled, as if a firework erupted in my ear. The ATV grinds through the dirt, kicking up clouds of dust.

We turn sharply uphill beneath a row of palms and behind "downtown Two Harbors." I instantly sit up. Whoa. Talk about night and day. There aren't any lounge chairs, umbrellas, or cabanas in sight now. Nothing but rustic plants and a smattering of bungalows cover the hills, with dirt trails crisscrossing between them.

"Where's everything else?" I crane my neck around. "The hotels and the houses . . ."

Cynthia laughs, an unexpected husky sound much deeper than her voice. "Banning House is the only hotel on this side of the island, and that's just twelve rooms. As for us locals, our cottages are scattered across the mountain here. We only have one hundred and fifty full-time residents."

One hundred fifty people. Far less than the total number of kids in my graduating class. I mean, I knew it was small, but not *this* small.

The first flash of doubt I've had today lodges in my brain. I shake my head, trying to rid myself of it.

After all, isn't that the reason I came here? To get away from everyone at home breathing down my neck, watching me, scrutinizing my every move?

Mission accomplished, Abby. You found an island with almost no human beings. Does Amazon even deliver here? I bite the inside of my cheek, a nervous habit I haven't been able to kick since preschool.

She hooks a hard right, winding higher up the mountain on a cactus-studded trail, and I spot the ocean on the horizon . . . again. This place is so small I can see both coasts at the same time. Two Harbors can't be more than a half-mile wide.

The doubt in my brain begins to spread like an ink stain.

"You're really going to be able to unplug here, Abby," Cynthia calls out to me. "It's very quiet, removed from the outside world. We barely even have Internet."

"Wow, that's . . . um, great." I grip the side of the ATV and say a silent prayer that she's exaggerating.

My phone dings as if purposely reminding me of all the people in the outside world I've just disconnected myself from.

Mom: How is it, honey? Everything okay?

Of course, her momtuition chooses to kick in at this moment. She wasn't totally on board with this idea, though after a talk with Dr. Gold, she acquiesced. Now she can probably sense I'm freaking out. The last thing I'm going to do is give her one more thing to worry about.

Me: Great!

I add a palm tree emoji before I send it.

"This is it!" Cynthia announces. She parks in front of a cute powder blue cottage overflowing with pots of succulents. On the wraparound porch, a wide wooden swing gently sways, as if a vacationing ghost is on it.

I'm halfway out of my seat when Cynthia tugs me back down.

"Wait—I forgot to tell you about Shanti, my African gray parrot."

It just keeps getting better.

An unkempt man with a nature-beaten tan and a beard emerges from the cottage. Also, there's a large parrot perched on his shoulder.

Cynthia motions toward him. "That's my partner, Chip. I asked him to bring Shanti outside so you could meet on neutral territory. African grays can be pretty hostile to strangers. I'm hoping if you meet her outside, we can avoid any issues." She gestures for me to follow her. "Ready?"

I flash the same smile I'd give someone with a horrible haircut who asked me how it looked. I suddenly feel very not ready. For any of this.

"Hi, Shanti," Cynthia purrs as we approach.

"Hi, Shanti." It's Cynthia's exact voice, inflections and all, but it came from the bird.

"Uh, hey, Shanti." I try to make eye contact with her, but Shanti purposely swings her head in the opposite direction, refusing to acknowledge my presence. Ouch.

"Don't worry. She'll warm up." Cynthia leans in to kiss Chip, and Shanti gets in on the action, nuzzling both of them. "Chip works for the island conservancy, if you have any questions about what to do while you're in Catalina."

He slings an arm around my aunt. I wonder if she told him why she invited me here. "Welcome to one of the few unincorporated areas left in the country. It's a little slice of heaven, even if it's gotten way too commercialized these past few years."

I'm about to laugh when I realize there's no trace of sarcasm in his voice.

I keep my distance from Shanti as I tag along behind them through a vegetable garden and into the cottage. It's tidy and bright, with so much natural sunlight, I'm surprised to see a roof on top. The living room brims with eclectic furniture and knickknacks that look like they were all carried here from different continents.

Cynthia taps my shoulder. "Ready to see your room?"

She glides down the hallway, and we reach her bedroom first, which smells faintly like weed, though maybe it's just some aromatherapy oil. Both seem equally plausible.

Cynthia steps into a bedroom across from hers. "And this is your sanctuary."

The curved wrought-iron bed is covered with a soft white comforter, and I resist the urge to immediately face-plant into it. The rest of the furniture is equally unfussy and straightforward. Whitewashed wood nightstands, a small writing desk, mismatched lamps, and a hand-painted dresser in a watery sea glass color.

Cynthia separates the billowy curtains to crack open the windows, giving me a view of the rugged mountainside, with a hint of ocean peeking out from behind. "There you go. You have no idea how much the energy transformed in here after I burned a little sage."

That must be that burnt woodsy smell clinging to the air. Mom warned me that Cynthia is "hippie-ish," but I figured that meant she'd give me a few wish beads and want to read my palm. (Spoiler alert: Too late. I already know my future.)

"There's room in the drawers, so you can unpack. And I put some fresh soaps in the bathroom for you." She hesitates in the doorway. "I'll give you some time to get settled."

I open my mouth to say thank you, suddenly feeling like those two words aren't nearly enough. *Thank you for reaching out at the exact right moment. Thank you for giving me a place to escape to when I needed it. Thank you for not asking me any questions yet.* But the words are stuck in my brain, and my brain is stuck in quicksand.

"Thanks for . . . having me," I eke out.

Her closemouthed smile teeters on pity. "Oh, I almost forgot. I have one more thing for you." She shuffles across the room in her bare feet and lifts a package wrapped in white parchment paper out of the dresser.

She hands it to me. "Something to help you on your path this summer."

I carefully open up the paper at the taped seams. Beneath it is a journal sealed with a hemp-braided rope. I suppress a groan and harness all my energy to raise the corners of my mouth. "Thank you."

"Reflective writing can help you sort through things. It's been a savior for me through some dark times." She rubs my arm with a consoling smile, and I almost recoil when I see it. I'm not sure how I missed it before, but she has a small dimple on the bottom of her left cheek. The exact same one I have.

And the same one Dad has. He used to tell me that a single dimple on the left side is a sign of good luck.

My skin tingles, burning up with the irony.

As soon as Cynthia leaves the room, I fall onto the bed hungrily and lock my arms around one of the fringy pillows, burrowing it close to my stomach.

There's this moment in *Mary Poppins* where chimney sweep Bert promises little Jane and Michael Banks that if they just blink their eyes and jump, they'll magically leap into a chalk drawing. After they do they open their eyes and find themselves still standing on the same exact London street. That's when Jane looks at Bert and asks, "Was something supposed to happen?"

I'm suddenly feeling a lot like Jane Banks. Was something supposed to happen when I got here? Were the delayed tears supposed to finally show up? Was I hoping I'd step on the sand and instantly know how to start dealing with all this?

Would it have been better to just stay home?

No, a voice inside me screams.

There's a difference between being homesick and missing something that no longer exists. And my home, at least as I know it, is definitely in the second category.

The journal catches my eye from the nightstand. Dr. Gold was always urging me and Brooke to write in one too. He used the word both as a verb and a noun. *Did you journal in your journal this week?*

Brooke did it religiously, of course, because she can't stand not to complete an assignment. But I would just stare at the blank page every time I tried, without a clue of what to write. Everything felt clichéd or not-quite-true, like I was writing what a person in my shoes was *supposed* to be feeling, though it hadn't actually passed through my own head.

After a few weeks of glancing at my blank pages, Dr. Gold still wouldn't let it go. "It doesn't need to be anything special or poetic. Just write down what's on your mind. You can even write it as a letter to me."

I've had six months of writer's block, but now I can finally imagine a journal entry for him.

Dear Dr. Gold,

Last week, I sat in your office while you opened a small white envelope and told me how I'm going to die.

Mic drop.
Abby

2

Before

Obviously, it happened right before Christmas. Because don't all extremely shitty things happen right around the holidays?

I ran up the front steps of my house, two at a time, shivering in my shorts. At least I beat the snow. I thought I had no chance when Coach Murphy hit minute thirty of the speech she always gives on the last volleyball practice before winter break. It was her attempt to pound into our brains that loading up on sugar, sleeping until ten, and zoning out on Netflix for the next two weeks did nothing for our volleyball game. Since those were the only three activities on my agenda, I spent the whole speech deciding what I would watch first and whether I'd start with peppermint bark or gingerbread cookies.

I was about to put my key in the door when I heard the

unmistakable sound of adult voices half laughing and half singing (off-key) the lyrics to "Deck the Halls." I whirled around and sprinted to the door at the side of the house instead.

Don't get me wrong. I loved Mom and Will's annual Christmas carol sing-along, but I preferred to make my appearance a little later in the night, after the adults were sufficiently liquored up. That way they were more interested in singing than asking me which boys I thought were cute, as if I was a fifth grader and not a senior.

I burst through the side door into the kitchen, right as the snow flurries started.

"Just in time!" Brooke chirped as she meticulously scooped cookie dough onto a baking sheet. On the rare occasion that I baked, I looked frazzled and disheveled, like a bag of flour exploded in my hands. But Brooke had on a pristine 1950s housewife apron, and could've been giving a baking demo on TV. "They're on round three of the spiked eggnog."

"Really? I didn't think they were that sloshed yet. It sounded like everyone was still singing the right lyrics." I grabbed a spoon and dug into the bowl of cookie dough. Brooke shot me a disapproving mom-like look.

"What?" I protested, mouth full. "You already have cookies in the oven. How many do Mom's friends need?"

"That all depends on how much eggnog they go through." She slid the bowl away from me. "And I want to save some for tomorrow. Brain power while I study."

"Study? For what? You don't have to go back for two weeks."

"I don't like going into a new semester blindly. And my Critical Reasoning professor is infamous. If I want to get any of the good internships at the DA's office, I need to impress him. I want to at least flip through a few chapters."

I gasped with faux horror. "And you're waiting until tomorrow?"

She ignored me and returned to scooping perfectly rounded cookies. I knew I was pushing my luck, but the little sister in me had to go back for one more spoonful. Plus, it wasn't hard for me to reach across Brooke. I tower over her and Mom by at least five inches. Brooke got Mom's height (or lack thereof), I got Mom's Italian olive skin, and we both got her bright green eyes. That was the only shared feature that suggested Brooke and I were even related to each other.

"Wait, stop!" She shot her arm across me, but didn't yank the spoon out of my hand. And she was grinning. "Listen."

We were on the opposite side of the house from Mom's party, but I heard it now too. Those were definitely the opening notes booming from the living room piano.

"Here we go." I grinned back at her.

Every year the same thing happened at the sing-a-long without fail. Mom's friend Tina—a shy, delicate wisp of a woman who could barely project enough for her first graders to hear her—was spontaneously moved to belt out a shockingly rousing rendition of "Santa Baby."

The second her thundering voice joined in with the piano, Brooke and I high-fived. We considered her performance to be the official kickoff of Christmas.

I grabbed my phone to text Nina that she better get over here before she missed everything, but my phone buzzed with a text from her first.

**Nina: You might as well forfeit now because the card
I got today is unbeatable.**

My fierce competitive side flared up. I grabbed Brooke's arm. "Do you know if Mom got the mail yet today?"

"If she did, it would be in the mail sorter next to the coffee machine. Like it always is."

Brooke and Mom tried out way too many organization tools. My all-time favorite was the set of bins Mom used to have on the small desk in our kitchen so we could sort bills, to-dos, and house chores. They were cute and covered in flowers and each one had a label—"Deal with Now" and "Deal with Later." I actually thought it was a great system, until Mom and Brooke pointed out that I was only putting things in the *Deal with Later* bin.

The mail sorter was empty so I raced to the mailbox and had already sifted through the stack by the time I got back inside. I shook off the snow, then held up the only envelope addressed to the family with the telltale thickness of a holiday card.

Please be better than Nina's.

And by better, I mean worse. We had an annual competition to see who received the phoniest holiday card. The one that bore no resemblance to the family in real life, but gushed, "Look how perfect and happy we are!" Nina won last year with a card from her neighbors. Apparently, their six-month-old baby refused to cooperate during the session with the photographer so they Photoshopped a happy baby in with their other two kids, hoping no one would notice. It was an impossible card for me to top.

Brooke eyed me while I giddily tore open the envelope. "You and Nina are sick."

"Really?" I snorted. "Then why do you ask to see the winner every year?"

The second I yanked out the card, my heart sank. A cute baby and a golden retriever nose to nose in the snow. Adorable. And definitely not a contender.

There was one more envelope at the bottom of the stack addressed to just me and Brooke. It didn't feel like a holiday card, but maybe I'd get lucky. I ripped it open and found a typed letter instead.

My pulse nearly stopped when I saw who it was from.

"Brooke," I rasped, my voice not sounding like my own. "You need to see this."

"What?" Brooke said, coming up beside me. "If you're trying to get me to make fun of a smiling family wearing matching pajamas—"

I shoved the letter at her and pointed to the last word.

Dad.

The color in Brooke's face changed. "It was addressed just to us? Not Mom, too?"

"Just us." I stuffed the letter back into the envelope.

"Wait—did you read it?"

"No." My pulse was back, and my blood beat fast and angry.

"Seriously? You're not curious to see what it says? Why he's writing us now?" She rapidly blinked at me, like she was trying to bring my face back into focus.

"Just the fact that it's a typed letter is reason enough to toss it in the trash." Setting aside the impersonal, too little, too late communication, I could rack my brains for years and still not come up with a good reason to do anything for him. Including reading this letter.

"What if he's finally telling us why he left?" Brooke's voice was hollow.

"The letter is a quarter of a page. Unless he's been doing secret CIA missions for the past thirteen years, he owes us a lot more of an explanation than that. It's probably guilt-induced garbage he's only writing because of the holidays."

Her eyes bounced up and down like her pupils were doing jumping jacks. She was definitely compiling an extensive mental list of the pros and the cons of reading the letter. I waited for her to finish up, drumming my fingertips on the kitchen counter.

"We should read it." She pursed her lips, solidifying her commitment to the decision. "Just to satisfy our curiosity. We can throw it in the garbage right after."

I hesitated. "Okay."

She smoothed out the crinkles in the paper from when I shoved it back into the envelope and held it out for both of us to read.

Dear Brooke and Abby,

I tried to think of a better way to do this, but I finally realized there is no good way.

I've tested positive for a fatal genetic disorder called Huntington's disease. The reason I'm telling you is because every child of a parent with the disease has a 50/50 chance of also carrying the gene.

Your doctor can explain how the testing process works to determine if you're a carrier.

I'm so sorry,
Dad

I read it again, convinced I missed something. Like a punch line.

"This is a prank, right?" I speculated, mentally scanning for anyone I knew who was messed up enough to think this was funny. "I mean, it was sent from a PO box. Who does that?"

"Someone who doesn't want us to find them." Brooke's eyes darted around the letter.

"Come on, Brooke. You really think he would write something that serious in a letter?"

"Why not? He left his two children and wife without saying goodbye."

She had a point, but this letter was so over-the-top that it couldn't be real. Like it was sent by some cyberbully trying out a new form of old-school communication. "Have you ever heard of Huntington's disease? It's probably not even a real thing."

Brooke dropped the letter and lunged for her phone on the counter. Her fingers flew across the keypad.

" 'Huntington's disease,' " she read, her voice sprinting through the words, " 'is an incurable, inherited disease that causes certain nerve cells in the brain to waste away.' "

"Time for Tina to switch to regular eggnog." Mom laughed as she breezed into the kitchen. "Is something burning in here?"

The chocolate chip cookies. I ran to the oven to rescue them, but it was too late.

When I turned back around, Brooke was pressing the letter into Mom's hands.

Mom started reading it just as the first lines of "Joy to the World" drifted into the kitchen.

3

*P*layback failure. Please check your internet connection and try *again*.

So, Cynthia wasn't exaggerating about the Wi-Fi at her place.

My plan for the rest of the afternoon was to lie here in this TV-less room, stream something, and zone out. Like I've done every day for the past week.

Abby's in shock.

Brooke's voice. Or maybe Mom's.

I will them out of my brain. Isn't that the point of me being here? To give myself some time to deal with this alone. Especially without *Brooke*.

I click open Hulu on my computer one more time, and the spinning rainbow wheel pops up so quickly it might as well be giving me the finger. My phone isn't much better.

One paltry bar of cell service. Enough for texting, but actually watching anything on it is out of the question.

I wander down the hallway with my laptop open, trailing a path through the living room and into the kitchen. It only takes a glance at the screen to sadly confirm that the Wi-Fi is equally crappy all over the house.

Cynthia is at the kitchen counter squeezing lemons into a wooden pitcher. As soon as she spots me, her face clouds with worry. "What's wrong?"

I twist my face around to give the impression that I'm not freaking out. "I'm trying to watch something on my laptop, but I'm, uh, realizing how accurately you outlined the Wi-Fi situation earlier."

"Oh yeah, it's terrible here." She casually crushes my vision of the next few weeks even harder than the lemon in her hand. "But I have a VHS player somewhere in the hall closet if you want to use it."

I wait a few seconds to see if she's joking. She's not. It seems rude to tell her I've never actually seen a VHS tape in the flesh. "Um, yeah, maybe."

She finishes mixing the lemonade and looks at me seriously. "So . . . now that you're settled, how do you feel about—"

My internal warning bell blares. "I'm sorry. I don't want to talk about it," I cut her off, trying to keep my voice calm. "Not yet, at least."

Where would I even start anyway? I found out how I'm

22

going to die. Okay, maybe not exactly how. But a rough sketch. Enough of an idea to know it's going to be agonizing. And it's going to happen sooner than I want it to. What more is there to say, because that seems like a real conversation stopper.

She smiles, and the dimple pops out at me like there's a spotlight on it. I guess in her case it *was* good luck. Unlike Dad, she's on the right side of this disease.

"I'm fine," I add again for good measure.

"Good. But I was just going to ask how you feel about a glass of homemade lemonade."

Oh. Oops. "Uh, yes. Sure."

She pours some into a mason jar and slides it over. "It's a North African recipe an old boyfriend introduced me to."

I take a sip, and it's the perfect combo of sweet and tart. I do my best to keep the conversation in this casual territory. "Wow. At least something good came out of an ex, right?"

"I think good or bad, you always learn something from the people you date. Don't you?"

I try to think if there's anything I learned from Reed. We broke up less than a year ago, but conjuring up his face in my brain is like tunneling back to a different lifetime. One filled with group movie dates and cuddling on bleachers, and corsages matched to prom dresses. He was part of a group of senior guy volleyball players that my own friend group had started hanging out with at the beginning of junior year. Little by little everyone paired off until it was just Reed and me uncoupled, like mismatched socks. He was cute, with dark hair he'd sweep out of his eyes, and a long, lean athletic body. I thought I *might* like him, but I couldn't tell if it was mainly out of convenience.

When we finally kissed for the first time, the two of us the only ones left on the couch in Nina's basement after all the other couples had already stolen off to various corners of the house, it was hard not to feel like a consolation prize. Inevitable instead of exciting. But then, when we pulled apart, he looked at me with a sweet smile and said, "You have no idea how long I've wanted to do that for."

I must have looked shocked, because he let out an embarrassed laugh. "The guys were going to kill me if I didn't at least try tonight."

"Really?"

"I told them you were off-limits a month ago. They've been waiting for me to get the balls to actually do something about it." I ignored the fact that he called dibs on me, like I was a piece of cake, because I was so surprised by the first thing he'd said. *A month ago.* I wasn't a consolation prize at all.

Our group fell apart the summer before the guys left for college. With our friends' relationship carnage already rotting around us, the two of us broke up by August. As much as it was fun being with him, we both knew we weren't the type of soul mate—high school sweethearts who end up getting married. Plus, I don't think either of us wanted to do the long-distance thing. After a few days of moping around, I was surprisingly fine. Though it did sting the first time he posted a picture from school with his arm wrapped around a girl.

I gaze back at Cynthia with a weak smile. "The only thing I've learned from an ex is that watching someone play *Grand Theft Auto* with his friends on a Saturday night is not my idea of a good time." I might be shortchanging Reed just a little.

"Well, maybe you'll learn something interesting from the next boyfriend."

My chest tightens. *Next boyfriend.* Right. How is that supposed to work? Is there a dating app for people who are gene-positive for Huntington's disease? Swipe right if you're in Stage One. Swipe left if you're in Stage Two.

If you're in Stage Three, you won't have the motor functions to swipe at all.

The glass in my hand suddenly feels heavy. "Actually, I think I'll check out the beach."

4

Before

It turned out the letter to me and Brooke wasn't sent by a cyberbully.

Somehow, Mom found a phone number for my aunt Cynthia, Dad's one sibling, who I hadn't seen since I was a kid. She and Mom used to be close, but they had a big falling out around the time Dad left. I never got all the details, but it had something to do with Cynthia trying to remain neutral in the situation, which was a pretty ballsy position considering one person was so clearly the blatant asshole.

But Mom managed to get her on the phone for what I was sure was an awkward conversation. *Hi, I know we haven't spoken in over a decade, but by the way . . . do you happen to know if your brother has this horrible disease he claims he does?*

Years ago, I would've pressed Mom to ask her more questions. *Does Cynthia know where he is? Does he miss us? Does he have a new family?* But at some point I stopped caring. And not in the way where you pretend to stop caring but secretly still do, like an ex you supposedly forgot existed but continued to cyberstalk. There was no reason to start getting curious about Dad again, just because he threw a grenade into our lives.

And grenade it was. Cynthia confirmed that, though she herself was completely fine, Dad had, in fact, tested positive for this gene. Which meant Brooke and I now had a fifty-fifty chance of inheriting a disease we'd never heard of.

Since this bombshell was dropped in our laps during Christmas, we couldn't get an appointment to see anyone until a week later. In the meantime a confusing tension sprung up in the house. Brooke spent hours clicking through websites, saving articles into a massive Google folder that she then meticulously took notes on.

"You should probably start reading some of this too," she commented one night as I passed her in the kitchen to grab my second bag of white cheddar popcorn. For some people stress and terrible news make you lose your appetite. I am not those people.

I eyed the screen, which was opened to a page of notes entitled "HD Symptoms."

"No thanks." I snagged a handful of holiday-colored M&M's to balance out my meal.

"You have to deal with this at some point, Abby."

"I am."

"By binge-watching Hallmark Christmas movies?"

"They're helping me process the news." I had watched one about a couple who fell in love in a cancer ward so it wasn't a total lie.

I didn't need to look at Brooke's research to get a rough idea of what we were up against, anyway. I picked up more every day from her and Mom's draining back-and-forth. Huntington's disease (or HD, as Brooke now referred to it, like they were new besties) usually strikes between your thirties and fifties. At first, maybe your hands occasionally shake so much you can't hold a glass. Or you can't remember someone's name for a moment or where you put your keys. You say awkwardly inappropriate things in casual conversation without realizing it.

And it only escalates from there.

Soon, you can't walk on your own; you can't speak without slurring; you can't get through a day without violent mood swings. You can't chew food without choking; then finally you lose control of every part of what makes you human until you die.

And you will die. Because there's no cure. Your symptoms just keep getting worse and worse, until it eventually kills you.

And there's a fifty percent chance I had it.

It was like calling heads or tails.

"Sixth floor," Brooke announced as we stepped onto the elevator. We were at a shiny new medical complex attached to the university hospital, on the way to meet our genetic counselor, Dr. Jeremy Gold. Apparently, this was the first step in dealing with this mess. He was the one who'd tell us if we'd be affected by this fuck-you of a gene, or not.

The doors opened to a wide pavilion still draped in holiday garlands and lights. It's always strange how decorations that feel joyful and festive up until Christmas suddenly seem tired and depressing just a few days later.

When I caught our reflection in the elevator mirror, I realized you could say the same thing about the three of us.

"Come on, Abby," Mom called from a few feet ahead, waiting for me. "Are you okay?"

I nodded, and she put her arm around my waist when I caught up to her. It was maybe the five hundredth time she'd asked me that today. Not that I could blame her. She was trying to put on a brave face for us, only slipping when she thought one of us wasn't looking. I wanted to tell her she didn't have to do it on my account, but I had a feeling that it was somehow helping her, too.

Brooke signed us in, and a few minutes later, we were whisked into a back hallway. Dr. Gold waited for us in the doorway to his office, shaking all our hands as we entered the room.

It wasn't exactly what I expected. For one, it wasn't an exam room, but an actual office, including a little cozy sitting area with a couch and armchair. It was toasty warm, and I took my coat and scarf off, immediately feeling overheated. "Are you okay?" Mom checked in again.

Dr. Gold wasn't what I expected either. He wasn't even wearing a lab coat. Instead, he was in a nice V-neck sweater, fitted slacks, and trendy socks that peeked out.

Once we got situated, Brooke pulled her laptop from her bag. "I brought this along. All the research I have so far."

He rolled his fancy ergonomic chair from behind his desk and sat in front of us. "Sure. You must have a lot of questions. And it's great that you've done some research. But I'll start at the beginning, so we can make sure you're getting the right facts."

Mom and Brooke gave simultaneous emphatic nods.

"As a genetic counselor I'm here to give you unbiased information so you can understand Huntington's disease and how this gene might affect you."

"Or might not," I felt compelled to add.

"Sure," he agreed easily. He launched into a general rundown of HD (okay, so Brooke had rubbed off on me). That it was like getting ALS, Parkinson's, and Alzheimer's, all wrapped up into a nightmare disease.

I stared at him, on the verge of zoning out, when Dr. Gold tilted his head at me. "How are you feeling about everything, Abby?"

"Um . . . I don't really know." I sensed Brooke rolling her

eyes. "It's hard to figure out how I'm supposed to feel when there's a fifty percent chance I don't even have it."

This whole thing could end up being . . . nothing. And until we knew, why get worked up? I wasn't usually the one shoving optimism down anyone's throat, but deep down I didn't think we had it. I just couldn't picture it.

"When do we get tested to find out if we have the gene?" I cut to the chase.

Dr. Gold tapped his pen on a notepad, like he was trying to be the movie version of a doctor. "We can't give you the results until we complete these sessions."

"And how long does that take?"

"Six months."

Wait, what? I swiveled around to share my shock with Brooke and Mom, but they didn't seem to be experiencing the same level of panic over having to live like this for the next six months. "And there's no way around that?"

"That's the required counseling period per the Huntington's Disease Society of America guidelines," Brooke reported in a tone that suggested this was yet another tidbit she had already shared with me.

Mom gently placed a hand on Brooke's shoulder. "Let Dr. Gold answer the questions."

He nodded. "Testing is not something to rush into quickly. That's why we do these sessions over six months. To make sure you're prepared."

"But . . ." I floundered in a sea of confusion. "I thought you were our genetic counselor. What are we doing at these sessions for six months?"

A funny expression crossed Dr. Gold's face. "Sure. Genetic counseling isn't just extracting DNA and reading test results. We're here to talk about the medical, emotional, and psychological consequences of finding out whether you're gene-positive."

Was he saying that we'd be sitting here *talking* for six months? And then it clicked.

Genetic *counseling*.

"Wait. . . . These are like actual counseling sessions? You're like a therapist?"

The horror in my voice was so obvious I could've sworn Dr. Gold almost smiled. He covered with a professional half cough. "In some ways, yes. I take it therapy isn't something you've tried before."

I wiped my clammy hands on my jeans. "No. My mom wanted me to go when I was twelve because she was worried that heading into puberty without a father figure would turn me into an indisputable ho-bag with low self-esteem—"

"I don't think I phrased it quite like that," Mom quickly interjected, her cheeks flushing.

"I'm not opposed to therapy," I clarified. "I think it can be helpful for some people." People who have an emotional issue they need to resolve. Not people who won't find out for *six months* if they have an emotional issue that needs to be resolved.

"Sure," he agreed. I was starting to realize it was his favorite word. "And this isn't classic therapy, anyway. My job is to guide you through the science and implications of the disease, and then at end of this process, you can decide if you want to get tested."

Did he just say "*if* you want to get tested"?

Why hadn't I at least *perused* Brooke's research?

"Um . . . I thought we had to get tested?"

"No. It's your decision if that's knowledge you want to have."

"We do," Brooke assured him.

Dr. Gold shifted his eyes toward her. "Sure. But that might change. And you each need to make your *own* decision about it. That's the point of these sessions. To confront how each possible scenario would affect you, whether you're negative, or one of you is positive, or both of you are." Brooke and Mom reached for tissues, identical tears springing in their eyes.

I sat awkwardly off to the side, looking down at my hands. I hadn't cried yet. At all. I knew they both thought it was strange. Mom snaked her hand behind Brooke and squeezed mine. I squeezed back.

Dr. Gold cleared his throat. "I have to tell you, it's considered very young to test at eighteen or twenty. We usually advise that you wait until at least twenty-five."

"Why?" Brooke and I asked at the same time.

"You can always get tested later. But you can't take back getting your results."

His eyes met mine. I came in here rushing to get tested because I'd assumed that would bring an end to this weird, terrible little chapter.

But what if it didn't?

"Even if you know you want to test, it might be better to wait a few years until you have a better idea how the results will affect your life, career, family . . ."

"If symptoms start hitting me at thirty-five, I'd say I don't have a lot of time to wait around," Brooke countered in her best lawyer voice.

"No one needs to decide anything today," Mom jumped in.

When it was time to go, Brooke and I grabbed the coats and scarves we'd scattered across the couch. But Mom remained in her chair.

"Hold on. One last question." Mom stared into her crumpled tissue, as if what she wanted to say was written on it. "My question is . . . now what? Where do we go from here? How do we get through tomorrow and the day after?"

Dr. Gold leaned forward. "Here's what you need to understand from now on. Not just you, Leslie, but all three of you. There's no right or wrong in dealing with HD." He let us absorb that for a moment. "Who you want to tell, whether you want to know, how you want to live with it. It is your call and your call alone. And there's nothing wrong with turning it off if you need to sometimes. Pretend it's not happening if that's what gets you through the day."

Pretend it's not happening.

Finally, an idea I was on board with.

Maybe therapy wasn't so terrible after all.

5

I walk out to Cynthia's front porch, determined to salvage this day, my laptop tucked snugly in my beach bag.

It's not until I close the door behind me that I notice a shirtless Chip sitting on the porch swing, looking like a homeless pirate with Shanti the parrot still harnessed to his shoulder.

"Howdy," he greets me, then turns to Shanti. "Don't be rude. Say hi to Abby."

Shanti deigns to look at me for the first time but says nothing. Chip gives me an encouraging nod, like *Go on*.

"Hi, Shanti," I venture. "How's it going?"

"I'm fine!" Shanti squawks in a pitch-perfect replication of my voice. She must have heard me say that to Cynthia inside. I cringe hearing how false it sounds.

Chip chuckles. "Nothing like having an African gray parrot around for some serious self-reflection, huh, Abby?"

I decide to cut to the chase. "Do any of the places down by the beach have public Wi-Fi?" I have headphones. It could work.

"No, ma'am," he replies heartily. Like it's a badge of freaking honor for the place. "They probably do in Avalon." The big town on the island.

"Right. How do I get there?"

"You gotta catch the Safari Bus at the stop, and then two hours later—bam!—you're there."

"Did you say it takes *two hours* to get to Avalon?"

He nods. "Catalina only spans twenty-two miles across, but it's a long, winding road to get there. And that's not a metaphor. You may get sick. It happens to the best of us."

"And this . . . Safari Bus you're talking about. That's the only way?"

"It's only about an hour by boat." That doesn't help me. Where am I going to get a boat? My mouth opens, but I have absolutely no response. All I can do is stare dumbly at the ocean.

Chip follows my gaze. "Beautiful, isn't it? You know what they say about the ocean, don't you?"

I'm not sure who "they" is or if the question is rhetorical.

His voice gets low and serious. "They say if you stare at the ocean long enough, you can see inside your soul."

"I'm fine!" Shanti squawks, mocking me in my own voice again. As if I needed another reminder of how *not* fine I am.

"Uh, sounds good. I guess I'm going to go to the beach then . . . and check out that ocean." I'm already halfway down the steps. Even without Wi-Fi, the sun is shining, and it's a better plan for the rest of the afternoon than anything else.

He points toward the road. "The beach is a straight shot down the hill. There's some fantastic plant life along the way. But if you see a bison and the tail goes up, walk the other way. They roam freely here."

Where the eff am I?

I start the trek back down the trail we took on the ATV. At the bottom of the hill, warm sand greets my flip-flops. The beach is more crowded than earlier, but thankfully not spring break–ish. No one is grinding on the sand or doing body shots off butt cheeks. (Not that I've actually been to a spring break beach, but that's my mental image of one.) Instead, the vibe is active. Kids splash in the shallow, clear water; couples maneuver stand-up paddleboards around the sailboats and yachts in the harbor; a large group heads out for a snorkeling excursion, their fins splashing in unison behind them. And even with all that activity, it's *quiet*. I guess that's what having no cars around does.

I reach a hut on the sand, which rents out beach equipment, next to a line of large open-air cabanas. A girl who looks about my age, and five inches shorter, raises her head from the receipts she's tallying. She's got the kind of style you can't teach. Her hair's pulled up behind a floral scarf and a loose, faded concert tank hangs over her bikini top. Her arms are adorned with a jumble of beaded bracelets and gold chains that glisten against her warm brown skin.

"Hi there." The British accent surprises me.

"A beach chair." I realize a second too late that she didn't ask "how can I help you," which is what I was expecting. I must have sounded like a crotchety old man. Or a complete bitch. Same difference I guess.

She doesn't seem fazed. "The regular kind or a lounger?"

"Uh, the chair is fine."

As she comes out from behind the counter, it's like the bottom half of her doesn't match the top: narrow shoulders and a chest giving way to curvy hips wrapped in a fuchsia sarong. "How's your day going?" she asks as she grabs a chair from a stack.

"Good," I lie, faking a smile to go along with it. You never realize how many people ask you in a day how you are, until you're actually not fine at all. But she doesn't *really* want to know how my day is going. Just like the barista at Starbucks didn't *really* want me to honestly answer her how-are-you greeting when I ordered my vanilla latte at the airport.

I hand her the cash, and she's back to her receipts within seconds, thereby dismissing me. I lug the chair away and drop it in the first empty spot I find, a few yards away from the beach hut. No sooner have I plopped down when my phone dings from inside my bag.

My stomach clenches until I see who it's from. Nina. A breath of relief escapes me so forcefully, I could power one of those sailboats in the harbor.

Nina: Wait, you left town for the entire summer???!

I can't help but smile at her punctuation overuse, a Nina texting staple.

Me: Sorry I didn't get to say goodbye. It all happened fast.

Understatement of the year.

Me: You're still leaving tonight . . . right?

I squeeze the phone in my hand tightly. Please let her answer be yes. I hope she's not doing something crazy like hopping the ferry here. I wouldn't put it past her.

"I'm not going" was the first thing she'd said to me when I saw her a few hours after I got my results, when she showed up on my doorstep. She'd already figured out that whatever was in that envelope meant this was a wake instead of a celebration.

I might have been in a fog, but I understood right away what she was telling me. She was offering to stay home with me and forfeit her graduation present. A two-month trip around South America, where her mom's side of the family lives. Considering her suitcase had been packed for a week and Nina is *not* a planner, I knew the level of sacrifice she was offering, even if I wasn't surprised. Nina is a natural do-gooder, the girl out in her galoshes after the rain, looking for slugs to save. And suddenly I'd become the slug.

I shook my head, and she understood right away too, the way you do when you've been best friends with a person almost your whole life. That it was the kind of "no" you don't argue with, not the kind that I could be persuaded from.

So, she came inside and gave me a long hug. When we pulled apart, her cheeks were wet and mine weren't. "I know there's going to be a time where you *do* want to talk about all this." She sniffled, her doe eyes leaking tears. "And when that day comes, I'm here for you. But I don't want to *not* talk until that day."

Then she got into bed with me and watched three Hallmark movies, giving me running commentary the entire time, gracefully acting as if I was part of the conversation instead of it being a one-woman monologue.

She came back the next day, and then the next, and just like that, *we* were okay, even if I wasn't.

> **Nina: I'm going. On the way to the airport now.**
> **You're sure, right?**
>
> **Me: YES.**

A few other texts come through, all in a rush. My stomach reclenches when I see Brooke's name. *No thanks.* I press delete without reading it.

I toss my phone into the bag and try to settle in. The chair is awkwardly upright, so I reach for the lever to recline it. It won't budge. I pull myself out of the chair and crouch down to yank on the lever, but it's still stuck.

"Let me give you a hand." I glance up, and a guy around my age, holding a huge bag of snorkel masks, is standing over me.

"That's okay, I've got it."

He ignores me, drops the bag of masks, and bends down next to me to adjust the chair. The unwanted gesture instantly lights up my misogyny radar like a firecracker.

"I said I've got it." I reach for the lever again.

He backs away with his hands up. "Sorry, I work on the beach. It's my job to help tourists."

"I'm not a tourist," I spit out, though that's not really accurate. But it sounds so insulting the way he said it. Like I'm holding a selfie stick and wearing an "I Heart Catalina" T-shirt.

He gives me a doubtful look. "I've never seen you before. I've spent every summer here for the last eight years."

"I meant I'm not *technically* a tourist. I'm staying with my aunt."

I can tell he's about to ask another question, but a group of seven-year-old girls excitedly wave to him as they pass by, like he's a celebrity, singing out, "Hi, Ben!" It makes sense. He's that type of unabashedly cute that little girls crush on hard. Thick brown hair, lips that curve into an easy smile. He gives them a salute, and one of the girls stops in her tracks and continues to wave until her friends drag her away.

I sink back down into the chair. "Your girlfriend?"

"My ex. We're on good terms, though." He picks up the bag of snorkel masks. "Who's your aunt, by the way?"

"Cynthia Freeman."

"Cynthia? Really?"

I lift my eyes to find him studying me. "Why are you looking at me like that?"

"I just don't see the resemblance. Cynthia is so pleasant." His lips quirk, and he strolls off before I can reply. Ugh. I can't handle any more human interactions.

I lean back in my still-unadjusted chair and let my eyes drift over the horizon, watching the boats bob in the distance. I take a few deep breaths, allowing my postcard-perfect view to calm my brain down. The beach was a good call. Maybe this *is* what I needed. To just *relax*. I burrow my feet into the warm sand and tilt my head to the sun, closing my eyes.

As soon as they shut, I'm instantly *back there*. In Dr. Gold's office.

He's sitting in the chair, right in front of me, holding up the envelope.

My envelope.

"Abby, I have the only printed copy of your results," he tells me. "It's not in any system. It's yours to use as you need to."

My eyes fly open, the breakfast burrito suddenly threatening to make its way back up, my breath coming in quick spurts. My body's out of the chair before I know it's happening.

Come to think of it, maybe a little activity is more what I need right now. Relaxation is overrated.

I make my way down to the shore, and a small frothy wave rushes out, nipping at my ankles. The water is so freezing it would probably send polar bears south in search of warmer seas, but as soon as it retreats, I want more.

I wade up to my calves, cringing with each step, then push myself even farther, ducking my body into the water. Eventually, I take the plunge, dipping my head under and swimming past the first row of buoys.

When I come up for air, the chair-police guy, Ben, catches my eye from the nearby dock where he's tying up a small boat.

"Careful," he calls out, that smirk still gracing his lips. "I know you're a local and all, but the tides can change quick. Seriously."

What is it with this guy? I may not be a Catalina regular, but I do know how to swim. I push past the second row of buoys and out toward the open water. It's as cold as the ice baths I take every few weeks during volleyball season, but it feels good. I glide forward, and before I know it, I'm out far enough to where my toes can't scrape the sand anymore. Past the point where the waves break, my body bobbing deliciously over them before they crest. It's like nature's version of an amusement park ride.

I lie back, floating, drifting where the water takes me. My

ears toggle in and out of the water. A few birds caw overhead. A smile unexpectedly spreads across my face, and I feel lighter than I have in months. My eyes flutter close.

And there I am again. In Dr. Gold's office.

On my right Mom grips my waist. On my left Brooke squeezes my hand. We were all hoping my envelope would say the same thing hers had. Negative.

Dr. Gold's eyes lock on mine before he opens it. I know what he's trying to tell me. That these are the last seconds I'd ever have the freedom to not know again.

His fingers break the seam.

And then real life literally comes crashing back.

I feel the pull of a wave a millisecond before I look up and see it about to crash on top of me. I brace for impact, trying to dive under the wave and failing miserably.

I come up for air before being sucked back in. Kicking furiously, I get back to the surface, steal another breath, and start swimming as hard as I can. The salt water murders my eyes. Shit. Doggy paddle it is. I do a head-up breaststroke until my lungs feel like they're going to burst.

When my toes touch sand, I sag with relief, staggering through the water the rest of the way, breathless.

I make it about four steps onto the beach before I decide to collapse for a minute. Or maybe "decide" is the wrong word since it's not any sort of active choice on my part. More like my quivering legs give out on me, and the rest of my body follows suit.

"Are you okay?" It's Ben. *Of course.* But this time his brow is furrowed, and he's looking at me with actual concern.

I must look insane. Drenched, caked in sand, my breath still ragged. I wish I could play this off right now. Let out a laugh and tell him *What do you know? That surf* does *get a little rough, ha-ha!*

But I can't.

"I'm fine," I mumble. My new standard lie.

Someone calls out to Ben from up the beach. He pauses for a second, like he's about to say something, but walks away wordlessly.

I'm fine. That's the weird thing with this disease. Technically, I *am* fine. Nothing is happening to me right now. And it might not for a long time. Twenty years. Maybe thirty. If Dr. Gold is to be believed, the point of these "in-between years," as they're called, is to actually live them.

The only problem is I don't have a fucking clue where to start.

~~~

I'm toweling off at my chair when a small commotion at the hut grabs my attention. A middle-aged man is yelling, and it's directed at Ben. The British girl stands between them.

"What the hell am I supposed to do now?" The man throws his leathery hands in the air. "You said I could count on her."

"I'm sorry, Tom. I thought you could," Ben answers. I try not to take too much pleasure in him getting reamed. "If it makes you feel better, it was a surprise to me too."

The man looks up at the sky in exasperation. "Why would that make me feel better?" He turns to an Asian guy with an impressive and chiseled but not-too-chiseled-that-it's-gross six-pack who's standing on the other side of him. "Curtis, Lucy, this is your problem now too. Thanks to Ben, there's only three of you. Hope you're all okay with no days off."

When the man huffs away, Ben turns to Lucy and Six-Pack. "I'm sorry. I'll cover more shifts so you guys can get days off."

"No worries, man," Six-Pack insists, being way too nice if you ask me. Which, obviously, nobody did. "I'm at the beach every day anyway."

"It's not your fault, Ben," Lucy adds, letting him off the hook too.

Once it's quiet again, I settle back down into my chair warily, not sure if I can handle any more "relaxation" today. I keep my eyes on the rhythm of the waves crashing, refusing to let my eyes shut this time.

So, this is it. This is my summer. Just me, my thoughts, and the ocean.

If you stare at the ocean long enough, you can see inside your soul.

Stupid Chip.

The Pit of Doom compresses in my stomach.

It first appeared a few months ago. As small as a seed. Every once in a while. But then it started popping up more and more, steadily sucking the air out of me a little at a time, pinning me down to my bed at home for days.

If I let it, it will eat me alive this summer.

I know it's impossible to outrun something living inside you, but I can try.

I just need to keep moving.

I drag my beach chair to the pile next to the hut, debating my next move. The guy in front of me hurls his lounger on top of the stack, and the whole tower of chairs crashes to the ground as he strolls away.

I catch a few flying toward me and then restack them as Lucy scuttles over.

"Twat," she mumbles in the guy's direction before turning to me. "I owe you one. It's been a day."

Yes, it has. "No problem." Thanks to my mastery of Jenga, I stack the chairs in alternating directions so they won't fall.

"You're hired," Lucy jokes, impressed.

"You found someone?" Six-Pack jogs up with an armful of rental equipment.

She grabs a life vest from him. "I was kidding."

"Actually . . ." My pulse speeds up, an idea forming. "If you guys do need someone, I'm kind of available," I finish in one breath.

"Wait, really?" Lucy eyes me skeptically.

"Yeah, I'm around the whole summer." I don't know if this

is a huge mistake or not, but clearly, sitting on the beach by myself all day isn't going to work. Neither is shutting myself in my room with a journal. And going home isn't an option.

Lucy brightens. "Are you sure? It's a lot of running around. You'll barely have any free time during the day."

This is sounding better and better. "That's fine."

Six-pack shrugs. "Sweet. You're hired. I'm going to take my break."

"Who's hired?" Ben questions, coming up behind me.

"Her." Lucy spins her head in my direction as she rewraps the scarf around her hair. "What's your name?"

"Abby."

"Abby's hired!"

I ignore the surprised look Ben shoots me. "I don't need to interview or anything?" I'm relieved but also slightly suspicious.

"Have you ever been arrested?" Six-Pack asks, shimmying into his wet suit. Such a shame to cover up those abs.

"No."

He gives me a thumbs-up, as if to indicate the interview is concluded.

Ben raises an eyebrow. "That's it? You have nothing else to ask her, Curtis?"

"It's not rocket science, Benny boy," Lucy huffs with mock exasperation. "Abby, can you count money and hand out beach equipment?" She's joking, but I nod, anyway.

"Can you adjust a beach chair?" Ben gives me a half smirk.

Lucy smacks him, which I'm grateful for because I think it would've been awkward for everybody if I had. "Don't be such a cow. It's your ass she's saving. *You* should be giving Abby a huge hug right now."

"Nope, I'm good." I quickly shut that down. He probably wasn't planning to, but I'm getting a slight summer-camp, touchy-feely vibe from the group, and I want to nip it in the bud, just in case.

"One more question— Wait, what's your name again?" Six-Pack asks.

"Abby," Lucy and I say at the same time.

"Can you start right now?"

"Sure," I answer with way more confidence than I actually have. But it's got to be better than my other two options for the summer: figuring out how to work a VCR or seeing inside my soul.

6

*E*very year during the two-week period leading up to our playoff tournament, it felt like I did nothing but eat, sleep, and play volleyball. Homework and a social life became things to squeeze in between twice-a-day practices and team dinners.

"In the zone," my coach called it.

"Tunnel vision," Mom called it after I forgot to wish Will a happy birthday one year.

For better or worse that's exactly what these past five days of beach hut training have been like. The days are full, running back and forth to the shore and getting up to speed on schedules, prices, rentals, and lessons. I'm so exhausted when I fall into bed every night that I don't realize I've closed my eyes. Until I wake up the next morning, the Pit of Doom greeting me before my alarm even goes off, and I jump up to do it all over again before it can pin me down.

I'm far from complaining, though. This job is proof that at least I'm functioning here. *More* than functioning. Considering that back home I couldn't get out of bed, I'll take it as a win.

Cynthia doesn't seem quite as thrilled. "You want to *work* while you're here?" she asked in surprise when I first told her. I think her vision for my summer was more along the lines of a meditative spa retreat, with lots of time for quiet reflection in nature. To her credit, she's said nothing about it since, still keeping her word to give me space.

My first Sunday in the hut is our most hectic day yet. Weekends are all hands on deck, and even so, it's hard to keep ahead of the crowds.

"Two smalls, a medium, and an XL," Lucy calls out to me as the line in front of the hut goes from busy to *insane*.

I pull the life vests off the rack and sign each one out, then help two children secure theirs and double-check the safety straps on the adults.

Lucy gives me an approving nod. "Well done, Abby."

I get a dorky surge of pride, finally feeling like I'm getting the hang of it all. Lucy is the one I man the counter with most often. She's been nice, but not in an invasively friendly way, like you might expect from someone the same age as you who you're trapped in a hut with all day. It's a quality I very much appreciate right now. Participating in getting-to-know-you conversations doesn't interest me in the slightest.

The line at the hut swells at lunch as a steady stream of people motor in on dinghies and skiffs.

"Where do all these people come from?" I wonder to Lucy as I speed clean a pile of snorkel masks. The only places to stay on this side of the island are a tiny bed-and-breakfast and a campground.

"Two Harbors is basically like an outpost in the Wild West." She motions to the hundreds of boats moored in the harbor, from fancy yachts and sailboats to dilapidated catamarans and bay boats. "For anyone sailing around this side of the island, we're the only opportunity for civilization. And public showers."

A gust of ocean wind blows through the hut.

"The checkout slips!" Lucy cries.

I whirl back around to the counter where a stack of receipts begins to flutter away. I clamp my hand down on them just in time and then stuff the pile into their labeled box. Like I was supposed to have done five minutes ago.

Maybe I'm not quite as up to speed as I thought.

After the lunch rush, Lucy sends me down the beach to collect abandoned rentals, my least favorite task. I grab the first six chairs I see and lurch back, lugging three chairs under each arm. I pick up the pace when I see Ben coming in my direction, high-fiving a group of kids as he passes them.

Since our little beach chair flare-up, we've had minimal interaction. I'm usually in the hut and he's on the sand, setting up chairs and umbrellas and, in general, socializing with everyone like it would kill him to breathe without also asking how your day is going.

He strides up beside me, just a few fins in his hands, while I stagger up the beach. "Wow. That looks pretty heavy." His voice is full of fake concern.

"I'm fine." Even if my arms were bursting into flames, there's no way I'm giving him the satisfaction of asking for help.

"You sure?" He pulls his lips together, hiding a smile. "Because if you need a hand, feel free to ask. . . ."

Before I can answer, an older man in a fisherman's cap interrupts us. "Hey there, Ben."

"Hank, how are you?" Ben gives him a hearty pat on the shoulder. "Did you find out if your brother's okay?"

"Yes. Turns out he doesn't need surgery after all."

"That's great. Glad to hear it."

"Is he a regular?" I huff once we're farther up the beach. Lucy told me I should learn who they are if I want to make better tips this summer.

"Hank? Nah. I just met him this morning. We were in line at the general store together."

I drop the chairs in a heap next to the hut. "You could become best friends with the stranger peeing in the urinal next to you."

"How do you think I met Curtis?"

If he wasn't so annoying, I would *maybe* smile at that one.

As if on cue, Six-Pack, known to everyone else as Curtis, jogs over. He's just finished teaching a paddleboarding lesson, and water drips off the tips of his hair onto his shoulders. He's technically in charge of the hut, but the title "manager" fits him about as loosely as his board shorts. I'm pretty sure he's said less than twenty words total to me over the past five days. At first I thought it was just that Lucy and Ben talk so much he couldn't get a word in edgewise. But during our only two-person shift, he greeted me by saying "Hey, New Girl" and didn't speak for the next three hours.

I try not to stare at his abs as he drags a towel across his body, but it's impossible. They're captivating. It's like an in-the-flesh biology lesson of how muscles connect to one another.

Curtis assigns us each a task, then grabs his wet suit off the rack. "I'm taking my break."

A "break" for Curtis means a twenty-minute solo kite-boarding session. It's a combo of surfing and windsailing, though according to Lucy, about a thousand times harder than any of those on their own.

"I'll take a break too," Ben echoes, before belatedly tacking on, "if that's okay with you guys?"

"Oh, please. Stop with the fake consideration. Just go." Lucy waves him away.

A few minutes later, I find Curtis cutting between the

waves, making it look easy, the kite waving wildly above him. Ben makes his way out to the end of the dock, filming Curtis with his iPhone. He's done that every day this week. Bizarre. Is it, like, something Ben plans to go home and watch at night? Is he obsessed with kiteboarding? Or maybe with Curtis?

It's just another one of the dynamics in this group that I don't get. They've all known one another for years—Curtis lives on the island year-round, and Ben and Lucy have spent every summer here since they were kids—so the three of them have the type of shorthand that naturally evolves from that much time together. A combination of shared memories, inside jokes, and random minutiae that I am light-years from catching up on.

It's okay, though. Their mutual obsession with each other keeps them from focusing too much on me. Even innocent chitchat only leads one way: to questions, to conversations I don't want to have right now. Better to stay quiet.

The beach clears out by four o'clock, in time for the last ferry departure, so Lucy and Curtis take off early, leaving me and Ben to close up.

"By the way," I say as I take out the stack of today's receipts. "I don't mind taking extra days. If people want more time off or whatever."

He gives me a long look. "Okay. Cool."

I grasp to change the subject before he can fire off a follow-up question. "Who's on with us in the morning? Curtis or Lucy?"

He scans the clipboard. "Curtis."

"You must be excited," we say to each other at the exact same time.

"Me?" we immediately respond in confused unison.

"You stare at Curtis's abs like you've never seen a stomach before." He smirks, clearly amused. My face flushes. "You know he's gay, right?"

"Yeah, I do know that." I've caught slash eavesdropped a few hushed conversations between Lucy and Ben about the guy from Long Beach "who ripped Curtis's heart to shreds then sprayed it like confetti across the Pacific Ocean." Apparently, it happened last spring and they're not sure whether he's really over it. "I also know that *you* scramble for your phone to film him every time he puts on his wet suit."

"You think that's why I'm filming him?" Ben's amusement triples, and he almost drops the clipboard. "Because I'm into Curtis?"

"There's some kind of obsession there." I shrug noncommittally, leaving some breathing room for error.

"I'm filming a documentary."

"About Curtis's abs?"

"No." He holds back a laugh. "Present company excluded, I don't think anyone would find a documentary about that very compelling."

"I'm sure there's an audience."

"Well, it's not my USC film school professors."

I glance up from the receipts. "Wait, that's where you're going in the fall?"

"Yeah." He says it casually, like it's no big deal to be accepted into one of the best film schools in the entire country. I slide this piece of information into the incomplete picture I have. Ben, the aspiring documentary filmmaker.

"I thought everyone in film school was dark and broody."

I expect a flippant retort, but instead his eyes settle on mine. "I can be dark and broody." I have no clue if he's being serious or not. I can't read him as easily as I thought.

We settle into silence for a moment, but I realize he didn't fully answer my question. And I'm curious enough to actually circle back to it.

"So, then, why are you filming Curtis?" I ask.

Ben looks at me in surprise. I'm assuming because it's probably the first question I've asked any of them that's not about work. "There's this class all the incoming film school freshmen take. It's legendary. It's what supposedly *breaks* you and immediately weeds out whoever can't take the pressure. The first assignment is to make a five-minute film using just your camera phone and basic editing software. It has to 'tell a compelling story from your summer.' Mine's a doc about Curtis training for the Kiteboarding World Cup."

"That's a—"

"Yes. Totally a real thing."

Makes more sense than my initial theory. Although a few ab shots wouldn't hurt anyone. "I'm surprised he's cool with being filmed. Is he going to have to . . . talk?"

"I can get him to open up. It's just about asking the right questions."

I file the sign-in sheets into separate folders, wondering yet again why Tom doesn't get a laptop for the hut. "It's that easy?"

"Sure, the questions are the gateway, but the reality is that people *want* to open up. The reward center in our brain lights up more when we talk about ourselves than it does with any other subject."

"That's pretty disturbing that we're wired to be narcissistic."

He shrugs. "Everyone has a story. Deep down most people just want someone to listen to them talk about it."

Another Ben puzzle piece clicks into place. All those conversations he has with strangers up and down the beach go deeper than him just being annoyingly sociable. He's collecting stories, the little details of each person, what makes them tick; he can't help it.

"So, what are these magic questions?" I ask.

His eyes flicker. "If I tell you now, how will I use them on you later?"

My stomach tightens. I have no interest in being Ben's new investigative study. "Good luck with that," I say lightly.

This is exactly why it's better to just stay quiet.

7

Before

The fluorescent lights of Target were slowly sucking out my soul as I wandered the aisles with Nina. She'd found out last week that she'd gotten into University of Colorado too, meaning our dream of living together was finally becoming a reality.

If we could decide on bedding, that is.

"I thought we weren't going to be those people with the annoying theme room," I said as Nina paused at a room display that could best be described as a rose garden on acid.

"I thought so, too," Nina agreed. Corkscrew curls bounced around her heart-shaped face, her adorable exterior the perfect disguise for a wicked sense of humor beneath. "Until I saw how cute this all was. What about nautical?" She pointed to a navy bedspread dotted with anchors. "We could add these red pillows."

"Why do we want to pretend to be on a boat?"

I was trying to be cheerful, but the session I'd just had with Dr. Gold was still sticking to my ribs. He'd spent the entire time running through all the HD testing rules. Someone put a lot of thought into how this carefully choreographed dance goes down. First, you had to be eighteen to legally test, so if we'd gotten this letter a year earlier, testing wouldn't even *be* an option. I also learned that once they finally drew your blood, there was a three-week waiting period before you could get your results. As if you hadn't waited long enough. Then Dr. Gold would reveal them by opening a sealed envelope, like some extremely fucked-up version of a dramatic awards show.

At the end of our session, I'd asked him the obvious question. "Why are there so many rules? It just seems extreme."

The expression on Dr. Gold's face made my palms sweat. "When the HD test first became available, an alarming number of people who found out they were positive committed suicide soon after. This timeline was developed to try to prevent that."

If I was looking for the stone-cold proof of what we were really up against, I'd just gotten it. This disease is so terrible that people would rather kill themselves than live with it.

"Ooh, how about this?" Nina pointed to a set of comforters covered in pineapples and psychedelic neon flowers. "We could be like the fun tropical room."

I blinked a few times. "Really? You don't think it's . . . bright?"

Her lips tightened, until a smile burst free. "Abby, it's ugly as fuck. I'm messing with you."

I laughed in relief.

She marched forward with the cart. "So, we agree on nautical?"

"Not funny."

As we rounded the corner to the next aisle, which hopefully had bedding options that wouldn't blind us, Nina's phone lit up. She read whatever was on it, then a strange expression crossed her face.

"What is it?"

"Nothing." She wrapped a curl around her finger innocently.

But a few minutes later I caught her looking back at her phone, her brow furrowed.

"Still nothing?"

She blushed until she was the same color as the nautical red pillows. "Okay. After you told me everything that was going on, I started reading a bunch of stuff about HD." Nina was the one person I'd told about Dad's letter. "I just wanted to understand everything better."

I nodded, touched but also weirdly guilty because I hadn't even done that yet.

"Anyway, I ended up signing up for notifications from that HDBuzz site, and they just sent me this."

She held up her phone and showed me an article about a drug being developed to stop HD symptoms. "Did you hear about it?" She stopped herself. "I mean, of course you've probably heard of it. But it just seems . . . positive."

Even though there wasn't a cure for HD yet, Dr. Gold had given us the rundown on a few potential drugs aimed at fighting the symptoms of HD. The one Nina was talking about was the furthest along in the testing process.

"Yeah. That's the big one. It reduced HD symptoms in lab mice, and it's now being tested on actual HD patients."

"I didn't realize they were so close. That's huge." She gave me a wide-eyed smile.

"It could be." I didn't add the rest. That researchers needed a lot more time before they knew if the drugs would work on people or for how long and with what side effects.

"I mean, not that you'll need any of these drugs anyway," she quickly added. "Since you're not going to have this."

She was parroting what I kept saying to her about it. If I was gung-ho on being optimistic, she would be too.

"Right," I agreed, but my voice shook slightly. I still couldn't picture myself being gene-positive. I really couldn't. But after this last session with Dr. Gold, something shifted slightly. Like I was finally beginning to understand how much I had to lose if my gut was wrong.

Nina pushed the cart down the aisle silently. "Is now a bad time to tell you that I see matching pineapple shower caddies on the shelf down there?"

I broke out into a real grin. Thank god for Nina. "Lead the way."

8

From the few words of Brooke's texts that my eyes catch before I delete them each day *(Fun . . . can't ignore . . . do anything you can't take back . . .),* I think she assumes I've come to Catalina for some kind of crazy YOLO bender. That I'm here scuba diving or windsurfing, a new adventure each day, maybe hooking up with a hot guy if he crosses my path, definitely making some questionable choices. That the envelope has turned me into someone who *goes for it,* or at least someone determined to have one summer of unadulterated fun before facing the music.

Little does she know I've worked almost every single day for the past two weeks. That slip of paper hidden inside that envelope didn't magically transform me into a spontaneous thrill seeker overnight. That work is the only thing that keeps the Pit at bay.

So, when Sarah, the bossy redhead from the restaurant, marched over to the hut a few days ago, asking if I wanted to be a cater waiter at the Two Harbors Food and Wine Fest with Lucy, Ben, and Curtis, I said yes.

Now, as I man the hut on the afternoon of the event, I realize why Lucy keeps calling it "the official kickoff to summer." The party isn't set to start for another few hours, but half the beach is roped off in anticipation.

"Let's wrap this up." Lucy twirls her finger in the air. "We've got to get ready for tonight."

Ben and Curtis jog back up to the hut, lugging the last batch of beach chairs on the sand.

"All right, Curty. You can't put it off any longer." Lucy bumps her hip against his. "What's your number?"

There's a long pause and then Curtis answers, "Ten dollars on four."

Lucy makes a "pshaw" noise. "I'm doing nine."

Ben stops stacking the chairs in front of him. "Are you seriously putting money in this year?"

"Obviously," Lucy confirms. "What's the point otherwise?"

I look up. "What's the bet?"

"Lucy . . ." Ben shakes his head, like she's his overeager little sister.

"You don't have to say." I flush. I rarely jump into their group conversations. And moments like this remind me that I've probably already solidified myself as the weird, standoffish outsider.

Lucy waves me off. "Oh, stop. It's not like it's a secret.

Every year at the Food and Wine Fest, Ben gets roped into being all the ladies' dance partners, from like age eighteen to eighty-eight. Everybody wants a piece."

Why am I not surprised?

"And we always make a wager on how many it'll be. Whoever's closest wins." Lucy lets out a throaty laugh.

Ben has the good sense to look somewhat mortified for about half a second, before laughing himself. "When you have hips like these, it's a crime to keep them to yourself." He does a few exaggerated gyrations to the music, but the kind where you can tell he's actually a good dancer.

Lucy snorts. "Is that how the kids are doing it up in San Fran these days?"

"I don't think anyone's doing that anywhere," Curtis murmurs.

"We've got to lock this down, Curty. Is four your final number? Because"—Lucy exaggerates batting her eyelashes—"I'm being extremely nice by telling you this, but I heard there's a large group of women staying at Banning House this week to celebrate their fiftieth birthdays."

"Damn." Curtis looks like he's giving this actual thought. "Ten."

I hike my usual route back to Cynthia's on autopilot, my brain occupied with plans for my immediate future. Like how fast

I can eat one of the burritos Cynthia stores in the fridge for me, shower, and change into the white T-shirt and black pants we're supposed to wear tonight.

But my plans are immediately derailed as soon as Cynthia's cottage is in sight. Chip is sitting on the front porch, shirtless and in the pair of bike shorts that he wears all the time. I have yet to see him on a bike.

I know from past experience that there's no point in fighting it. It's much easier to accept that the next ten minutes of my life will not involve a burrito or a shower. They will be spent debating a bizarre topic of Chip's choosing that would probably be much more interesting if you're extremely high or a botanist.

He breaks into a grin when he spots me. "Hey, Abby!"

"Hi, Chip."

"If you had to marry one person from the Bible, who would it be?"

This is weird, even for him.

I grit my teeth. "Are we talking modern times or biblical times?"

"Biblical."

I tap into the deepest part of my faith to pray for a miracle that this conversation will somehow end.

Just then Cynthia pulls up in her ATV. I must be more spiritual than I thought.

"Abby!" She hops off and strides toward us. "They let you off early today?"

"Because of the wine fest."

"Right, right, right. Fabulous. Why don't you go on in-side, take a shower, relax a little, and then we'll head over there together?" She winks at me because that's the type of thing Cynthia does.

Seeing her so excited at the idea of spending time together sparks some major guilt.

Cynthia misreads my expression, because she immediately adds, "Or if you're not up for it, that's okay too. You can have a nice, long evening to relax, right?"

"No, I . . ." I shift my weight from one foot to the other. "I'm working the party, actually. They asked everyone in the hut to be cater waiters."

She raises her eyebrows in surprise. "Wow, you've been going nonstop, Abby."

"I don't mind."

Cynthia gives me a long, appraising look. "I trust you know what's right for you. Your time here this summer is whatever you decide you want or need it to be." She sweeps her hand out toward the ocean. "However you take it, it's a gift."

"Thank you," I say, then add, in case it hasn't been clear, "it's really nice of you."

She shakes her head slightly. "No, I meant your time here. All time is a gift."

Like Catalina itself, the festival has a dreamy, rustic vibe. Palm trees sparkle with twinkle lights. Paper lanterns hang between tables on the beach, and tiki torches dot the sand, which makes it look like it's shimmering. Even the ocean is lit up by the lights of the sailboats docked up and down the shore.

When all the waiters are convened in the kitchen, Sarah huddles us up. "Okay, guys. Don't overthink this. The only thing you have to do is make small talk and shove food in people's faces."

That sounds unpleasant for everyone involved.

I grab my tray and follow the other waiters out to the beach. The first guests I reach are a well-heeled couple with sweaters tied around their necks. Definite sailboat people. It's only been two weeks, but I've mastered the differences.

"How's your night going?" the man asks genially.

"Uh, good." I try dipping a toe in the small-talk pool. Thankfully, the hut is so chaotic I never have to schmooze with the customers. "And you?"

"Oh, this is our favorite night of the year. We've been coming to Catalina for ages, since we were kids. We just love it."

They wait for me to answer, eyes wide, eager to share in the Catalina love affair.

"What brought you out here?" the woman finally asks.

Um, a fatal, incurable genetic disease. Would you like peanut sauce with your beef satay?

It's moments like this that I wonder how the hell I got

here. Why I'm on this island, passing tiny skewers of meat to strangers instead of being back at home holed up under the covers streaming every Netflix show known to man. Then I imagine Brooke peeking in on me from the doorway, and I have my answer.

"Just wanted a place to get away to this summer," I half lie, before I can mercifully dart away.

Unfortunately, it takes what feels like an hour to unload my tray, whether because of my social ineptitude or because the beef satay is not a major hit. It hasn't escaped my notice that Ben's goat cheese crostini are flying off his tray like wildfire.

Finally, someone snags my last appetizer, and I can head back to the kitchen to restock. I find Lucy standing at the edge of a metal counter, filling wineglasses and placing them on a tray.

"Here." She slides a glass across the counter to me.

"Are we allowed?" I'm on board so I'm not sure why I sounded like I'm about to whip out a badge.

"Of course. Half the staff has helped themselves. This is a party for everyone, trust me." She takes a sip from the wineglass in front of her. "Anyway, I'm assuming it's better if we at least taste the wine, so we can properly describe it to the guests."

I give her a small smile and take a swig so I can avoid another narc-like comment. I've never had fancy wine before, but this stuff goes down way easier than the wine in a box that sometimes shows up at parties back home. "Yum. It's really fruity."

"You mean aromatic with notes of pear?" Lucy raises an eyebrow, her accent making her seem even more refined.

"You sound like you know what you're talking about."

She erupts with a quick burst of laughter. "I don't. Once, at a house party last year, this kid opened up a bottle of wine from his parents' bar. I thought it was rubbish. Threw it down the sink. Turned out the bottle was worth five *thousand* dollars."

My eyes pop.

"There's some crazy rich people in Laguna." Lucy shrugs. "It took a little bit to get used to. Not at all like my neighborhood in England. Not that *that* was a riot, either."

I take a few more sips. "Now that you mention it, I am getting some very . . . intense *floral* flavor profiles. Don't know how I missed that the first time."

"Now you got it." She clinks her glass with mine.

I down the rest and refill my tray with skewers. When I walk out of the kitchen this time, I'm a little lighter.

Lighter quickly progresses to loose and limber. I'm not drunk, but I definitely get why it's called "a buzz." My body is warm and tingly, and my brain is along for the ride. Back on the sand, I pop from group to group, less fearful that each innocent question is going to out me somehow.

Dr. Gold talked about alcohol as a coping mechanism, not that he was recommending it. But I get it now, the way this wine replaces the icy dread of the Pit of Doom with a warm coziness in my belly.

Lucy and I have one more glass of wine an hour later, then I cut myself off and stroll back to the beach with my tray. I've never been hard-core wasted before, but from what I've witnessed with a few of my friends, the switch from fun to teary to meltdown happens so fast you don't see it coming. I have enough mental clarity to recognize this is probably not the best emotional timing to give wasted Abby a trial run.

The music suddenly cranks up, and the waiters on the beach start clearing out the tables to transition the area to a dance floor. I think that means the food service is officially over. As I look for Sarah to give me the okay to clock out, I migrate away from the main party area to the bar on the restaurant patio. It's usually full of people during the day, but with everyone on the beach tonight, it's quiet back here. A few of the general store workers huddle at one end of the long thirty-foot bar. Meanwhile, Ben is perched on a stool at the other end and *not* on the dance floor. I wonder if Lucy and Curtis are renegotiating their bet.

"Just wait, it gets better. . . ." Ben is midstory to the bartender, Marcus, who's laughing hard enough to cry. "Man-

Bun Marcus," as Lucy calls him, is basically worshipped at the hut, due to the fact he sends us free food and drinks at least twice a day. Also, both Lucy and Curtis have a massive crush on him.

I absently head toward them, the conversation drawing me in.

"Not only did she cheat on me *and* bail on working here all summer . . ."

Ah, he's talking about the mysterious fourth person who never showed up, who is, apparently, an extremely recent ex-girlfriend of his. The plot thickens.

"The really shitty icing on the cake is that when she called to tell me, she said I knew what I was getting into if I dated her, so technically the breakup was *my* fault."

"Maybe she's right," I volunteer from where I stand a few feet away, the words out of my mouth before I can stop them. I'm about as surprised I joined this conversation as Ben is.

"What?"

"*Did* you know what you were getting into?" I ask.

Ben scowls. "No! I mean, yes, I knew she had some issues, but I wanted to help her."

Marcus belly laughs and heads to the other end of the bar.

"I think I know what's going on here." I'm aware I've fallen victim to the wine chats, but I'm powerless to do anything about it as I sit down next to him.

He tilts his head. "I'm listening."

"You're a fixer guy." I say it with confidence, even though

I only threw it out there because Brooke dated a fixer guy once and Ben reminds me a little of him.

"A fixer?" He leans forward, his attention fully captured now. "What does that mean?"

"It means you love the drama of swooping in, fixing a broken girl, and saving the day."

He opens his mouth to presumably argue with me, but something stops him. He doesn't quite gasp, but I definitely hear a sharp inhalation of breath.

"Holy shit," he mutters, his eyes widening. "My tenth-grade girlfriend was supersmart, but she popped Adderall like Tic Tacs. I mean, that's not *why* I liked her, but I did think I could help. . . ."

"Mm-hmm," I murmur.

"My eleventh-grade girlfriend was an amazingly talented ballerina who'd been battling an eating disorder since freshman year. And now this ex. She had crazy trust issues that I tried to get her through, even though she was convinced I was cheating on her. Why do I keep doing this?"

He said it more to himself than to me, but nonetheless I feel the need to respond. "Because every fixer wants to be the hero of his own movie."

He stares off into the distance like he's doing some serious soul-searching.

"Um, are you okay?" I have one butt cheek off the barstool, ready to bolt if this turns dark.

"I'm fine," he answers absently. "I'm just trying to come up with a good title for my hero movie."

I snort. "Any success?"

"Nothing that I feel comfortable committing to yet."

"*Bad Judgment*?"

He grins. He has a great smile. No wonder every family on the beach is obsessed with him. "Too nineties Schwarzenegger."

"What about *The Fixer*?"

"Sounds like a Mafia movie."

Hmm. He might be right. "How about *Mommy Issues*? If you're a fixer, you definitely have those." I have no idea if this is true, but given how much time my AP psych teacher went on about Freud, it seems like it applies to everything.

"Nope," Ben counters. "No mom issues. She's a psychologist, so she's very big on talking things out."

"And yet it took a complete stranger to actually figure you out."

"Apparently." His eyes are lit with amusement. "I'm done being a fixer, though. I'm not going to let it happen anymore."

"You probably shouldn't set your expectations so high," I warn him. "Start small. Like dating a nice pathological liar."

He breaks out laughing, and then suddenly I am too. Really, truly, feel-it-in-my-ribs laughing. An unfamiliar signal lights up my brain like a sparkler. It takes a second to recognize what's happening because it's been a while.

Fun. I'm actually having fun.

"No, I'm going to go cold turkey on this one," he insists. "After eighteen years with a psychologist parent, I know the drill. There's a reason behind every pattern of behavior. And the only way to change it is to figure out the reason."

I lean forward. "Any clues?"

He's about to answer when he stops short. "Did you know your eyes get greener at night?" I shift in my stool as he studies my face, and it feels like this is the first time he's actually *seen* me since I got here. "They're like a mood ring."

Before my cheeks have time to flush, I tap his chest with my finger. "You do realize, you've got a much bigger problem now."

The corners of his lips rise. "Really?"

"If you're not a fixer, then what's going to be your new angle?"

"Shit. You're right. Any ideas?"

I pull my head back, sizing him up. "Emotionally Unavailable Guy with a Secret?"

"Too much work. What about Shy Guy?"

"Please. You could never pull that off."

"Good point."

"Cocky Know-It-All?"

His mouth twitches. "It feels like you've turned this into a different game."

We're still for a beat, as if someone pressed pause on both of us. "Ben!" An attractive-adjacent woman interrupts. She's decked out with a tiara and sash that reads "I'M NOT 50! I'M 5 PERFECT 10s!"

"How's the birthday going, Mel?" Ben asks.

"Almost perfect." She winks at him. "But I need a partner to tear it up on the dance floor with me."

"How do you know Ben is a good dancer?" I can't stop myself from chiming in. When has he danced in front of this random woman?

Ben hops off his barstool and shakes his head at me. "Oh, newbie, everyone in Catalina knows I'm a good dancer."

He takes off with Mel, and that's my official cue to get out of here. I'm dreading the hike back to Cynthia's, though. I've never worn flip-flops this many days in a row, and the blisters between my toes are bigger than my actual toes.

I spot Curtis hopping into an ATV with a small trailer hitched to it and hobble toward him. "Curtis! Wait!"

"Hey, New Girl."

"Could I get a ride?"

"Sure."

Not surprisingly he says nothing as we swerve up the path. Normally, that would be fine with me, but apparently, my wine chats aren't comfortable with silence.

"Did you have fun tonight?" I yell above the whooshing air.

He gives a half nod.

"Do you work at the festival every year?"

"Yup."

"Do you think you or Lucy is going to win the Ben bet tonight?" It's not lost on me how annoying I sound.

"I'll win. Even my mom ends up dancing with him by the end of the night."

"Which one was your mom?" A vision of a woman grabbing a beef skewer pops into my head. "Wait! I think I met her. There was a lady who came up to me, and I didn't *know* her know her, but I felt like I kind of did. Is she a real estate agent?"

"Yes."

"Wow, you guys are nothing alike!"

We pull up to Cynthia's cottage. "Most people say we look pretty similar."

"No, I mean, you do. It's just she's super outgoing and chatty. And you don't . . . you know . . . talk," I finish awkwardly.

Curtis just smiles as I hop off. "Until tonight I thought you had me beat, New Girl."

9

Sunlight blitzes my room through the curtains, which I apparently forgot to close last night. I wrench the comforter over my head, but it's pointless. My throat is raw and dry, and the empty water bottle on my nightstand is making me salivate.

I peel myself out of the bed, more exhausted than usual, thanks to the Food and Wine Fest. It was worth it, though. If nothing else, I know I'm still capable of laughing. At least with Ben. Or with wine. The jury's still out on which one.

I throw on what's becoming my hut uniform—bathing suit, loose cutoffs, shirt, and a fleece hoodie because the morning fog is no joke—right as my phone vibrates with a text.

> **Nina: Just got an email from U of C. We need to coordinate our housing forms roomie! Fill yours out!!!**
>
> **Abby: Will do.**

There's no way I'm operating at an awake enough level to deal with that now. I rake my hair into a ponytail and fly toward the kitchen like a homing pigeon. Water and carbs are calling me.

Cynthia's already awake, puttering around with the juicer, which explains the acidic, citrusy smell in the kitchen. She's got the bay window cracked open, and a breeze flutters through the room, kissing my bare legs.

"Morning," she greets me, more muted than her usual chipper self. I guess it was a late night for everyone.

"Never trust the man!" Shanti pipes in from her cage in a dead-on impression of Chip.

I mime a fist bump to her. "Power to the people."

Cynthia motions for me to sit at the table and then pushes over a mason jar of green juice. It smells like an herb garden and not necessarily in a delicious, savory way. More like an earthworm kind of way. But I'm so thirsty I start chugging. I wait for the overwhelming taste of dirt, but there's some kind of honey-and-lavender combination that makes it sweet.

"Thank you. I've always been scared of green juice, but this is amazing." I'm already halfway through it.

"It's very hydrating." She leans against the counter and takes a long sip before adding, "I assume you need it after last night."

I scramble through my brain to understand what she's referencing.

Oh. The wine I drank last night. "Nothing like a little wine buzz to make you forget about your problems," I joke

80

without thinking. It's the first time I've brought up my . . . situation.

"This isn't a joke, Abby. There's a strong link between substance abuse and trauma. You might think you're just temporarily self-medicating, but it's a vicious cycle." Not even a hint of lightness peeks out from behind her eyes.

Suddenly I feel like a five-year-old who's been caught stealing cookies after dinner.

"I only had two glasses." Great. Now I *sound* like a five-year-old. *It was only two cookies, Mom!*

Her frown deepens. "I know this is your journey, and I meant what I said when I invited you here: I want to give you space."

"And I appreciate that." I can already feel the walls closing in around me.

"But I was hoping you'd take this as a chance to start processing everything."

"I am." Would I even be able to get out of bed every day if I wasn't *somewhat* dealing with this?

"How?" She drops into the chair across from me, elbows on the table, eyes zeroed in on me. "You're working nonstop, dodging Brooke's calls, drinking . . . As far as I can tell, you haven't talked about it *at all*."

"Because there's no point. Not when I'm still wrapping my brain around it."

"I think you have it reversed. Talking about it can *help you* start getting a handle on it."

My face is hot with irritation. She makes it sound so simple. "Look, I get that you're just trying to help me, Cynthia, but you really don't know what it's like to be on this side of things."

"What side of things?"

Her feigned ignorance slays me. "HD! You tested negative."

"Actually, I don't know if I am. Negative."

I lower my glass down with a thud. "What do you mean? You told my mom you were fine."

"I am fine." She motions to herself, like *Look at me.* "That doesn't mean I got my results." She takes my empty mason jar and rinses it out in the sink, as if this is a casual conversation and not earth-shattering news. "I'm older than your father, so it seems likely if I were positive, there would be symptoms by now, but you never know. My mother didn't have symptoms until her late fifties, though obviously we didn't realize it was HD at the time. She was living in a home for Alzheimer's when she passed away."

I'm still stalled on the first part. "And you didn't find out if you had the gene?"

"I decided not to. At the end of the six months, I stopped the counselor before she opened the envelope."

For some reason this infuriates me ten times more than anything else she's said all morning. "Then I rest my case. You *definitely* don't know what this is like."

"Do you feel as piss-poor as I do right now?" Lucy croaks when I walk up, shifting her limp body in the wobbly beach chair.

She's the only one working at the hut, and by working, I mean she's in the fetal position on a beach chair, wearing huge sunglasses and with a death grip on her coffee. The paper lanterns from last night are windblown and raggedy. The twinkle lights are crooked. The sky is as gray as a corpse. No surprise, the beach is empty.

"Not too bad. I left when the dance floor started heating up." That is definitely the lamest sentence that's ever come out of my mouth. "How late were you out?"

"Late enough that my brain feels like jelly being squeezed from a doughnut." She flops her legs out from the chair and buries her feet into the sand. "I should've texted you to bring me some of Cynthia's famous green juice."

The aftermath of the juice churns in my stomach. I reach for the stack of yesterday's credit card receipts to add up, because even math seems more appealing than talking about Cynthia.

"I'll do it." Lucy motions for me to hand her the pile, just as I'm pulling up my phone calculator.

She sinks back into the beach chair and flips through the thirty-plus receipts. In under a minute she tosses the stack back to me. "It's $302.47."

"How did you do that?"

She shrugs. "I'm a numbers nerd. I've dressed up as a math

pun every year for Halloween since I was four and went as a slice of pi."

"Wow. I mean, obviously the math genius part is impressive, but coming up with fourteen years of math pun costumes couldn't have been easy."

She groans. "Maybe I should've added those to my Berkeley application."

I frown. "I thought you said you're going to Santa Cruz."

"Only because I got wait-listed at Berkeley. If I haven't heard from them in the next two weeks, I'll let you know what settling feels like." She gives a dull smile. "Where are you going?"

"University of Colorado."

"Was it your first choice?"

"I didn't really have one." When the volleyball coach at Colorado recruited me, it was a massive relief. I was the only one of my friends not glued to College Board every night or comparing glossy mailers and booking college tours, the entire process so overwhelming, I hadn't even known where to start. The fact that Brooke already went there, and Nina would hopefully be going too, made it even more of a no-brainer to say yes to that volleyball coach.

But now, standing on this beach, that decision feels like it was a million years ago.

And actually showing up on campus, moving into my dorm, meeting my teammates—it feels like it's a million years away.

The Pit of Doom suddenly spins around my stomach like a globe.

"Are you okay?" Lucy studies me over the top of her sunglasses.

"Yup." I flip around to face the counter so she can't see me gulp down a few deep breaths.

Luckily, Ben shows up a few minutes later, instantly distracting me. Even though he's showing signs of wear and tear from last night too—his eyes not quite as bright, his hand raking through his bedhead—he looks *better* than usual. Maybe because after last night, he doesn't quite annoy me like he did before.

He gives Lucy an amused once-over. "Hungover, Luce?" She grunts out a nonreply before Ben turns to face me. "I was looking for you last night. Did you leave early?"

"I guess." I double down on my lameness. "Why were you looking for me?"

"I wanted to tell you about this girl I met."

I'm not sure why, but I'm suddenly glad I left when I did.

Lucy half lifts her head. "Is it the redhead you were talking to? With the yellow dress and the big—"

"Yes."

Lucy gives him a thumbs-up. "Nice."

"But . . ." He pauses for what I assume is dramatic effect. "I didn't get her number because I thought about *you*, Abby."

Lucy perks up, like she missed something between me and

Ben. I redden, even though I know he's talking about our fixer conversation, not about me in general.

"I was serious when I told you I wasn't going to let it happen again," he continues.

I can't believe he actually listened to me. "And?"

"I realized there were a few warning signs. Like in the span of five minutes, she mentioned twice that her roommate is jealous of her *and* she said she only has guy friends because 'girls are always mean to her.'"

"Never trust a girl with no girlfriends," Lucy and I say at the same time, then grin at each other.

"The point is, this girl's entire body morphed into a giant red flag. So do you know what I did?"

"Proposed?" I guess.

His lips part in a half smile. "I was wondering if you'd still be funny in the morning."

"I was wondering the same thing about you." I flash him a saccharine smile. "So did you guys set a wedding date?"

"Yup. She wants to be a winter bride," he deadpans, and I crack up. I guess even without the wine buzz, he can still make me laugh.

Lucy takes off her sunglasses. "I'm lost. Did you hook up with this girl or not?"

"Nope. I made up a polite excuse that wouldn't trigger her and walked away."

"Good for you," I tell him, grabbing a basket of sand-covered snorkel gear.

He folds his arms across his chest. "That's it?"

Lucy hiccups. "Were you expecting a medal for leading a girl on and then ditching her?"

"No, I was expecting Abby to gloat a little more about being right."

I give him a big smile. With teeth. "Okay, fine. I'm a genius. I nailed you so hard."

A half-second later, I realize what I just said. I blush so intensely I have to put my hands to my cheeks to cool them down.

Lucy snickers. "Now *that's* a story I want to hear."

"That's not what I meant," I sputter.

Ben's eyes meet mine. "I know what you meant."

A flutter erupts in my stomach. Which is weird. Because even though I can admit that Ben's attractive, I'm not attracted to him *like that*. That part of my brain is definitely shut off right now.

"It probably wasn't only what I said that made you ditch her," I tell him, determined to U-turn this conversation. "Don't forget that you also *just* got cheated on and dumped."

"I didn't forget. . . ." He cocks his head. "But what does that have to do with you nailing me?"

Lucy cracks up again, and it's my own fault I detoured us here. "What I mean is that maybe you weren't into the red flag girl because you just went through a bad breakup."

"Nah. I'm way over that." The brightness in his eyes dims, as if his body momentarily lost power. "Haven't you ever been stuck in the middle of such a chaotic shitstorm, you know you'll only find your way out if someone forces you to?"

"Yes," I answer too quickly.

Ben's eyebrows shoot up, and I feel a follow-up question coming, but a few guys in board shorts and tank tops interrupt, returning some chairs and a volleyball.

Ben easily switches gears and greets the group. "How'd it go?"

"Great. It's a nice setup down there," one of the guys answers, gesturing down to the volleyball court that's been erected at the far end of the beach. Ben and Curtis put it up a few days before the Food and Wine Fest. I keep telling myself to check it out after work, but I haven't yet. This is the longest hiatus I've taken from volleyball in years.

When the guys shuffle off, Ben tosses me the volleyball. Instinctively, my hands shoot up to catch it, like I've done thousands of times before, but as soon as the grainy leather presses against my fingertips, I drop it like it's covered with fangs.

The Pit unfurls for the second time this morning.

"Nice catch," Ben jokes. "You fit perfectly on our team."

"Team?" My chest tightens.

"Our hut team," Lucy explains, her eyes closed. "There's a Fourth of July volleyball tournament. We do it every year."

I ignore the lifeless volleyball leering up at me from the sand.

Ben flicks his eyes to me and adds, "In case it wasn't clear, we suck."

"I forgot to ask." I again attempt to steer the conversation in a different direction. "Who won the bet last night?"

"Curtis." Lucy groans. "You know, Benny, maybe if you'd spent less time chatting up bitchy girls, you would've squeezed in a few extra dances with some more *mature* women."

Ben pats her knee. "You're grumpy, Luce. Go home and sleep it off. Abby and I got this."

Lucy moves faster than she has all day.

It's past five, and I'm closing out the register when I feel Ben's eyes on me. I whirl around and confirm my suspicion. "Can I help you?"

"Just wondering about the chaotic shitstorm that landed you on this island."

I knew right after I'd said it that he'd bring this up again.

"Was it a breakup?" he guesses.

I laugh, which is messed up considering the real reason, but he's so far off it's funny. "No."

"Why, then?"

I hesitate, and the energy between us gets weird.

I can practically hear Cynthia's voice in my ear again. Per her questionable suggestion, if I just *talked* about it right now, told Ben the whole story, I'd miraculously open the door to start processing this mess.

But would talking really help? I haven't had to tell anyone yet. Brooke and Mom were there when I found out, and Nina knew without me having to say a word. So just figuring out where to start is an emotional minefield.

And there's no going back. Even if it *did* make me feel better in the moment, Ben would never be able to *unsee* that part of me. Last night was the first time I've managed to act more like myself around him, Lucy, and Curtis, and it felt good. Breaking news like this would guarantee that they'd treat me differently—not *bad,* but not like *me,* either.

"There was no shitstorm. Cynthia invited me to stay with her, and I thought it would be a good way to spend the summer."

He searches my eyes like he's trying to dig a tunnel to the bottom of them. "Okay."

I twirl the last padlock to the hut, and Ben follows me out.

"Why are you bringing that with you?" I motion to the kayak he's dragging behind him.

"I like to cuddle with it at night."

I make no effort to conceal my horror.

"Jesus, I'm kidding. I'm going kayaking. Best time of the day. It's better after five when no one else is out there." He pauses. "Want to come?"

I consider my choices.

Option A: strap myself in a boat with someone who

prides himself on stealthily prying personal stories out of people.

Option B: go back to Cynthia's, where she will no doubt force me to finish the conversation we started.

Option A it is.

10

According to Ben, it's easier to launch the kayak from one of the less crowded coves, so we trek to the back side of the island. There's a curved, rocky shore that he bee-lines for, dragging the two-seat kayak into the water.

"Hop in." He holds it steady for me. "You've done this before, right?"

"Yeah. A few times." I assume the canoe I paddled around in at camp when I was younger counts. "I'll get the hang of it."

That's an acceptable enough answer for Ben, who hops into the seat behind me. He pushes us off the sand, and we float deeper into the water.

"The main thing with a tandem kayak is that the paddlers have to catch the rhythm together. Otherwise our paddles clash and we won't go anywhere. On the count of three, we'll do a forward stroke on the left side," he directs. "That way we get on the same pace from the start."

"Shouldn't you be in front so I can watch you?"

"The more experienced paddler sits in the back. Ready?"

I hold my oar up, poised for his count.

"One, two, three!"

I drag my paddle through the water, which requires more muscle than I anticipate, but I rise to the occasion. We don't move forward, though. We make a kind of lopsided semi-circle.

"Try to keep the blade vertical," Ben says. "When your hand reaches just behind your hip, slice the blade out of the water."

After another few tries, each one subsequently worse than the one before it, Ben states the obvious. "You've never been on a kayak, huh?"

"I went on a canoe a few times at camp." I grit my teeth, annoyed with my own incompetence.

"At least I know your tell now."

"What tell?"

"You mess with the hair behind your right ear when you're lying."

"No I don't."

"You did the same thing when you told me why you came to Catalina."

"Then it's clearly not my tell because that was the truth." I wonder if they sell hats at the general store. "Can we get back to paddling?"

"We haven't even started yet," he cracks. He counts to three again, and I slice the blade through the water. We jerk forward. On the next count of three, we propel forward another inch, with the additional threat of capsizing.

I'd like to make it out of here with my ego partly intact. "Maybe we should go back."

"I want to at least get across the cove. There's this family of turtles we might be able to see over there."

"If you're trying to motivate me, you're going to need to up the incentive a little."

He counts to three again, then says, "They're not just any turtles. These guys were my inspiration when I was ten."

"You wanted to be a turtle?"

"No," he laughs. "They helped me tackle my first and only identity crisis."

I'm less interested in the turtles than the identity crisis part. It's impossible to imagine any version of Ben—even a ten-year-old one—as not completely self-assured and in control. "Okay, my curiosity is mildly piqued."

"Flash back to eight years ago. My dad had just moved here, and my mom was bringing me to stay with him. It was our first father-son summer postdivorce."

"No brothers or sisters?"

"I have a sister, but she was already eighteen. Had her own

plans. So, my mom takes me out here and drops me off at his place. And by *place,* I mean the boat he still lives on. But I was pissed at both of them for making me bounce between Marin and Catalina."

"You weren't even a little excited about living on a house-boat? That sounds kind of awesome."

"It is. But this was before I realized that. As soon as my mom left to go back to Marin, I ditched my dad and started exploring the island solo. And that's when I found the turtles. I sat there for hours watching them crawl back and forth, up to the rocks, then down to the water. Moving between their homes like it was no big deal. It was just part of their lives."

"You saw yourself in the turtles. That's sweet." I smile. "Also, I think you've got a million-dollar idea here for a kids' book about divorce."

"I made them my first documentary subjects instead. You should've seen how impressed my science teacher was with my video when I got back to Marin."

"I bet you named them, didn't you?"

"The turtles? Of course. I was ten."

I laugh, and the kayak wobbles.

"Ben! We're moving!"

I'm not sure how I missed the fact that we've paddled at least three hundred feet from the shore.

Ben laughs behind me. "You were way too in your head about paddling. Distraction was my last-ditch effort."

We finally emerge from the cove into the wide ocean, and

it's like we've completely left civilization. How is this place only an hour from Los Angeles? There's not a boat around for miles, not a person—just shimmering open water.

I inhale a deep breath and then another, my shoulders basking in the sunlight. "This is amazing."

"It's what I wait for all year. When I was younger and people would ask what my favorite season was, I'd always say summer. Exactly because of this."

"Everyone always says summer."

"I don't know. Christmastime gets a lot of hype. What's yours?"

"Fall," I say, like *Obviously.*

"And you just answered one of my documentary questions."

I'm so surprised that I stop paddling. "You trapped me?"

"I mean, you walked right into it."

"But what does that even tell you about me?"

"Fall. I'm going to guess you're one of those people who's just as happy staying home as going out. Routine feels good, but you like getting to start fresh, because deep down you're a procrastinator."

Huh. Not bad.

We navigate over a few soft waves before my curiosity gets the best of me. "All right, let's hear some more."

We trail along the coast as Ben launches questions at me, from "What's your spirit animal?" to "What's the most illegal thing you've ever done?" By the time he gets to "What's the worst thing you've ever eaten out of politeness?" (Mom's ill-fated turducken one Thanksgiving), I think I might be a convert. It's kind of fun figuring out how he dissects these seemingly random questions to peer inside someone's brain.

Or maybe he's right. We're all wired to love talking about ourselves one way or another, and I'm just as narcissistic as the next person.

We're almost back to the cove when Ben moves on to a lightning round.

"Pick a side. Messy or clean?"

"Messy."

"Half empty or half full?"

I groan. "Empty. But I wish I could be a half-full person."

"Sweet or Salty?"

"Both. Haven't you ever heard of kettle corn?"

"Fate or free will?"

The question stops me midstroke.

I wait for my stomach to bottom out, for the Pit of Doom to swell, but something about the gentle gliding of the kayak, the drive to stay in the rhythm, Ben's presence behind me that fends it off.

"Fate," I reply, flat and resolute. "All the important things are mapped out from the start, and there's nothing you can do about it."

Like your DNA.

"So we're just playing out a movie that's already been written?" I can tell by his voice my answer surprised him.

"I guess. Yeah."

"And if you leave your house and get hit by a bus, you don't think leaving five minutes later would change anything?"

I think about this. Even being gene-positive, there's no guarantee it will kill me. I could, like Ben said, get hit by a bus or washed out to sea in a kayak or eat a piece of bad lettuce that kills me before symptoms of HD ever hit.

"That bus is going to hit you one way or another." I feel his eyes burrowing into my back. "Clearly you don't agree."

"Life deals you shit you can't avoid, but it's not like you don't have choices along the way. You can take them or leave them, but even bad things can lead to good things."

I cover my groan with a cough. "Like what?"

"Like Audra bailing on this summer and you showing up at the hut instead."

A blast of warmth hits my face, even though the sun is setting.

Shit.

I *cannot* let myself like him like that. I may not have a clue as to how to start "processing," as Cynthia calls it, but I'm fairly certain that letting myself fall into that kind of situation with Ben isn't the answer.

We reach the cove and haul in the kayak a few minutes later.

"Thanks for taking me. That was actually . . . really great."

I don't add that it's the most relaxed I've felt since I got here. That, surprisingly, talking *did* feel good, even if it wasn't the type Cynthia meant.

"I do it every day. You've got an open invitation."

"I might take you up on that."

11

I balance my phone against my ear while I pour coffee into a thermos. Cynthia will be up any minute, and I'm still avoiding her since our flare-up after the Food and Wine Fest a few days ago.

"Hey!" I'm thrilled when Nina picks up. So far, we've only been able to text, but hearing her voice instantly boosts my mood.

"How are you?" Before I can answer, she stammers, "Never mind. Dumb question. I'm sorry."

"It's okay. I'm good." I'm eager to dissolve the awkward tension. "Or at least, better than I was when I first got here." I tiptoe to the front door and sneak out, the relief of avoiding Cynthia hitting me as I start down the path. "How are you?"

"Uh . . . fine. Good. I mean, not great. But not terrible. I'm . . . good."

Guess this is going to keep being awkward. I wonder if these are just natural growing pains, or if our friendship will never be the same. If she'll always feel like she has to pretend around me. If everyone who I tell will pretend around me.

It's silent for a moment. "Please tell me a funny story," I blurt out. "Without worrying if it's going to make me upset. Just . . . be you."

"I'm sorry," she says quickly. "I don't want to say anything stupid that makes it worse."

"I promise I'll tell you if you say something that pisses me off."

"Okay." She exhales like she's been holding her breath. "Funny story. I'm on it."

She proceeds to tell me about her cousin's hot friend, who she met yesterday while touring around, but who thinks her name is Nikki. "I can't correct him now, right? He called me Nikki during the entire four-hour tour."

"Go with it. That can be your alter ego down there."

She laughs. "Tell me what's happening with you."

"Your stories are better. I haven't seen any hot tour guides."

"I don't know. . . ." Her voice lowers an octave. "It seems like Ben is touring you around the island in his kayak *a lot.*"

Since our first kayak ride earlier this week, Ben and I have gone every day after work, always somewhere new, to parts of the island that only the locals know about. I've texted Nina a few photos from some of the best spots.

I shake my head as I take a gulp of coffee. "Not the same thing."

"I have a few notes for your next round of photos. Less ocean, more Ben."

"Stop. It's not like that with us."

"Are you blind? He's hot. You should let yourself have a little fun while you're there."

"Obsessing over some random guy is the last thing I need right now," I snap, the edge in my voice surprising me.

"I'm sorry." Her voice immediately breaks. "Of course your head's not there."

"No. I'm sorry." She's quiet. "Seriously, Nikki." This earns me a half laugh.

But when we hang up a few minutes later, just as I'm arriving to the hut, I still feel bad. I know Nina just wanted me to share a guy story so everything could feel normal between us. And maybe she's right that I deserve to have fun. But what she doesn't understand is that, hot or not, kayaking with Ben is about my *sanity*. I'm not going to ruin that for a hookup. Being with him, out on the water, makes me feel like I'm . . . *okay*. At least as okay as I've been since I got here.

Which is why I internally panic when Ben walks up and tells me he needs to cancel our kayaking plans at the end of our shift.

"Sorry, Abby, my dad just called and . . . needs me for something." His eyes are dark, jaw clenched.

I smile tightly, covering my massive disappointment. "No worries."

He gives my arm a nudge. When I look up, his eyes are on mine, serious and intent. "Tomorrow, okay?"

"Okay."

The end of the afternoon comes too quickly. And without kayaking I have nothing to delay me from going home, each step up the path to Cynthia's bringing me closer to the follow-up conversation I've been avoiding for a week. *Maybe Cynthia won't even be home,* I let myself hope.

This theory is immediately debunked when I reach the front of the house and find her and Chip puttering around out front in the vegetable garden. Sneaking by is not an option right now.

Cynthia looks up from the tomato she's just plucked from the vine. "Hi, Abby. Do you have a minute?"

"Yeah, sure." I chew the inside of my cheek like it's gum as I climb up the front porch. Brooke has told me on multiple occasions that I'm allergic to confrontation.

She brushes a lock of sweaty hair off her forehead. "I was out of line to speak to you the way I did after the party."

"Um, okay. Thank you. Me too." I wait for the other shoe to drop.

"I overreacted," she continues. "Whenever you're ready to deal with this, I'm here."

The tension in my scrunched-up shoulders cautiously descends from its home by my ears. "I appreciate it."

"Good news, ladies!" Chip calls from across the garden. He's wearing a straw hat that has a tiny built-in fan right above the brim. He raises up an enormous melon. "First cantaloupe of the season!"

He walks the melon over to Cynthia. She examines it carefully, rolling it around in her hands like clay.

"Beautiful. Perfectly ripened. Muskmelons are challenging to grow. They need a long season and a lot of space." She says it like it's an extremely profound observation. "If you crowd them or try to rush them into ripening, they'll never open up."

"It looks delicious," I tell her.

She gives me this grave look in response. I don't know much about melons, but maybe that wasn't an appropriate reaction.

Unless . . . Wait a second. *Oh.* Am I the melon?

"But every now and then, they *do* need a nudge. Last year the melons refused to ripen, so I put a hoop tunnel over them to try and keep the insects out." Cynthia points to the chicken wire tunnels with plastic covers over the tomato plants. "By giving a little help, I was able to let them ripen at their own pace."

Yup, I'm definitely the melon.

"Or maybe they would've turned out okay, anyway, even without the tunnel?" I can't help but counter.

Cynthia and I eye each other like two chess players. "Could be," she finally admits.

"Well, if we've learned anything from these hothouse cucumbers," Chip pipes up, handing me a large basket of them, "it's that not all crops need to be babied in order to harvest."

If I'm not mistaken, Chip just scored me a point. When Cynthia turns back to the cauliflower, he winks at me, then says, "So, Abby, settle an internal debate I'm having: Should we be calling cereal a breakfast soup?"

I don't miss a beat. "Would that make oatmeal a stew?"

He smacks his palm to his forehead. "Mind blown."

In the most shocking turn of the day, I think I've actually missed being around Chip.

12

There's an area in the back of Cynthia's house where the breeze kicks up perfectly. Instead of facing the front of the island, the view is of the western side—all overgrown hill-side, with bits of ocean peeking through. I discovered it after climbing out my window one of my first nights here, when the room felt too small. Now I use it whenever I get that feeling like I'm going to suffocate if I don't breathe real air soon.

Or when I call Mom. The calm vibes I aim for during our phone calls come more naturally when I'm out here.

"Abby." Mom picks up the phone after the first ring, slightly panicked. "Are you okay?" Her requisite first question. Each time, she asks it like *this* might be the time that she'll find me hysterically bawling on the other end.

"Hey, Mom. Yes." I settle into the small hammock chair

that hangs from the eave of the cottage. "I'm fine. Just wanted to call and say hi."

She lets out a breath of relief, and I launch into a few stories about work, like I always do, keeping it light. Mom does her part and acts thoroughly entertained.

This is more or less how our conversations have gone since I got here. Not just because it's easy, but because what else is there for either of us to say? It all feels too big and yet entirely pointless at the same time.

"Are you sure you're okay?" Mom repeats. "I promise you, you don't need to protect me, Abbs. I would rather just know the truth."

"That's not what I'm doing. Really. Things are going okay."

"Oh, fudge nuggets! I spilled my tea. One second." Mom's version of cursing never fails to make me smile. Once, in her first year of teaching fourth grade, she almost let a swear word fly. She was so freaked out, she forever changed the way she spoke, inventing these phrases so she would have time to catch herself before the wrong word came out. Judging solely on the amount of times Mom screams "Shitake mushrooms!" and "Shut the front door," I believe she used to have quite the potty mouth.

She comes back a few seconds later. "How is everything with Cynthia?"

"Good," I answer tepidly. "She keeps hinting that I should

go to this six a.m. yoga thing she's leading this weekend on the beach."

Mom lets out an incredulous snort. "I cannot picture Cynthia up and active at six in the morning. She was always such a night owl—last woman standing, dancing in her platform heels."

"Really?" Cynthia is usually in bed by nine o'clock here. Not that there's any raging nightlife to speak of, anyway.

Mom's voice brightens. "It was always a new adventure when we'd go out to visit her in LA." Mom and Cynthia used to be close years ago, back when she and Dad were dating and first married, but it's still weird to hear her talk about Cynthia like this, like someone she *knows* on a deep level. Especially considering that for most of my life they haven't spoken at all.

"Please tell her I say hi." She says that every conversation we have, but it's the first time that it actually sounds like she means it.

"I will, Mom. I'll call you soon."

"Oh—speaking of calling. I got a message here from someone in the registrar's office at Colorado. Something about missing documents."

Those housing forms Nina mentioned. The ones I had mentally shoved into Mom's good old "Deal with Later" bin. "Right. I'm on it."

After we hang up I let myself sit there a moment. I know I should go inside, wait out however long it takes the crappy

Wi-Fi to download whatever forms Colorado has sent my way, and fill them out. Just get it over with.

But when I hop back into my bedroom and spot my laptop, chills rock my body like the air in my room dropped twenty degrees, and the Pit springs to life. Goddammit. Every time I try to think about anything to do with college, volleyball, life off this island, I can't breathe.

Frustrated, I will myself to open my in-box, but the Pit keeps expanding like a sponge in water, my throat getting dry, my heart rate picking up, the room vaguely spinning.

Just then my phone dings. I look down, expecting one extra text from Mom, but instead it's from Lucy, inviting me to join them at a bonfire right now.

I blink a few times, and a second text comes in from her.

Lucy: BTW, we're celebrating.

Celebrating what, I have no idea, but a deep lungful of air greets me at the thought of meeting them. I close my laptop, then decide to leave my phone on the bed. No need to stoke the Pit any further tonight.

I smell the bonfire before I see it.

Smoky ash mixes with the scent of eucalyptus leaves, which soak the whole island at night, as I crunch through the narrow trail to the firepits perched on the hillside of a campsite. I take my frustration out on the shrubs and bushes I have to push through, shoving them out of the way like they're punching bags. Am I seriously incapable of downloading a form on my laptop without hyperventilating?

Curtis sees me first from his spot coaxing the fire and gives a half salute, which I take as a warm welcome. When Lucy turns she's all lit up from the inside.

"I got in!" she announces, jumping over to greet me with an effusive hug.

I look at her, still uncomprehending.

"Berkeley! I got in off the wait list! I just found out!"

Her dream school. I smile in excitement for her, even as my stomach drops at the mention of college, right after my own failed attempt at the Colorado forms.

She's watching my reaction so closely, though, and I don't want to ruin this moment for her. "That's amazing, Luce!"

"I know!" she crows, her confidence unwavering. She immediately starts jumping and shrieking excitedly, and my smile becomes more real.

Ben walks up, wearing a beanie slung back on his head, and it gives him such an unexpected edgy vibe that I almost do a double take. I mean, obviously he's good-looking; that's been established enough by Nina and the string of teenage girls who drop by the hut in search of new life vests. But tonight there's suddenly something else there.

"Hey, Abby." He slings an arm around me in greeting.

His hand skims across my bare shoulders, and a ripple of heat shoots down my spine. I was telling Nina the truth before about me and Ben—that I'm not even close to the right headspace to think about him like that.

Unfortunately, I now realize that my body strongly disagrees with my head on this matter.

Lucy's jumping has morphed into a solo dance party sans music, and Ben looks down at me conspiratorially, his lip curling up at one side. I never noticed until now that this isn't the same smile he gives everyone else. That grin he doles out like candy to tourists and friends alike. It's this little side smile—head turned, eyes flicked toward me—that makes me feel like we're the only two people in the world in on the same joke. "Has anyone ever gotten this excited over engineering?" My breath catches into a laugh, but Lucy is undeterred.

"Oh, Benny, you have no idea. You want a good topic for your next doc? Come to one of the robotics club national conventions. They go *off*."

Ben pauses for half a second. "That's actually not a bad idea." He immediately reaches for his phone and starts typing things into his Notes app.

A few minutes later Curtis proclaims the fire ready for business, and we get busy assembling s'mores. As I skewer a few marshmallows, the Pit of Doom thankfully recedes to a mild simmer, and I relax into the chair next to Ben.

Meanwhile, Lucy is still chattering about what her life will look like at Berkeley.

"And then I'll minor in environmental engineering starting my junior year."

"When did you decide all this?" I gently rotate my marshmallow over the flame, trying to get that perfect golden glow.

"I got obsessed with engineering when we moved to the States. My new school had this maker space, and you could, like, use power tools and build things that you'd designed. It was like math coming to life." She gets sick of waiting for her marshmallow to toast and annihilates it in the flames.

Ben nudges my marshmallow kebab with his. "You haven't decided on your major yet, right?"

"Nope." I tap his kebab right back and deftly turn the focus back on him. "Which means I have no homework over the summer, like you."

His eyes are a deep amber in the glow of the fire. "Nah. I'd be filming something like this anyway, assignment or not."

Another person who has it all figured out. Then there's Curtis who isn't even *going* to school in the fall. He's taking a gap year to take his shot on the kiteboarding competition circuit. I'm starting to feel like the only one here who doesn't already have some deep-seated life passion. I guess I always assumed I'd discover one at some point after high school. A super tiny voice inside my head wonders darkly if I'll even have time now.

"For fuck's sake, Ben. Stop looking at Abby like she's a puzzle to solve." Lucy's voice brings me back to reality. I look up, my cheeks rosy from more than just the fire.

Ben puts his hands up in defensive surrender. "I'm not."

"Please." Lucy turns to me. "I only recognize it because he's done it to me before too."

"How do you think I feel?" Curtis asks in mock outrage, and they all burst out laughing.

I laugh right along with them until I feel a twinge of guilt. We're all becoming actual *friends*. And they don't even know why I'm here this summer. I know Dr. Gold would say it's okay to keep this private; normal, even. To wait to share this until I feel ready. *There is no right or wrong.* But it doesn't take away the icky feeling that I'm lying about who I am to them. Pretending I'm just a regular girl spending the summer at the beach.

God, I wish I was that girl.

The one I used to be, the one who took for granted how *uncomplicated* life was.

"Hey, guys, the party can start!" A voice in the darkness interrupts my spiraling thoughts. I look behind me to find two guys coming up the trail.

Curtis squints to see them across the fire. "Sanchez, hey. And is that Berk?"

"Guilty." A guy with curly hair and a wrestler's body, broad shoulders, and skinny legs raises his hand. The other one—Sanchez, I'm assuming—wears a guitar backpack and Birkenstocks. Now that they're closer, I recognize them both as counselors from the sleepaway camp out in Emerald Bay. They come into town on their days off.

Ben greets them both, and Lucy throws him a death stare. "Traitor!" But then she breaks into laughter as she turns to me. "You know that volleyball tournament on the Fourth I was talking about? It's always counselors versus beach hut."

"Can you call it a tournament when one team loses every year?" Berk asks, already throwing shade. Maybe it's just my crazy competitiveness, but I actually feel annoyed.

"This year we have a secret volleyball weapon," Lucy taunts him. She pauses for a dramatic moment. "Abby."

How does she know?

For a second I freeze, but then I realize she's just messing around.

Ben throws a wry smile my way. "Don't count on it. She can't even catch a ball."

I want to tell him I actually kick *ass* at volleyball, thank you, but instead, I reply tartly, "From what I hear, you can't either."

Ben's eyes flash with amusement, but something more intense sizzles underneath.

Lucy interrupts, "Guys, this is Abby, who we thank our stars for arriving on this island. If only to put this one in his place." She gives an exaggerated nod toward Ben.

"Abby, I like you already," Berk remarks, stepping closer

to me. Something tells me this is a dude who makes his way through a lot of the female counselors by the end of summer.

Lucy slings an arm around me. "In your dreams, Berk."

We all end up huddling around the fire on mismatched beach chairs. Berk passes around a joint that I avoid, unsure if it will settle the nerves in my stomach or enflame them, and Sanchez whips out his guitar. Within minutes everyone is belting out "Free Fallin'."

Next to me, Ben isn't singing. Instead, he's filming the crackling fire with his phone.

"Why are you filming if Curtis isn't kiteboarding?" I whisper.

"B-roll." His eyes stay focused on what he's filming. "It's extra footage to intercut with the main action. I won't know if I need it until I'm editing. Sometimes it's not until I watch everything that I realize the story I was trying to tell isn't actually the story at all."

He points the camera at me.

"Is this for b-roll too?" I smile.

"Sure," he replies. A beat later he adds, in a lower voice, "Also, you're highly filmable."

I blink a few times. "What does that mean?"

He keeps the camera on me, his eyes fixed on the screen as he talks. "Sometimes people who are beautiful in real life just fall flat through a lens." He pauses for a second. "You're not one of those people."

Is he calling me beautiful?

My stomach dips, and *yeah,* my body is really not getting

this memo. Our eyes meet above the phone before he quickly moves the camera away from me and pans around the fire.

Later, Curtis douses the fire in water and we all begin gathering items to head out.

Berk is suddenly beside me. "I can walk you back, Abby. Buddy system."

It doesn't make sense because he's got a forty-five-minute walk back to his camp that he should do *with* Sanchez, but as I start explaining this to him, Ben approaches.

"Don't worry about it, Berk," Ben interjects smoothly. "Abby and I will go together."

Our group separates at the base of the campsite, with Ben and I splitting off to the trail that leads toward Cynthia's and the back of the island, while everyone else heads toward the front.

"You don't really have to walk me all the way back," I tell him once Berk is out of earshot, in case he was just saying it for show.

"I don't mind. Do you even have a flashlight?"

I shake my head. Of course not, and I left my phone on my bed.

Our footsteps are quiet, and the crickets are the only sound around us. I'm used to words filling the space between us, but everything feels more charged out here in the darkness than it does during the day.

The moon is hiding as we approach the front steps to Cynthia's.

"Here we are," I announce unnecessarily.

"Careful." Ben puts one hand on the railing, the other on the small of my back to guide me, and the small slice of contact takes me aback. I instinctively swivel around, our faces suddenly inches from each other.

I'm about to make a joke, something to diffuse the tension of us being so physically close, but the look on his face stops the words in my throat. His eyes are suddenly dark and focused on mine, like I've caught him off guard, and the intensity of it catches *me* off guard.

Before I know what's happening, his lips are on mine, soft but firm, setting off a series of fireworks in my stomach.

His hands glide up, one cupping my jaw, the other in my hair, and it's so fucking instinctive that I seem to fuse to him, my lips parting and his tongue sliding over mine. He's so sure, so confident—like he is at everything—but there's a gentleness, too, as his thumb traces my jawline, his fingers running through my hair, his body warm against mine. I hear a soft noise that I realize a beat too late is coming from me, and it unleashes something in Ben, his grip tightening, his lips more insistent, and just before my brain completely short-circuits, an SOS message suddenly rings through loud and clear.

You can't do this right now.

I pull back suddenly, the force of it taking us both by surprise. "I can't."

"What?" His breathing is shallow, and he looks at me as if he's heard me wrong.

"We just . . . We can't do that." I exhale, my own breaths shaky. "We can't."

It was too intense. Too fast. Too much better than I ever could've fantasized.

Why is the best thing happening at the same time as the worst?

He's still watching me, his eyes dark, trying to put the pieces together. "There's someone back home," he guesses in a flat voice. "That's where your brain goes sometimes."

"No. That's not it." The words are barely out of my mouth before I regret them. I should've lied and said I do have a boy-friend. Now I have to give him a *reason* why I just shut down a kiss I'm sure he could obviously sense I wanted.

If I needed confirmation I couldn't handle anything like this right now, I've got it. I hold my arms tightly across my chest, as a barrier; just in case my body decides to stage a mu-tiny against my brain.

Several long, silent seconds tick by. How can I explain this to him? If my sanity here on Catalina was built on a tripod, he, Lucy, and Curtis would be the legs. I'm not in a place where I can afford to mess that up.

"I'm sorry. I just think it's better if we're friends," I finally tell him.

When it comes to Ben, I'd rather have some of him than none of him.

"Jesus, you don't have to apologize. It's my bad. I, uh, mis-read the moment." He looks me straight in the eye, and my knees weaken for a second.

"Are we still good?" I ask, my voice a little desperate.

"Yeah. Of course." He takes a few steps back, and his lips kick up into a half smile that rips my heart out. "Friends."

13

Before

Ice pellets slugged me in the face outside of school the moment I pushed my way through the big double doors. That wasn't surprising. But Brooke, parked next to the curb, calling out to me from her window, definitely was.

I hopped in and warmed my hands against the vents. "What are you doing here?"

"Wow. I'm happy to see you, too."

"Shut up. You know I'm happy to see you. I'm just surprised you're in town." I threw my arms around her and breathed in her favorite coconut lotion.

She set the windshield wipers on the fastest speed possible. "Do you have to get home, or can you can hang out?"

"I can hang out. What do you want to do?"

She grinned.

"Help me!" I shouted at Brooke, almost peeing my pants from laughing so hard.

She was doubled over and could barely peel the hot pink vinyl crop top off my head.

"You looked hot in that!" Brooke wiped the tears off her face. "That's definitely in the top five."

Brooke ingeniously created this game a few years ago, and it was now impossible to go to Cherry Creek Mall without playing. The rules were simple: Whatever outfit I chose, she had to try on, and vice versa. No exceptions.

Today, she chose a vinyl crop top and faux fur harem pants for me, which was only mildly less embarrassing than the leopard jumpsuit she originally considered.

I flashed her a big, toothy grin. "My turn."

"Do your worst." She narrowed her eyes to slits, challenging me.

I pulled out my outfit from where I'd stowed it under my coat.

When she lifted her eyes, her jaw dropped. "Abby, that's from the tween department!"

"I know."

A few moments later Brooke emerged from the dressing room, and the laugh that erupted from me was so loud, a store employee felt it necessary to peek in.

"Everything okay in here?" the salesgirl chirped. Her sparkly name tag read "Ali B."

"Everything's great." I dug my nails into my thighs to stop laughing.

I fully opened the dressing room door so Ali B. could check out Brooke in all her glory. The child size–fourteen sequin dress fit perfectly, except for one thing: Brooke's C-cup boobs spilled over the top of it. They were almost all the way out.

"You look great, sweetie," Ali B. cooed. Brooke definitely looked way younger than she was, but there was no question this girl worked on commission.

Brooke, remarkably straight-faced, adopted the high-pitched voice she invented when we used to play hair salon. "I'm just looking for something cute for school." She turned to the side. "I think I need a smaller size."

Ali B. nodded manically, like her head was stuck in that mode. "Um, sure. I'll grab one."

We closed the dressing room door and collapsed on the bench, howling.

We were still laughing as we wandered along the top floor of the mall sipping iced boba teas, per our tradition.

"God, I needed that." Brooke exhaled.

"So, why are you home? Did you come back to meet with Dr. Gold?" I asked. We'd recently started doing solo sessions with him, and she'd been driving in and out for them.

"Yeah. Tomorrow afternoon." Under the bright mall lights, her dark circles were even more noticeable.

"How's it . . . going? With Dr. Gold?"

She shrugged as she took a long sip. "Have you read any of those HD message boards he talked about?"

I gave her a *what do you think* look.

"Everyone on there calls it 'the Devil's Disease.' And it seems like every other post is about how HD ripped that person's family apart."

I forced myself to engage. I could tell she really needed me to. "Because the people in the families got different results?"

"Because of everything. Two siblings get tested and one decides they don't want to know, or siblings get opposite results, fights about caretaking—"

"That's not us, though. We're going to be fine."

"You don't understand how bad this can get, Abbs. I'm scared if we're not a united front on this the whole way through . . . we won't survive it."

I stopped midstride. "Even when you get on my nerves and I drive you crazy, we're still a united front. We'll be fine."

She opened her eyes as wide as she could, her move when she didn't want tears to spill out. It was jarring to see Brooke this fragile. I never played the role of consoling cheerleader in our relationship. In any relationship. But ever since we got Dad's letter, she always seemed on the verge of breaking. Like a sneeze would topple her over.

I chewed the inside of my cheek while I searched for some inspirational words. "Maybe you should stop reading those boards. . . ."

"Maybe you should start," she snapped.

Ouch. We both shifted our gazes to the shiny ceramic tiles beneath our sneakers.

"I'm sorry, Abbs. That came out really bitchy."

We meet eyes and share a shallow smile. "We'll be fine, Brookie. I promise. I mean, look at us! We embody united front. We're so sweet to each other."

I flashed her a covert picture I took of her in the sequined dress, her boobs smashed up to her neck. Brooke busted out a laugh, and then I started up again too. It wasn't until we were back in the car that we gained a tiny bit more control over ourselves.

"Do you have to go back tomorrow?" When she drove in from Boulder for Dr. Gold appointments, she never stayed long. I was hoping for at least one more day.

"I'm not sure."

"What do you mean?" I asked. "Don't you have classes?"

"Not exactly." She pulled out of the parking garage. "I dropped the semester."

14

When I arrive early at the hut the morning after the bonfire, I realize it's Ben's day off. So naturally, I spend the entire day trying to flatten the tornado sweeping through my stomach. I've accepted that things are going to be weird, and I just want to get this first post-kiss interaction over with. By the time Curtis, Lucy, and I close up, I'm scared my heart palpitations are audible.

The three of us head over to the restaurant, where Ben is meeting us. It's the day before Fourth of July, and the patio is as packed with tourists as the restaurant inside. I have to crane my neck to do a quick sweep of the room.

I finally see him. He's in the back bar area, leaning against the pool table like he's a freaking model.

The nosedive my stomach takes is more than enough proof

that I was right. I am *definitely* not in the right headspace to deal with this.

I follow Curtis and Lucy over to the pool table.

"Hey, Abbs," Ben greets me with a casual fist bump.

Vague annoyance ripples through me. It's like he's one step away from calling me "dude" or by my last name, like I'm some random buddy of his. Which I guess I am. By my own request.

"Hey!" My voice smacks of false brightness.

Lucy holds her pool cue like a weapon. "Anyone up for a game?"

The only thing I want to do with that cue is whack it over my stupid head.

"Don't hustle her, Luce," Ben laughs. *Laughs.* So easy for him. I guess he's not replaying last night like it's the only channel his brain is tuned in to.

"I wasn't," Lucy replies with mock offense.

"Math angles," Curtis explains to me. "She's unbeatable."

"You make it sound like I'm cheating." Lucy brushes him off. "Understanding congruent triangles and the law of reflection is not cheating."

"I'm going to get a drink," I respond to absolutely no one.

When Man-Bun Marcus delivers my strawberry lemonade, I stir it with so much vigor, I spill half of it on the bar. A hand I instantly recognize passes me a napkin.

I look up at Ben and give him the biggest smile I'm currently capable of. I will not mess this up more than I already have.

"I was thinking about White's Landing for tomorrow," I throw out casually. "Or is that too far to kayak?"

"I can't go tomorrow."

A thud lands somewhere between my heart and my stomach, even though I have zero right to it. "Oh."

He lowers his voice. "It's going to be crazy here tomorrow with the Fourth and everything. My aunt and uncle are coming in, too, and I have to see them at some point."

"Oh," I say again, because that's all I can manage over the gravel piling up in my throat.

"We can do White's Landing when they leave, though."

I wait for the side smile or a hand on my shoulder or a joking nudge. I'd even take another fist bump. Just some kind of personal contact. "Sure."

I can barely see him through my thick fog of regret as he wanders over to the jukebox. All I wanted to do was save our friendship. But as he flips through the songs, never once looking back at me, I'm terrified that I've ruined it.

I ditch my drink and weave my way toward the door, hiding among the clusters of tourists so no one sees me leave. I allow myself one last glance at Ben before I duck out.

Yet another big mistake.

He's still at the jukebox, but two girls have now joined him, flipping through the songs, laughing and chatting. Of course the prettiest one is wearing a USC T-shirt. *Awesome.* They'll have so much to talk about. I don't think he's being overly flirty with her. He's just being Ben.

I'm a human version of the puke emoji.

I torture myself and watch for a few more seconds, how the girl practically purrs as she talks to him. She'll probably try to hang out with him all night. Maybe she'll even give him her number so they can hang out tomorrow or at school in the fall. Because why not?

She can do whatever she wants. There aren't any brain-killing genes lurking in her perfectly normal body. She's free.

Sometimes the unfairness of it all takes my breath away.

~~~~~~~~~~

I reach the lit-up porch a little later and find Cynthia inexplicably hanging upside down from a long, silky sling suspended from the top railing. I have no idea what she's doing, but it spurs my first genuine smile of the day.

"What's happening here?" I laugh.

She pops her eyes open, and like an acrobat, flips herself to a seated position in the hammock contraption. "Aerial yoga. Want to try it? It's a great relaxation practice."

I drop my bag. "You know what? Why not?"

"Look at you, so adventurous," she teases.

I'd slather myself with mud and visit a shaman in the Amazon if I thought it would somehow lead me in the right direction. My way of processing has blown up in my face, and I'm ready to feel better, even if it's just by a few ticks. I've been here weeks, and I feel like I'm still barely holding my head above water.

Cynthia gracefully steps out of the sling and stretches the fabric for me to sit on top of it. "There's something exhilarating, but still calming, about defying gravity. It was a lifesaver for me when I got sober."

Oh. I suddenly see our conversation after the wine festival in a new light. *Cynthia had an issue with alcohol.*

She flips a lock of gray hair out of her eyes. "Yes, that was me projecting my shit on you the other morning. I'm not proud."

"You were worried. I get it." I wobble back and forth on the sling, flailing in an attempt to balance myself. "How long have you been sober?"

"Twelve years. I'd been falling apart long before that, but it was a perfect storm that finally pushed me. My fiancé and I had just broken up, my mom had died, I'd stopped speaking to your dad. . . ."

I'm confused—I didn't realize Dad cut everyone out of his life. But maybe he hadn't. . . . Cynthia just made it sound like not speaking was *her* choice. So, then, why didn't she back up Mom more when he left us? I know Cynthia would tell me the whole story if I asked, but I can't bring myself to.

I turn my focus back to the sling. "How am I supposed to sit in this thing?"

She spreads the sling wide and helps me into an upright position. "This is my favorite calming pose."

Without warning, she spreads the fabric underneath me to form a small hammock, but I immediately lose my balance and flip over on my side.

Cynthia chuckles. "You'll get the hang of it." She props me up like a baby who hasn't learned to sit yet, and lifts the sides of the sling to form a snug cocoon.

"How did you do it?" I ask, clutching on to the sides so I don't flip over again.

She knows I'm not talking about aerial yoga. "The first year was hard. Making that choice to get out of bed each day."

I swallow. Maybe Cynthia knew what she was talking about a little more than I gave her credit for.

"It doesn't all happen at once. It's baby steps. Convincing myself to go to an aerial yoga class, try something new—that was a step. Then actually sitting in the yoga sling for the first time was another step. You have to take it little by little."

She carefully guides me so that I'm lying down and suddenly weightless. My muscles lighten up with it.

"Do you want to borrow my grounding stone?" she asks.

"Maybe. If I knew what that was."

She smiles. "It's something that literally connects you to the ground, to the earth, and that energy helps you stay centered. You have to play around with it a little. Some people like to breathe into it. Amethyst is my favorite."

She opens her palm to reveal a small purple crystal.

I instantly recognize it.

She places the amethyst in my hands, and I curl my fingers

around the deep, purple ridges, a few of those missing pieces about Brooke snapping into place. Her . . . Cynthia . . . *Dad* . . .

"Are you okay?" She can probably hear my heart racing.

Breathe. I close my eyes and let myself forget everything back home. A few seconds later my pulse slows back down. Maybe she's on to something with this aerial yoga situation.

"You can't let it only live *here* all the time." She puts her hands on the top of my head. "You need to find some techniques that let you release it. Like this . . ."

I shift my weight and hear Cynthia yelp. I twist over onto my stomach, do a full somersault, and land with the sling wrapped around half my body. Cynthia's eyes are wide, but it's hard to tell if she's impressed or extremely embarrassed for me.

She helps untwist me from the sling, as if I'm a tetherball. "Okay, maybe aerial yoga isn't the best release for you. But I'm sure we can find something that is."

I start to laugh, and then she does, and this time, her dimple doesn't bother me.

15

If anyone's ever worried about having a blah Fourth of July, they should immediately book a trip to Two Harbors. It's like a red, white, and blue tsunami swept through here last night. Every boat in the harbor is fully decked out. Patriotic pennants line the beach, and the water is full of people lounging on inner tubes and floats.

A volleyball whizzes by my head, and I duck behind a rack of life vests. Ben runs past me to catch it, and I take a step back in case another fist bump is coming my way. I refuse to let myself wonder what happened between him and that girl from USC after I left the restaurant last night. I need to be spending less time focused on him and more time focusing on myself. Period.

He tosses the ball to Lucy, who laces her fingers together and barely pops it over toward Curtis. They've been practicing all morning for their big game this afternoon against the counselors. If their pathetic attempt at passing is any indication, they are about to get their asses handed to them.

"It's almost game time," Lucy announces after another failed rally. My stomach instantly fills with butterflies, the Pit stirring to life, which is ridiculous, since I'm not even playing. I'm not even planning to *watch*. I was going to use the half hour we had off to slip away and grab some food.

Suddenly an earthquake of sound erupts, and in the distance I spot a herd of campers marching down the trail toward the beach, chanting "We Will Rock You."

"That's obnoxious," I comment as I spot Berk leading the pack. I have a strong feeling they'll be singing "We Are the Champions" on the way home.

Lucy just grins and bumps the ball in the air to herself. "You coming to watch, Abby?"

I could make an excuse right now. Or . . .

Baby steps.

I follow the three of them down the beach to the volleyball court I've been avoiding for weeks. The nerves in my stomach increase with each step. I haven't been this physically close to the court since I got here. But as I approach it, it's oddly anticlimactic. Nothing happens. My nerves don't dissipate, but they don't explode, either.

I settle into a spot right in front and shift in the sand, struggling to get comfortable. After several failed attempts, I give up. It's being on the sidelines that feels weird.

Lucy, Ben, and Curtis warm up on the court, which mostly consists of them joking around and chasing after the ball. Meanwhile, across the net, Berk, Sanchez, and a female counselor wearing red, white, and blue wraparound sunglasses are taking it much more seriously. The campers are pumped up on the sidelines, already cheering, "Berk, Berk, Berk!"

Maybe it's because of the crowd beginning to form, making it feel like a real game with actual stakes, but a rush of competitive excitement slices through me.

"Warming up for a big game of cheering, Abby?" Berk calls out. I look down and see that I've instinctively begun doing my usual pregame stretch, pulling one arm in front of me one way while I twist my body the other. What I really want to do is smack the smug smirk right off Berk's face, and for a quick second, I look over to Ben, Lucy, and Curtis and debate joining them. I have no doubt they'd be thrilled for the extra help.

But it's *baby* steps. It's enough that I'm even sitting here. What I don't need is for the Pit to rip open wide like a crater as a hundred people watch me try to spike a ball.

The counselors win the coin toss, and the girl throws up a sloppy serve that flies just over the net toward Curtis. He jumps up and spikes it hard.

Right into the net.

I cringe, squeezing my fists together. He jumped way too soon. If he'd taken off two seconds later, he would've been on top of the ball and nailed it.

The next two plays are no better.

When it's 5–0, I uncurl my fists, and my nails have left a cluster of U-shaped indentations in my palm. My words of encouragement are drowned out by the campers chanting, "Scoreboard, scoreboard!" We have to turn this around. Curtis, Ben, and Lucy might not care about winning, but for some insane reason, I do.

Berk's next serve falls deep to Lucy, and she miraculously manages to bump it to Curtis, who seems to accidentally dink the ball over the net. Sanchez dives and misses, and it's finally side out. Beach hut's serve.

Ben tosses the ball up and claps it with his palm. Since he didn't follow through, there's no topspin, and it bounces right off Sanchez's arms and back to the beach hut side. Curtis is closest to the ball, dives for it, and whiffs it.

"Time-out!" Curtis yells, his voice strained. He gets up from the sand, but he's clutching his right hand. The three of them congregate right next to me on the sideline to examine it.

I leap up and take a closer look. "What happened?"

Curtis tentatively lets go of his right hand, which is beet red. "I jammed my thumb."

"Oh shit." Ben's eyes widen. "Are you okay?"

Curtis shakes his hand out, massaging it. "I think so. But . . ."

He doesn't need to say anything more. Curtis can't risk injuring his hand in the middle of his kiteboard training, especially not over something like this.

Ben claps his shoulder. "Don't worry about it. We'll forfeit." He arches an eyebrow at me. "Unless you want to play, Abby?"

I'm about to say no, but there's a tingling in my fingertips I haven't felt in *weeks.*

"Don't force her if she doesn't want to," Lucy says. "Forfeiting and getting our asses kicked is kind of the same thing, anyway."

I gasp. "No, it's not! Forfeiting is much worse than losing."

The counselors are staring us down from across the court. "Are we ready, guys?" Sanchez yells out.

Ben shifts the volleyball between his hands as he watches me. "What's it going to be, Abby?"

The energy from my fingertips spreads through my entire body. I'm practically vibrating. Before I know what I'm doing, I grab the ball from Ben. "I'll play for Curtis," I hear myself say.

Berk is near the net, and he immediately starts trash-talking. "Ooh, Abby's on the court now. The so-called secret weapon . . ."

I ignore him. Sanchez is up to serve, so I move up a few inches. When his hand smacks the ball, I can tell it's headed exactly where I predicted. I explode straight up and slam my palm into the ball. It lands with a resounding thud on their side of the net.

Ben turns to me, eyes wide and surprised, like he's trying

to decide if this was a fluke or not. "Wow. Good one." Lucy openly stares at me like I'm Wonder Woman.

"Side out!" is all I say, as if the reason they're gaping at me is because they're confused about whose ball it is. But it's my serve now, and I'm in the zone.

I step into position and spin the ball in my hands. It's my serving ritual, and also my chance to preview the other team's setup. I bend my knees and toss the ball into the air. As soon as my palm connects with it, it blasts over the net like a missile and lands exactly where I wanted: on the sand between the girl and a completely shell-shocked Berk.

Ace. And I haven't even warmed up. Hot *damn,* that feels good. I think I found that stress relief Cynthia was talking about.

I slam another serve over the net with even more heat than the first one. This time I aim for the top of Berk's head, knowing he'll panic. As soon as he realizes the ball is coming straight at his face, he wildly throws his arms up. His fingers graze the bottom of the ball, and it shoots way out of bounds.

Lucy gawks at me. The campers have quieted down. Ben blinks several times. From what I know about him, this means I've rendered him speechless—a rarity.

It takes six serves for the counselors to finally return one. It's not pretty, but Sanchez manages to get the ball over the net. I'm ready for it, though.

"I got it!" I yell, and cushion the impact of the ball on my forearms. "Lucy!" I pass it to her, and she bumps it back over. The ball sails back and forth a few more times for the longest rally of the game. Unfortunately, it ends with Ben spiking the ball a millimeter out of bounds. Side out. Their serve, but we're now winning by two points.

Berk is up. He's stopped trash-talking, and I catch him licking his lips nervously. I rub my hands against my knees with more excitement than I had during our championship game last year. I take a step forward and crouch into position as he tosses the ball into the air. Too easy. I spike it hard cross-court, and the counselors scramble uselessly.

Side out. Lucy's serve.

"Abby!" Lucy shout-whispers. "I thought—"

"Take two steps back," I cut her off, handing her the ball. "And aim more for the bottom of the ball when you punch it."

Lucy nails the ball exactly where I told her, and it's a great serve. We win another point and then another. I'm shocked a few minutes later when Curtis calls out that it's already game point. Ben's up to serve. He turns to me with an inscrutable expression. "Any pointers?"

"Rotate your hips and pound it harder."

His lips twitch. "Are we still talking about volleyball?"

I hurl the ball to him, a laugh escaping me. "Let's see what you've got."

He backs up, then tosses the ball up into the air and smacks it dead in the center.

I move closer to the net because Berk has a predictable

spike I've been dying to block the entire game. Adrenaline shoots through my body. Right before he jumps I meet his gaze, then I fire up like a rocket, and we meet at the top of the net. Just as he tries to spike, I stuff it right back over to his side. The ball drops to the sand next to him.

We win. I pump my fist as I jump up, before Lucy and Ben both rush me, like we just won an Olympic gold medal. When we finally pull away, Curtis barrels over. "Abby, you were on fire!" I got five whole words from him. And he didn't even call me "New Girl." I take this as yet another win.

Lucy and Curtis go on a victory lap, high-fiving everyone on the sidelines, and I'm inclined to join them, but Ben stays put.

"That was kind of amazing." His eyes search my face, as if he's trying to crack open a safe. "Why didn't you want to play before?"

I blurt out the most plausible reason that pops into my head. "I thought it might be obnoxious." I pause, then add, "I'm actually playing for Colorado in the fall." The words feel almost true for the first time in a long time.

Ben's brow furrows as he recalibrates this information with what he already knows about me. "You're just full of surprises." His eyes settle on mine in a way they haven't since we kissed, and I quickly blink away.

"Are you watching the fireworks with us tonight?" I ask. Lucy invited us all to watch from her mom's porch.

"Of course. Where else would I go?"

I shrug, pretending I'm not on a serious fishing expedition

here. "I didn't know if you already had plans with your family or . . ." I stop myself from asking him out loud about the girls from USC.

He gives me a look, like he can see straight through me. "No. No other plans."

I know it shouldn't matter, but my victory smile returns.

I'm still on an adrenaline rush from the game when I get home that evening. I take a long shower, mentally replaying a highlight reel. When I get out I even catch myself grinning in the fogged-up mirror, which is ridiculous. It was a random beach game with zero stakes, other than pride.

But out there I actually felt like *me*. The version of myself before the envelope. It's like the game untwisted one of the knots in my stomach and cracked open a little more space to breathe.

My laptop stares at me from the desk, like a puppy that's been neglected far too long. It may start whimpering soon. I have a few minutes before we're all meeting back up to watch the fireworks, and I'm suddenly inspired to get at least one task out of my mental "Deal with Later" pile. Maybe it's another baby step that will release even more breathing room.

After waiting the requisite five minutes for my browser to whirl to life, my in-box appears on the screen. I quickly type "COLORADO" in the search bar.

Nine emails pop up.

Nine.

How did I miss that many? Okay, I know how.

The first few emails are automatic ones from the registrar, with subject lines like "MISSING DOCUMENTS." But the most recent one is a personal email sent by my new coach herself.

Crap.

I take a breath and click it open.

Hi, Abby,

I just got word from the Head of Athletics that your registration paperwork has not been completed. Are you still planning on attending Colorado as part of our team? If your plans have changed for next year, please let me know immediately.

These forms must be turned in by Friday, or the school will cancel your enrollment and you will have to forfeit your spot on the team.

Best,
Coach Jacobson

My heart races as I click back to the other emails I missed. Housing forms, legal forms, financial forms. They'd actually sent me most of these documents after spring break, and I'd planned to deal with them—you guessed it—*later.* Like after I'd gotten my results and could really focus.

So that never happened.

I click back to Coach Jacobson's email. The deadline to send back these documents is Friday. Two days away.

Are you still planning on attending Colorado?

Of course I am.

Her question throws me off-kilter, though; like it's calling my previous decision into question. I know I've been procrastinating sending these forms since I got here, but that was just because I didn't have the mental bandwidth to deal with it.

Right?

The knot that the volleyball game untwisted coils itself back inside the Pit.

When I decided to go to Colorado, I didn't have all the facts I do now. What if part of me has been wondering this whole time if college still *is* the right choice for me?

If that envelope means that I'm supposed to change things?

My phone jingles incessantly with the hut text chain.

I can't pretend to be dazzled by fireworks. I'll make up an excuse. That's my less guilt-inducing word for "lie."

After weeks of pushing away all thoughts of my future, I now have two days to decide what my next four years will look like.

Cue hyperventilating.

"Okay, breathe," Nina says after I've miraculously gotten her on the phone a few minutes later. I catch the undercurrent of bass in the background; she's stepped outside of some kind of club to talk to me. "Why do you think you shouldn't go? I mean, I know why, but what specifically?"

I hesitate. I need to talk to *someone* about this, but with Nina, or anyone else, so far I've only succeeded in talking *around* HD. Once I open the door with this college mess, will the other question marks I've been ignoring about the future begin to fall like dominoes?

"I just wonder if it's worth four whole years of my life being stuck in a classroom or on a volleyball court if . . ." The words catch in my throat.

"You don't know how many you have left?" Nina finally supplies softly.

"Honestly, yeah. If symptoms start hitting me when I'm thirty-five, I don't know if I'll get a chance to have a real career. Isn't that why you go to college?"

"No, that's why you go to grad school."

I smile in spite of myself.

"I thought we were going to college to make a lot of extremely bad decisions together," she tempts me.

"We *were* . . ." Outside the window I can hear the fireworks show starting.

"What if symptoms *don't* start as early as you think? What if they don't come until you're almost sixty?" Nina's basically as much of an expert in this disease as I am. "That's a long way away. Then what?"

"Then I'll regret not going to college and having a career." I fall onto the bed and curl myself up around a feathery pillow. "So basically, it's down to guessing what I'll regret the least."

Nina is silent. I think of all the plans we made about living together, the dorm room décor, the fantasies we've indulged for months of what it would be like. What it would *still* be like if that envelope had said anything else.

Or if I hadn't opened it at all.

"This is so fucking shitty." I've never said it out loud. I think I might finally cry, but the muscles in my neck cramp up instead. "I hate this."

"I know. I'm so fucking angry, too." Nina's voice cracks. "I couldn't even go to church with my grandparents because I didn't trust myself not to start screaming at the priest that it's all bullshit."

Somehow her anger makes me feel better, not worse. "What should I do?"

"Selfishly, I want you there with me, but I get it if it's not what you want right now."

"I don't *know* what I want anymore. Or what I'm supposed to want."

She lets out a small sigh. "Look, none of us have a clue what's in store for us, right? But if you spend all your good years focused on the bad years, then you've kind of defeated the point of them."

I close my eyes, knowing she's right. We're both silent.

"Are your eyes closed?" Nina finally whispers.

"Yes."

"Good. Then you know I'm right."

16

The next day as I smile at customers, hand out fins, and lead groups to palapas, my conversation with Nina swirls in my mind the entire time. I don't want to focus on the bad years, but shouldn't I at least consider them?

When Man-Bun Marcus delivers my favorite strawberry lemonade and Ben's usual of club soda and fresh grapefruit juice from the bar, I'm surprised there's only fifteen minutes left till closing. I guess existential crises really make the day go by fast. Or maybe it's the ticking clock in the back of my brain. When there's a deadline, suddenly days sneak past you, slippery and fast, impossible to hold on to; like a fish in a tide pool.

Is that how my *life* is going to start to feel at some point?

Ben sidles up next to me to file the day's receipts. He's close, but not *too* close, stopping short of even miniscule physical contact. Still, I get that instant jolt to the veins I always do when he's near me.

I think it's better if we're friends.

That's what I said. And that's what we are.

"So, what's wrong?" he probes out of nowhere.

I take a long sip of lemonade to buy time. "What do you mean?"

"You've been chewing the inside of your cheek all afternoon."

It's deeply unsettling spending hours with someone as observant as Ben, though if I'm being honest, there's also something . . . *intoxicating* about it.

"I don't know," I stall. "I was just thinking about things. . . ."

"Things? Like what?" His eyes narrow, almost imperceptibly, and he gives me the side smile. It's about damn time. *Please* let that mean the post-kiss weirdness between us has finally faded.

Suddenly, our conversation in the kayak about fate pops into my head and the words tumble out. "If you knew you were going to get hit by a bus at forty, would you still go to college?"

His eyebrows rise in surprise. "Why are you asking me that right now?"

Shit. I should've kept my mouth shut. Just because I can finally sort of talk about HD with Nina, doesn't mean I'm ready to spontaneously bring it up with Ben. Hence, my bus analogy. "It's a dumb question. Never mind."

"No, it's not. It's just . . . weird you're bringing it up *now.*" He disappears somewhere in his mind he hasn't let me see, and I forget about my own shit for a moment. "I've had the same question in my head all week."

I was *not* expecting that. He moves toward the palapas, and I follow him. "About if a bus was going to hit you?"

"Not that exact same question. Just the college part."

"Are you thinking about not going to USC?"

"Some things changed." We begin clearing out a palapa, moving the chairs back to their original positions. "I got an email from the assistant director of that documentary I worked on."

It was on one of our less busy, middle-of-the-week two-mans that Ben told me about the documentary crew his film teacher managed to connect him with at the beginning of senior year. They were shooting a documentary about the opioid epidemic and lack of rehab beds in San Francisco, and Ben got to tag along as their production assistant in exchange for school credit.

"They're about to shoot another one." He lifts up a small table to return it to its place, and his muscles flex like their sole purpose in life is to distract me. "There's a new rehab in New Hampshire that's trying this unconventional treatment for heroin addiction. They're going to do a mini-doc about it, and they offered me a job."

"Seriously?" My jaw hangs open.

"I mean, not like a real job. A production assistant, like I was last time. It's low budget so low pay, but I'd get a shitload of experience."

"When did this happen? Why didn't you tell me?" I feel a pang of possessiveness, like I should've been the first to know. *Hypocrite,* I chastise myself.

"Last week. Out of the blue. And you're actually the only person I've told so far."

"Oh." I pretend this doesn't send a thrill through my body.

"This documentary could be huge. It's hard to pass up being part of something that could actually save lives." He speaks quickly, fervently, his words running together. "And then on a purely selfish level, won't I learn a lot more helping to *make* a film than I will sitting in a classroom *hearing* about it?"

"What if you deferred for a year?" I suggest, wishing I had that option. If I miss this deadline, I give up my spot on the team and have to reapply to college all over again. No guarantees.

"I've thought about it. But who knows what will happen between now and then?" He leaps down to the sand from the palapa. "I could get hit by a bus."

He reaches out his hand to me, and the second I grab it, little bonfires flare under my skin. He pulls me up to stand, and I hold on to his hand a few seconds longer than I probably should.

"What about you?" He steadies his eyes on me. "Are you suddenly questioning your pedestrian safety, or is this about Colorado?"

"Not Colorado specifically." We meander across the sand, and I formulate my words carefully. "It's more that I didn't realize what a huge decision it was when I accepted. It goes way beyond the next four years."

"I mean, yeah. I get it. It's the first life-changing decision we've ever had to make."

Life-changing.

He latches the padlock to the hut and tosses me an oar. The sun is still high in the sky, but its strength has dissolved, leaving just a shell of warmth on the empty beach. We tread down to the shore, where a kayak is waiting for us.

"You're saying you want to make your days count," he finally says.

Yes. "Um, that's not exactly what I said—"

"But that's what you meant by my death-by-bus fate, right? Which, by the way, seemed unnecessarily brutal." The glint in his eyes cranks up my body temperature.

"I bet you never jaywalk again."

He stops right next to the kayak, leaning against his oar. "What do you want *right now*?"

He refuses to take his eyes off mine.

I turn my attention to the kayak because it's too hard to look at him straight on. It's like being locked in a jail cell with a beautiful view. "I don't know."

"I just think most things come down to that in the end. Or they should. What we want in that moment. I don't have any scientific proof or anything, but it seems like you regret things way less if you do what you want, without letting all the other bullshit cloud your decisions."

We slide the kayak into the water, our paddle strokes immediately in sync.

We're halfway through the narrow entrance of a wide cave, like we're diving inside the mouth of a sleeping beast, when Ben asks, "So, if you don't go to college, then what would you want to do instead?"

I freeze midpaddle. As much as I've debated the choice today, I haven't even considered the alternative. "I have no idea."

"You must have at least thought about it."

I stiffen and grip the oar tighter. Only now do I realize how fundamentally different our situations are. Ben has two equally great options and is trying to figure out how to get the best of both worlds. I'm scrambling to find *any* option that feels right.

Light crisscrosses through the rocks as we emerge from the cave, the water shimmering around us, like it's laced with jewels. It suddenly feels infinite—how many corners of the Earth there are, little magical pockets like this one that I never even knew existed before a month ago.

"I want to see more of the world." I pause, sifting through a pile of words to find the right ones. "Before I can't."

"You mean, because of a job and family and stuff?"

I'm grateful we're in the kayak so he can't see me wince. "Right." I suddenly drag my oar out of the water. "Hold on."

Ben stops paddling. "What's up?"

151

I can't explain this sudden urge I have to *do* something, *feel* something, anything, different today. I may not have all the answers, but I know what I want. Right now.

"I want to swim back."

"Is it something I said?" Ben jokes, not realizing how close he is to the truth.

"Nope. I just want to try it." I stand carefully and shimmy out of my shorts and tank quickly, catching his eyes on me as I do. They flash with a raw urgency that transports me back to the porch, his hands around my waist, his lips on mine . . .

Now I have a second reason to jump off this kayak. I need to get out of here before I do something stupid.

"We're a half-mile from shore," he tells me.

"I'll be fine."

Before he can say anything else, I step onto the seat and dive into the sea.

The water is cool and delicious on my sweat-soaked skin. I focus on my breaths, calibrating them, feeling the way my pinkies first slice through the water with each stroke, my legs powering me like a motor. I've always taken swimming for granted. That my body would just know what to do. When will the day be that I suddenly can't make my legs kick like that anymore? Will I know it's the beginning of the end?

I can sense that Ben is kayaking behind me, keeping close in case I need help, but I don't look back and I don't stop until I reach the shore.

When he glides in a few seconds later, I help him beach

the kayak, as if me jumping ship was a totally normal thing to do.

"You know," Ben starts, and I can tell whatever he's about to say, he's been mulling over since I deserted him. "I think if something is important enough to you, you'll get to it at some point. Even if it happens later. After college or kids or whatever."

I stop pulling the kayak and stand to face him. "But if you wait until later, it might not be up to you anymore. Sometimes things happen that turn your entire life upside down. And it doesn't matter what you do or how you fight it because you have zero control."

I'm out of breath and wait for him to say something, but he's looking through me, as if his brain is a million miles away. He must feel my eyes because he gives a quick smile, like he's been caught.

"You're right." He keeps his voice light, but it's impossible not to hear the sadness underneath.

It never occurred to me that Ben—confident, joking, happy Ben—might have secrets of his own.

17

Before

"*A*re you feeling suicidal?"

I still wasn't used to the fact that this was how Dr. Gold now started all of our sessions.

"No," I reply, adjusting the pillow behind my back. Today was a one-on-one session, and the loveseat felt too big without Brooke sharing it.

He waited until I got comfortable before he continued. "Now that we're getting closer to the end of the counseling period, I wanted to check in about testing. If you still want to move forward . . ."

"Yes. That's what we decided." Had a few doubts popped up into my head from time to time? As Dr. Gold would say, *Sure.* But the stress of these past few months was only getting worse. "It feels pointless to drag it out. I don't want this hanging over my head forever."

"Sure. But you *could* decide to hold off until the end of college, at least," he suggested reasonably. "I just want to throw that out there as an option again."

"Is that when most people do it?"

His eyebrows converged as he pushed his Warby Parker glasses up the bridge of his nose. "Most people choose not to take the test at all. Only about ten percent of those at risk go through with testing."

"Why?" I croaked. How was that the one statistic Brooke had never mentioned?

"Mainly because there's nothing you can do. You can't get a surgery, do chemo, remove an organ. It's a hard reality to face." One thing I liked about Dr. Gold was that he didn't pull any punches. People don't take the test because they're scared the result will fucking suck. What more was there to say?

"The question is how much knowledge you want at this point. Because if you go forward, it's a decision you'll never be able to reverse."

For the record, one thing I hated about Dr. Gold was that he didn't pull any punches.

I charged into Brooke's room that night to find her perched on her well-worn desk chair, an HD message board lit up on her laptop screen.

"Did you know most people choose *not* to get tested?"

"Yes. Of course I know." She continued scanning the messages, her tone clipped and edgy, like it had been the last few weeks. Maybe she regretted dropping the semester so she could "actively process this" since we can't *actively* do anything until we get our results.

"Dr. Gold said ninety percent of people don't choose to test," I repeated. "That doesn't . . . make you think that maybe they all know something we don't?"

Apparently, this still wasn't surprising enough information for Brooke to warrant eye contact with me versus the HD blog. "I think that data is skewed. There was a lot more stigma attached to HD years ago. I bet if they just controlled for younger people, the percentage who test would be higher."

I was about to argue further, but her pencil-straight posture was wilting before my eyes. This was exactly what she'd warned me about. Fighting, arguing. We needed to be a united front, and it's not like I sauntered in here flashing a peace sign.

She finally looked up and exhaled, uncurling her hands from tight fists. In her left palm was a small purple crystal.

"That's pretty," I commented, hoping it might supply me with the subject change we needed.

"Thanks." Her cheeks colored.

"Where did you get it?"

"I can't remember."

She dropped it in her desk drawer next to the small orange-

and-white bottle of pills Dr. Gold prescribed after she had an anxiety attack last week.

She followed my eyes, her jaw tensing. "You know anxiety and depression can be an early symptom of HD, right?"

Was *that* what she'd been torturing herself over? "Brooke, no." I crouched down and wrapped my arms around her tightly. "Your anxiety isn't a symptom of HD. We're under a lot of stress. Anyone would feel this way."

"I know. It just scares me." She leaned into my hug, a few tears escaping out of the sides of her eyes. "What if that's why Dad left? Maybe he was feeling really depressed and didn't realize it was an early symptom. It explains why he did something so irrational."

Unlike me, Brooke's never stopped searching for reasons why Dad left.

"Plenty of people suffer from depression and manage *not* to abandon their children. Why are we even talking about him?"

She swivels back around to her laptop screen. "No one's asking you to forgive him, Abbs. But you should at least be able to *talk* about him."

I stretched back up. "Should I get the popcorn going?" Brooke had already agreed to watch a Hallmark movie with me if I let her yell feminist pointers to the main characters.

"Sure." She curled her lips into a joyless smile, and we trotted downstairs. I threw a bag of popcorn into the microwave, and we stood in front of it, dazed, watching the intense heat pressure the kernels until they finally exploded.

18

*E*very time we used to go out for ice cream, Brooke and Mom would get annoyed by how long it took me to pick a flavor. They each had their favorite, same thing every time, but I would drive the people behind the counter crazy, asking for sample after sample and hemming and hawing until Mom would say we were leaving if I didn't make the decision *in the next five seconds*. The stress of it would lead me to blurt out whatever was on the tip of my tongue, and I usually left wondering if I'd picked the wrong flavor.

I wake up the morning of the day my college decision is due with newfound sympathy for everyone in that ice cream shop. I still haven't figured anything out, and at this point, I'm annoyed with myself.

I'm done talking about it.

I'm done thinking about it.

And yet I'm paralyzed to pull the trigger one way or another.

Even though I technically have until five o'clock to turn in my forms, I was hoping to wake up this morning with a gut feeling of what to do. Instead, my gut is torturing me with the silent treatment.

My phone dings a few times from the nightstand. The beach hut text chain is already blowing up because Ben, Lucy, Curtis, and I are going ziplining in Avalon today. It's one of the few days we all have off this summer while Tom mans the beach hut with the crew from Avalon. We figured we should do something fun to make it count.

I get out of bed, and the Pit of Doom pools in my belly ominously, like a thundercloud ready to wreak havoc. The house is dark and quiet when I peek my head out, Cynthia already gone for an early morning meal drop-off. I head into the kitchen, knowing I'll find a breakfast burrito or sandwich in the fridge. But the Pit looms too large.

Deep breath. No breakfast it is. Not even coffee sounds good.

I go back to my room, restless, my pulse picking up a bit. I'm supposed to meet everyone in an hour. In the meantime I should just focus on making this decision.

The problem is, neither choice feels entirely right.

Shut up, Dr. Gold. I know I walked straight into that one. But I'm onto him now. *There is no right or wrong* is a just a nice way of saying you can't win either way.

Nerves slosh in my stomach, and sweat begins to pool under my arms. I crack open the window to let in some breeze, but it doesn't help and I have to pull my hair up, fanning myself.

Maybe the fact that I'm feeling this stressed about the decision is a sign I'm not ready for college right now.

My chest tightens, and I keep fanning my face, sweat springing up along my forehead.

Or maybe it's a sign I just need to stop questioning things, stay on my original path so I can keep some semblance of normalcy for now.

My heart starts beating quicker, harder, like it's trying to break out of my chest. For a second I have the insane, fleeting thought that I want that grounding stone of Cynthia's.

I just need to make this decision.

How'd that last decision work out for you?

My knees buckle, and the room whirls around me like a carousel. I reach out and grab the wall for support, trying to catch my breath—it's suddenly coming so fast.

Outside. I hop out the window to my usual spot, trying to take in a few deep breaths, but they're coming up short and spiky, bristling against my lungs, as if they're covered in thorns. I close my eyes to steady myself, and the memory of the envelope fills my brain. . . .

I'm back in Dr. Gold's office, that last moment I had, the moment his fingers pressed against the seam, about to tear it open.

I had one more second. The words almost made it out.

And then it was too late.

He ripped the paper from the envelope and looked me right in the eye. "I'm sorry Abby. Your test is positive with a repeat of forty-two."

Positive.

Dr. Gold's eyes, full of apologies. Brooke's shocked inhalation. Mom's body shaking against mine, both of them crying like I was already dead.

My eyes pop open again. My knees give way, and I slide to the floor. I can't catch a breath. The more I try, the less I can. *What the fuck is happening?* My heart pounds mercilessly, another breath too short, the world closing in on me as darkness seeps into the edges of my vision. I need to call for help, but I can't. I can't breathe.

Pure terror clutches me. *I'm having a heart attack.*

"Abby." I lift my head up to find Chip running toward me. He crouches down, his eyes full of concern. I need to explain to him, but my heart is racing, my air supply too tight.

"Can't . . . breathe," I eke out. "ER."

"Abby, look at me." His eyes bore into mine. "You're going to be okay. I'm here."

He's too calm. Why is he just sitting here when he should be calling 911, getting help? I gasp out another short breath. "I . . ."

"Don't talk." He keeps looking me right in the eye, speaking matter-of-factly. "You're having a panic attack. That's all this is."

I want to argue with him, but I can't get the words out. He gets right down next to me and grabs my hand, holding it tight. "There's only one way to get through this, and that's deep breaths. I'm going to help you, okay? Take a deep breath . . ."

I'm wheezing, practically choking. I can't do it.

"We're going to do it together, Abby. Just count with me. Breathe in for seven, and out for eleven. Let's try again. In for seven . . ."

I'm able to inhale for a few seconds, the exhale scratching out of me too fast before I hungrily try to suck down another breath.

"Again." He counts it out for me, his eyes glued to mine. "That's right. Keep breathing like that. That's all you have to do."

I do what he says. I only focus on the breath.

One two three four five six seven . . . and exhale.

"I'm staying right here," he tells me, his voice steady. "I'm not going anywhere."

One two three four five six seven . . . and exhale.

"You're okay. You're in a safe place. I've got you."

One two three four five six seven . . . and exhale.

On and on we go like this. Eventually, the breathing gets a little easier. I pick my head up, the sweat turning cold on my back as I continue counting my breaths. The abject terror has left.

After a few more minutes, my breathing almost fully regulates, my heart no longer jumping out of my chest. It's like a small miracle.

Chip never breaks his focus from my eyes, his hand still clutching mine. "That's right. You're okay."

I nod, still breathing deeply. I've somehow made it to the other side.

Which is the cue for embarrassment to wash over me.

I look up at him. "Chip . . . I . . ."

"Everyone has their shit, Abby. Everyone has their own darkness."

We sit there like that for a while—maybe five, ten minutes—until I feel almost fully back to normal. In fact, I can't believe *how* normal I feel, considering I was just lying on the ground, convinced I couldn't breathe. It's like when Mom steps in the doorway of my room after I've frantically cleaned it, with no trace of the chaos that lived there only moments ago.

Chip finally releases my hand. "Thank you," I tell him, my voice a little shaky. It feels tragically inadequate.

"I'm happy I was here. Those are hard to come out of alone."

"How did you even . . . know I was out here?"

"Shanti." I finally notice Shanti through the window. "She led me right to you."

First Chip saving the day, now Shanti. I burst out laughing, which surprises me, but Chip smiles. "Good. There you go. I always feel relieved once these pass too." He's right. I've got a slight buzz, like I've just taken an espresso shot or come off an intense volleyball victory.

My phone vibrates next to me, one ding after another.

"Are they expecting you at work right now?" Chip asks.

"No, I'm supposed to go ziplining with everyone. I probably shouldn't now, though."

"Why not?"

"Um, because I just had a panic attack?" I know if it were Cynthia, she'd suggest staying home and taking a therapeutic Himalayan salt bath.

But Chip is cut from a different cloth. "It's done now. You're okay, Abby. Go clear your head and fly through the trees. The expression 'free as a bird' exists for a reason."

Shanti tactfully does not comment on the obvious irony.

I make it to the Cyclone, the high-speed boat that treks between Two Harbors and Avalon, a few minutes before it's due to leave.

Ben spots me from his seat in the front row of the boat with Lucy and Curtis. When he stands up to let me by, his white T-shirt stretches across his chest tightly, and our bodies practically press against each other. His eyes find mine, I have the weirdest impulse to just stay here awhile and hold on to him.

Maybe I'm exhausted from my roller coaster morning, or

maybe the panic attack somehow chipped away the top layer of my impulse control, but before I know what I'm doing, my head finds his shoulder and my body connects to his.

It's like sinking into bed after a long day. His chest stiffens in surprise before he relaxes, his hand softly resting against the small of my back. We've had almost no physical contact since our kiss, and I wonder if he's missed this as much I have.

The Cyclone engine roars to life, and the moment is over far too soon.

I take the empty seat between him and Lucy, but that half second of contact has suddenly left me craving more. My body seems to lean all on its own until it rests against his.

He looks down at me for a full beat.

"You okay?" His eyes narrow as he studies my face.

"Yeah," I reply casually, and nestle slightly closer. *No big.* It's nothing a *friend* wouldn't do. A few seconds later, I feel a quiet rush when his arm settles around my shoulder. I've started a game I probably shouldn't have, but it feels too good to stop now. He's a drug I can't stop chasing.

"Put your hair in a pony!" Lucy shouts to me over the engine. "Or it'll be in knots when we get there. This thing gets some serious speed."

"Wait—Abby's a Cyclone virgin?" Curtis asks, giving a rare grin as he leans forward from his spot at the end of the row.

I take the hair elastic Lucy hands me. "I'm an Avalon virgin, too."

The three of them share an amused look I can't decode. Like when I was little and Brooke and Mom talked about something way over my head.

"Avalon is a hot mess," Lucy rants, not for the first time.

"Hey there," Curtis says, mock offended. His family lives in Avalon most of the year. He just comes out to Two Harbors for the summers.

"A hot mess with a grocery store," Ben murmurs to me.

"Wait, what?" My eyes widen, and I'm instantly extremely present. "There's a grocery store? Like a real one?"

Ben flashes a smile, as if my ignorance is adorable to him. "And a movie theater. And a"—his voice drops like he's about to say something really disgusting—"spa."

I reel backward. "That's just wrong."

Lucy grins. "Congratulations. You're officially a Two Harbors girl, Abbs."

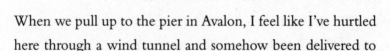

When we pull up to the pier in Avalon, I feel like I've hurtled here through a wind tunnel and somehow been delivered to an alternate universe.

"Take it in slowly, Abby," Ben half jokes. "You've been in Two Harbors for an entire month. This is a lot to absorb."

He isn't kidding. One restaurant after another line the block with trendy beach wedged in between. Tourists pour out of old-fashioned candy stores and ice cream shops. The smell of fish and chips lingers in the air like it's the official scent of Avalon. It's full sensory overload, the noise of it all screaming directly into my ear after spending a month in quiet Two Harbors.

"Wasn't I right?" Lucy waves her hands in the air. "Hot mess."

"Has everyone done this before?" Alex, the lead guide, asks us when we've all convened at the top of a mountain. We're at one of the highest points of the island, the zipline stretching across a deep canyon, dotted with shrubs and eucalyptus trees. Up here the landscape is peaceful and familiar again, not a souvenir shop in sight.

We all nod, and Ben leans into me, even closer than usual, with that knowing half smile and whispers, "Have you, really?"

Whatever game I started on the boat, Ben's ready to keep it going.

"Yes," I murmur.

"Did you learn this at camp too? Or is it actually something you've done for real?"

"For *real*," I hiss back. "Watch and learn."

We line up on the platform, and Alex double-checks our harnesses and helmets, while his partner, Aron, breezily hops on the zipline and sails over to the other side. The two of them are buddies of Curtis, doing us a favor for the day, both of them young and surfer-ish meets rock climber.

"We're going to do the lines tandem today, so partner up," Alex tells us.

Ben raises an eyebrow at me, like it's a straight-up dare. "We doing this?"

Don't do it, Abby. Bad idea. "Sure."

"You going to be able to catch the rope at the end?" Ben asks me in a low teasing voice.

"You don't think I can catch the rope?"

His lip quirks slightly. "I never know what to think about you."

Alex straps us into what he claims is the most basic tandem position, which apparently means I'm on Ben's lap.

"Safest thing is for you to wrap your arms around her," Alex instructs Ben. "And Abby, you grip the handles. I'm cool with you taking one hand off, but not both. Unless you want to die."

My mouth drops open.

"Just kidding," Alex says in the least funny way possible.

We step to the edge of the platform, and Ben's fingers graze the top of my ribs as he rests them on my waist.

"Are you nervous?" His warm breath in my ear triggers a flutter through my stomach.

"No, why?"

"Your whole body just tensed up." His hands tighten

around my waist a little more, like he *knows* exactly what it is that's having this effect on me. It doesn't help that we're strapped into a contraption that could double as a sex swing.

"Nope, I'm good."

Alex radios to Aron that we're ready. "All right guys. Bon voyage."

I count to three, then Ben and I jump off the platform together.

The surge of adrenaline is immediate. Ben's hands grip tighter around my body, and the treetops whip by us in a blur. Chip was right. This is exactly what I needed after a morning on the ground. As I soak in the thrill of flying through the air, I must look like a dog with its head hanging out the window.

It's jarring when the handles suddenly smack up against the brake on the cable and we bounce back a few inches. I spot Aron on the platform, rope in hand.

"Catch it, and I'll pull you in," he calls.

"Don't miss," Ben murmurs low in my ear, soft as velvet, triggering another full wave of sensation through my body. Dammit, is he doing this on *purpose*?

I easily catch the rope. "I told you I've done this before," I gloat, and Ben laughs into my hair.

Once Aron pulls us in, we wait on the platform for Lucy and Curtis, and it's as if the adrenaline of our jump has peeled off yet another layer between us.

At least that's the way *I* seem to be feeling. I lean against him, my back firmly against his chest and stomach, and he wraps both his arms around me. I close my eyes for a second, soaking it in like sunlight.

"Guys?" Alex is calling out to us for our next turn. I straighten up and realize Lucy and Curtis have already come and gone.

We get hooked up to the line, and Ben and I jump off into the sky again. The chilly air sprinkles my arms with goosebumps, even though I'm warm with Ben's body pressed against mine.

"Look down," Ben says into my ear. The Pacific Ocean comes into view through the mountaintops. The water sparkles and shimmers, as if there are sapphires floating on top of it.

We glide off the line and onto the platform, our bodies still sticking to each other like magnets, the two of us continuing to pretend it's completely normal that his arms are still wrapped around me.

By the time we dive into our final line a few minutes later, everything falls out of focus, except for what's directly in front of me. This line is the longest, and we pick up more and more speed the farther we propel. I loosen my grip on the handles. Just a little. I take one hand off, and the flying sensation is even more intense.

I realize right away it's a bad idea.

My balance gets thrown, and the wind swings my body around to face Ben. I have no control over my legs when they suddenly lock around his body like handcuffs. We sail down the zipline, moving way too fast for me to untangle my body from his. I reach behind me with my free hand for the handles to use as leverage, but the force of the wind jerks my body forward instead. The momentum spins us in circles, and our bodies press closer together. When we hit the brake on the cable, our noses are touching, our eyes locking together.

Ben reaches his hand toward my face. For the second time today, I have full-on heart palpitations.

He's going to kiss me on the zipline.

And I want him to.

His hand reaches right over my head. It's now painfully obvious that his target is the rope. Not my face.

He catches it, and Aron drags us onto the platform. Lucy and Curtis seem thoroughly entertained by the last thirty seconds.

"That was some serious zipline porn," Lucy cracks.

Ben smirks. "Abby mentioned she was looking for a new career."

"I figured it was the next logical step after losing my Avalon virginity." I catch his eyes, and they're electric with something I can't put my finger on, something that makes my stomach dip nervously.

"Let's get you guys unharnessed," Aron interrupts. He releases us from our straps, our bodies no longer forced together. The sudden lack of warmth is like a quick jab to the ribs.

"I've got your phones," Alex calls, handing over the bag we dropped them in before we harnessed up.

When I spot the time on my phone screen, the lightness I felt on the lines steadily dims, reality creeping out of the hiding place I'd stuffed it in at the very back of my brain. College. The deadline. My stupid gut.

Plus, there are two missed calls and a text from Brooke.

I do my usual move of deleting without reading, but I accidentally catch a few words first . . . *you see the news?*

News? What news?

I'm now dying to retrieve the message, but this is probably a Brooke tactic to get my sudden attention. A text version of clickbait.

I scroll down to the other text I've missed, from Nina.

Nina: Did you see this??? Game changer? I feel like this might make your decision for you?

My pulse quickens. Maybe something actually did happen. Maybe Brooke wasn't just trying to bait me.

There's a website link to a CNN report, but like everywhere in Catalina, there's zero Wi-Fi here and not enough cell service to actually open it.

I spin to find Ben still beside me. "Is there Wi-Fi anywhere around here?"

"Not really. It's pretty bad across the island. Maybe you can find something at one of the fancier hotels."

I check the time on my phone again. The Cyclone leaves in twenty minutes. Not enough time to start running around finding hotels and begging for Wi-Fi scraps. I'll have to wait until we get back.

We trek toward the harbor, and I barely notice the shops and restaurants this time, my face glued to my phone, searching for random pockets of Wi-Fi and doing mental calculations. If the Cyclone gets us back by four, that still gives me an hour to figure out what this news is and to make my decision.

Finally, we reach the pier and I force myself to keep from racing down it. I still have time. There's no reason to freak out.

Until there is.

The Cyclone isn't at the dock.

"Did we miss it?" I cry frantically to no one in particular.

"Ah, crap. It's Friday," Lucy grumbles. "Having the day off screwed me up."

"Dammit." Ben scrubs a hand across his face. "Me too. Last one leaves at two on Fridays. It's done until tonight."

"So what does that mean?" *Deep breaths. Everything will be fine.* "How will we get back?"

"Safari Bus?" Curtis suggests.

My head spins. "That will take two hours!"

"Not to mention, the Safari Bus makes me want to hurl," Lucy adds unhelpfully.

I know I haven't made a choice about college yet, but I don't want to reject it by default because I'm stuck in Avalon. Especially if there's something Nina thinks will affect my decision. *Why did I think it was okay to cut it this close?*

Ben puts a hand on my shoulder, the touch jarringly intimate, and tugs me away from the group. "What's going on?"

His eyes are intent and focused, and for a second, they calm me, as if I'd just done one of Chip's deep breathing exercises. "I *really* need to get back to Two Harbors. Like, now."

He nods, not asking me a single question, then starts heading farther down the pier.

"Where are you going?" I call after him.

"Getting us a boat."

The pressure in my chest releases a bit. If we rent a boat, I could still get back in time. Hope seizes me as Ben enters the Avalon version of the beach hut.

"What did they say?" I pounce when he returns a few minutes later.

"I know the guy in there. He's got a powerboat, and he'll take us right now."

I exhale in relief, suddenly so giddy my impulse is to leap on Ben with a full-body hug. Instead, I pelt him with the biggest smile of my life. "You're amazing."

His side smile lights a match up and down my body. "I knew you'd realize that at some point."

A little over an hour later, the fire is out, and my hope has begun to wilt. By the time Ben's friend got the boat ready and herded us on, it was already past three thirty. Now it's approaching four thirty, and Two Harbors is still nowhere in sight.

"How much longer do you think it's going to take?" I whine to Lucy, like an annoying kid in a car. "We've already been on the boat for an hour. That's longer than it took us to get to Avalon."

"Right. That's because the Cyclone is a super-high-speed boat. It cuts the time in half." She consults the coastline, as if the rugged landmass jutting out gives her a clue of our location. "We probably have another forty-five minutes or so."

My heart jumps into my throat. I look back to the driver, willing him to *Go faster, go faster.*

At 4:50, I realize it's futile. I slump in my seat, the adrenaline of the day sucked out of me, leaving me just a dry, lifeless husk.

This is what I do. Let decisions happen around me instead of making them myself. The choice I've agonized about for the past forty-eight hours has suddenly been taken out of my hands.

The clock strikes five. And just like that, I'm not going to college.

19

I don't know if I'm happy or sad when Two Harbors finally comes into view.

Ben and Curtis hop out to tie up the boat, and three quick dings jangle from my phone. All the texts I've missed since we left Avalon. All from Nina.

> **Nina: Did you read it?!!**
>
> **Nina: Have you decided?**
>
> **Nina: ???? You're killing me.**

What is this link?

I clamber out of the boat with no explanation to anyone and rush down the pier, straight to the restaurant patio, the one spot where I can usually get a blip of decent Wi-Fi.

Yes. Here we go. I click open the attachment, waiting as it downloads, not moving an inch in case it messes up the connection. Finally, it pops up. An article from CNN.

A medical breakthrough for HD.

I blink until my eyes are clear enough to read every word of the article.

It's not a cure. Not yet. But it's still major. It's the first round of results of that drug Dr. Gold told us about, the one they started testing on people with HD, to try to prevent or reduce their symptoms.

And, apparently, it worked *even better* than the doctors thought it would. They're calling it the most promising research on HD in twenty-five years.

I focus on the last line. *If this drug continues to live up to its promise, it could be approved in the next fifteen years and curb up to eighty percent of HD symptoms.*

The next fifteen years.

Holy shit. No wonder Nina was blowing up my phone all day. If this drug is approved by then, *before* my symptoms are even supposed to hit . . .

I might get a chance for a mostly normal life after all.

Or, at least, closer to one than I thought. This drug could take me up into my sixties, almost symptom-free.

My legs give way under me, and I sit down in the nearest empty chair.

I've been so focused on whether my in-between years would be long or short, trying to guess how much time I had, what that meant for me, I never thought about the *what if* of a breakthrough like this.

A total game changer, says the lead scientist. The freaking *lead* scientist.

I look up through the blinding brightness of the light bulb that just exploded in my head. What if I *don't* need to change the entire course of my life because of that envelope?

Finally, I'm starting to grasp what Ben meant the other day. I need to do what I want right now, without letting anything else cloud it over. If I make every choice trying to guess what I think *might* happen with HD, I'll never get it right. I should keep living the way I would have before this envelope ever intruded. Starting with college.

The clock on my phone clouds the joy of this epiphany: 5:32 p.m.

The deadline has come and gone.

Disappointment hits the back of my throat, hot and bitter. I've realized what I want seconds after it's been taken away. Once again.

Something inside me snaps, though, my frustration with myself boiling over.

I sprint up the hill to Cynthia's as if my sneakers have jet packs attached to them, throw open the door, and run to my room, more empowered with each step. There's not a second of hesitation as I look up the email and dial the number at the bottom.

She picks up on the first ring.

"Coach Jacobson?"

"Yes?" Her voice is clipped, like her time is perpetually limited.

"Hi, this is Abby Freeman. I'm going to be a freshman on the team in the fall."

"Oh, hello, Abby."

I take a deep breath. "I'm sorry I didn't respond to your emails. I had to deal with some family issues that were . . . complicated."

"I'm sorry to hear that." Her voice is sandpaper. She doesn't soften at all.

"I feel horrible for missing the deadline to turn in my forms."

"Does that mean you still want to join us?"

"Yes." Silence. I'm not above begging if I have to. "I really, *really* do."

She sighs. "I know this can be a hard transition for some."

What does that mean? Is she saying I can still come or not?

"Listen, I think you'll be a good asset to our team. Our best outside hitter just graduated."

I hold my breath.

"How about this? I'll deal with the admin office if you get the forms into me tonight. No later, or my hands will be tied."

"Deal." I do a silent version of Lucy's happy dance. "Thank you, Coach Jacobson."

"See you in the fall, Abby."

As soon as I disconnect with her, I call Ben. He has a Wi-Fi hotspot he uses to transfer film files, and I have a feeling I'll need it to actually upload these forms.

"Can you come over?" I ask before he even gets out the second syllable of "hello."

"Now?" There's surprise in his voice, and I hear Lucy and Curtis chatting in the background.

"Um, as soon as you can? With that Wi-Fi hotspot thingy you were telling me about." He's silent for so long, I think he's hung up on me. "Hello?"

"What's up with you, Abby?"

"Please? I'll explain when you get here."

A half hour later, I hear Ben at the front door talking to Cynthia, and I bounce off my bed like it's a trampoline. I've already filled out all the forms; I just need the Wi-Fi hotspot so I can upload everything and send them.

"Thank you so much." I practically accost him the second we're in my room.

"No problem." He eyes me, cautiously reserved, as if he can't make sense of this bright, enthusiastic Abby in front of him. I don't blame him. I went from draping myself over him on the ziplines to freaking out to boisterous enthusiasm in the course of a few hours.

"Do you have the hotspot?" I sound jittery, like I've been waiting all night for my drug dealer.

"I brought it." He makes no move to hand it over.

He's not going to make this easy, but I respect his tactics. He's got leverage, and he's not going to waste it.

He folds his arms. "So, what's going on?"

For once I can give him the truth. At least most of it. "The deadline to turn my forms in to Colorado was at five o'clock today. So when we missed the Cyclone, I thought I'd lost my chance to go."

"And that's why you took off up the hill like it was a fifty-yard dash?"

"Yes. But I just called the volleyball coach, and she said it's all good if I turn everything in tonight."

His smile injects an unexpected warmth through my body. "Good for you, Abbs."

I clear my throat and reach out for the hotspot. "Can I?"

"The texts you got today. When we were pulling into Two Harbors . . ." Of course Ben noticed that. "Who were those from?"

"A friend . . . ?" We're on shakier ground now. How do I explain Nina's texts without everything else that comes with it? Or more so, explaining how much I haven't told him yet this summer?

"A friend." He nods slowly, his expression darkening.

"Yes, she's a friend," I clarify, and my face immediately

flushes, embarrassed by my sudden compulsion to establish that my "friend" is a girl.

He takes a step toward me. Close enough that it's impossible not to inhale his scent. Which I do. Cologne companies would kill to bottle his spicy-woods-and-salty-ocean combo. The electricity that's been circulating between us all summer blazes as he moves closer.

"Here you go." He holds out his hand.

I blink a few times. The Wi-Fi hotspot. Right.

I exhale deeply. *Focus.*

I sit at the desk and begin uploading all the documents. Ben lounges on my bed, elbows propped up behind him, watching me as I upload the forms, the tension crackling wildly between us in the silence, intensifying with each second that passes.

Finally, the last form uploads. I stand and turn to face him, my cheeks flushed. I hand him back the hotspot, and he tosses it onto the bed next to him, the energy whipping between us even more intensely now, like we're about to burst into flames. My body is trembling, but I don't know if it's on the inside or if he can see it. *Please be on the inside.*

He stands to meet me. "I've got one more question."

I'm about to tell him he's pushed his luck too far, but he takes another step closer so we're inches apart, and I forget how to speak.

His voice is low, but I hear every word. "Are you really not feeling this between us?"

I swallow. No guy has ever been this direct with me before. "Ben, it's . . ."

"It's what?" His eyes flash in frustration. "I can't figure you out, Abby. Sometimes it seems like you want this too. And other times . . . I can't get a read on you." His eyes drill into mine. "Just tell me, and I swear, if it's what you want, I'll leave you alone the rest of the summer." My stomach clenches at the thought of it. "Tell me what you want right now."

The only sound in the room is my heart thumping. I look up at him and lose whatever last shred of resistance I had. "You," I whisper.

His lips kick up in surprise just before I press my mouth to his, and the electricity that's been mounting between us since our first kiss combusts. He wraps a hand around my waist, the other sliding behind my neck, into my hair, pulling me closer to him, like now that he has me, he's not letting go.

"I have been wanting this all summer," he says into my ear, flooding my body with heat.

Every part of me is tingling, my mind blissfully abandoning all thoughts that aren't related to Ben's hands on my skin, his tongue against mine. It's like someone gave him a user's guide to my body that he stayed up late studying for days on end.

No one has ever made me feel like this.

I didn't know I *could* feel like this.

"Abby." Cynthia's voice rings from the other side of the house.

We break apart, and Ben's eyes are dark, a little wild. I'm sure mine look the same.

"Abby, I made you a turmeric latte," Cynthia calls out.

I have never been less inclined for a goddamned beverage in my life. "Just a sec." My voice is ragged and shaky.

Ben takes a half step back, both of us still breathing hard. "Fuck, Abby . . . that was . . ."

Insane. Life-changing. Fill-in-the-blank adjective that will never do it justice.

We look at each other for a few seconds, before I finally say, "I better go out there."

He nods and pulls me close one last time, his voice soft in my ear. "See you tomorrow?"

As we exit the room, my heart sinks just a little. Because I have zero doubt *that* was the kiss I will forever judge all future ones on.

20

The bounce in my step the next morning is probably visible from space. I saunter down my usual path from Cynthia's to the beach, my newfound optimism suddenly turning the whole island more vibrant, like I'm Dorothy from *The Wizard of Oz*.

"*Someone's* in a good mood," Lucy says as I enter the hut.

Out of the corner of my eye, I catch Ben's lips quirk. I mean, he's part of the good vibes, but not all of it. There was the matter of an earth-shattering medical breakthrough. *Egomaniac.*

We both play it cool in front of Lucy, barely acknowledging each other beyond hellos, and that's fine by me. I don't know exactly what our kiss last night unlocked, but I'm not going to start worrying about what this thing between us is—or isn't. I'm not going to start worrying about whether I can kiss him without telling him about HD when that may not even matter as much as I thought it did. If I learned nothing else yesterday, it's that I can't make choices in the *right now* if I'm stressing about how things *might* turn out later.

And *right now,* all I want to do is just roll with whatever happens with Ben and enjoy the ride.

The whole morning Ben and I do a fun little dance around each other.

He finds an excuse to put his hands on my hips as he walks behind me.

I innocently ask him to spray my shoulders with sunscreen and spend a few more seconds than needed when he asks the same.

I catch him watching me as I help a customer.

He catches me watching him as he hoists a kayak over his head.

"I need oars!" Lucy calls out to me that afternoon.

I zip behind the hut to grab them, and my heart rate instantly spikes. Ben is crouched down on the sand, gathering up the snorkel gear. It's the first time we've been truly alone all day, in the cool shade behind the hut, no eyes on us.

He looks up at me with that side smile. "Hi, there."

"Hey, yourself."

When he stands up, our bodies are practically touching,

and it's like I can't quite catch my breath. His eyes flick to the side quickly to confirm we're alone before he drops the bag of snorkels and lifts his arm, backing me against the wall of the hut, his palm splayed on the wood shingles.

It's so fast, I don't have time to overthink it. My body instinctively arches in response, my head tilting back and eyes closing. I expect to feel his mouth against mine, but his lips find my neck first, blazing a path to my jawline. I shiver despite the fact that it's a perfect seventy-eight-degree day and slide my fingers into his hair, pulling him close. Finally, he reaches my mouth, and I practically sigh in relief. The kiss starts gently, his other hand cupped against my cheek, but as his tongue swirls in my mouth, it turns hot and urgent so quickly, I get light-headed.

If last night's kiss was like a combustion of a month of tension, this one is more deliberate, inviting, teasing, as if he's giving me a detailed preview of all I have to look forward to this summer. *Yes, please.*

When Ben finally pulls apart from me, I can't for the life of me tell how long we've been back here. He keeps his arm up, my body still gently pinned, like we may start a second round of this, as if there isn't a line of people probably waiting for us on the other side.

And that's the precise instant that Curtis rounds the corner. He stops so suddenly when he sees us, sparks should be flying up from his heels.

There's no use denying what just happened. I can just

imagine what we look like—flushed cheeks, swollen lips, faces inches apart. Even if I wanted to, there's no getting out of this. No sidestepping and pretending Ben and I were *just talking, ha-ha*.

For a second I think we're about to get in trouble. Curtis is the manager, after all. But instead he breaks into a full grin. "Finally."

"Finally, what?" Lucy says, coming around from the front of the hut. Her eyes widen. At least Ben has the good sense to lower his hand from the wall, but instead of putting it at his side, he wraps his arms around my waist, pulling me close. Our bodies are on fire next to each other.

"Oh, you mean the heads have *finally* been removed from the arseholes." She turns to Curtis, gloating, and taps him on the chest. "It's before August, my friend. Pay up."

"Fine," he says, sighing. "Ten?"

"Please. You know we said twenty. I'll grab it from your wallet."

"Wait—you did an over/under bet on us?" I squeak, mortified at Ben and I being a conversation topic.

Lucy shows no remorse. "Of course. Another week or two, and you would've cost me. Thank god you all got it together."

Ben and I look at each other, and I'm sure my cheeks have permanently been stained red. Which Ben takes as license to lean in for one more kiss, this one quick and sweet and laced with affection.

"You guys are gross," Lucy gripes with a huge smile on her face.

The dynamic between me and Ben adds a new dimension to everything over the next few days. We still kayak, but now his hands graze my body as we get in and out. When we're all huddled around a bonfire, I lie against him, feeling his soft laughter on my neck. He'll take his phone out and film something, but the subject ends up being me more often than not.

I take a day off, and we spend it together, trekking down the no-access road that he swears we won't get in trouble for being on, and ending at a small, hidden, secret sliver of a beach. We glide into the water together, hands intertwined as we snorkel along the cove. Nothing but cool quiet as we float around practically weightless, like we're in outer space, except that everything is clear and blue and fish dart around the rocks as if they're playing hide-and-seek with us.

When we come back to the shore, we realize we forgot towels. I wedge myself in the warm sand, and Ben plants his elbows on either side of me, kissing every drop of salty water off my stomach, my arms, my neck, until the sky gets dark around us.

Our closeness somehow knits the four of us tighter together, too. At the end of the next busy weekend, we all stay on the beach long after we've closed. We blast the music and dance and jump in the sand, and Ben films us because it's magic hour, which means it's the time of day where the lighting is luscious and we look like the most natural, gorgeous versions of ourselves. He keeps the camera going as he pulls me in close and kisses me, the pink marshmallow sky behind us, and I wonder if anything will ever be as good as *this*.

I have a feeling when I look back at this part of the summer, these moments will always be extra bright, like over-exposed film, bursting with so much color that it all fades to bright.

21

Before

"The black will look better with the gown, but the nude works better with your dress, so you can really go either way. . . ."

It was day fifteen of the final three-week waiting period before Brooke and I could get our results. Our blood had been drawn. It was being tested for HD in a lab somewhere right now.

And Mom and I were talking about shoes.

"At least the black ones are flats," I pointed out. "One less thing to worry about with tripping as I cross the stage."

We'd just picked up my cap and gown and were headed for manicures, the last item on our list of errands before my graduation tomorrow.

"Wait—hold on." Mom turned her focus to the road, stressed out like always, whenever she approached the highway.

Mainly because she usually waited too long to get over and then couldn't edge her way in. Today was no exception. Two cars honked at her as she tried to snake into the lane. "Son of a beesting."

Once she was firmly merged onto the highway, she turned back to me. "Nina gave you her extra ticket, right? For Will?"

I nodded, trying to shake off the weird bitterness I hadn't felt in years. That this would be yet another milestone Dad had missed. After years of not caring, after not even giving him a second thought, his letter hadn't just opened up a new wound—it had ripped open an old one I thought was long scabbed over.

"I think I'm starting to hate him again," I admit, resting my head against the car window. "But worse. Worse than ever before."

Mom sighed quietly. "I get it, sweetie, I do. But this isn't his fault."

I bristled. "Seriously?"

"Genetically, yes, it's his fault. Everything that happened *before,* that's his fault. That he has this brilliant, gorgeous, wonderful daughter that he doesn't know, that's his fault."

"No arguments here," I muttered. Who else's fault would it be?

"And if you want to hate him for that, you have every right." She paused for a second, her eyes flicking to mine. "But he had no control over this HD gene." Her voice caught, and she looked away from me. "No more than you will when you get your results."

Suddenly my stomach plummeted, and I doubled over.

Mom shot a worried look my way. "Sweetie, what is it?"

"I don't feel good," I said in a quick burst. My grip tightened on the door, like I was holding on for dear life. She rolled down the window, to give me air, but it felt like we were racing down the highway at rocket speed, whooshing by trees and cars too fast.

Or was it everything else coming too fast? Graduation and blood tests and results envelopes. All these things that felt so far off months ago, and now we were hurtling straight toward them, the days ticking down before my eyes like a New Year's Eve countdown, the ghost of Dad lurking in the background.

Mom crossed three lanes of traffic until we were safely pulled over on the shoulder. "Take a few sips." She passed me her water bottle, but I couldn't bring it to my mouth, my hands were shaking too bad.

"Oh, sweetie, I know." A few tears snuck down her cheeks as she stroked her fingers through my hair, down my arms, like when I was little. "It's a lot. My poor baby. It's too much."

I sucked in air like I'd been holding my breath underwater and miraculously clawed my way to the surface. "It's like I'm on a train I can't get off."

Mom wrapped her arms around me and whispered in my ear, "You can get off if you want to. Just say the word."

22

A week after the kiss, Cynthia invites Ben to celebrate her thirteenth "birthday" of sobriety at the house with us.

He fits right in, amiably chatting with her and Chip throughout dinner, trading favorite secret local Catalina spots. I nod along, but it's hard to focus on the conversation when Ben is gently massaging my shoulder, and my brain is overflowing with thoughts that don't involve talking.

I manage to lure my mind back to the table just as Cynthia asks Ben, "How long will you have in Marin before you move to LA?"

"I'm not sure. It depends on when I decide to leave here I guess." His eyes burn into the side of my face, but I focus on twirling my pasta. If I start worrying about what happens when we leave the island, I won't be living in the *right now.*

"I'd like to make a toast." Chip raises his glass. "To Cynthia. You amaze me every day. You somehow manage to be both tough and gentle. Strong and vulnerable. A fighter and a lover. A very good lover, I might add." *Ew.* "Congratulations on thirteen years!"

A beaming Cynthia lifts her tangerine rosemary mocktail to clink ours. "Thank you. To have you all here—"

She doesn't finish. It happens quickly, the glass falling from her fingers and crashing into a million pieces on the floor.

I freeze.

The glass jerked right out of her hands.

Ben is out of his seat immediately, but Chip and I stay glued to our seats, our eyes meeting across the table.

Please let it be an innocent accident. Please don't let this be the first sign. The first symptom. The beginning of the end.

"It's okay," Cynthia assures us, her eyes communicating what she's not saying.

Ben looks between the three of us, like it's dawning on him that there's something more going on here. I quickly jump up to help him and Cynthia clean the floor, then follow her into the hall where we're out of earshot.

Cynthia answers me before I've even asked the question. "It's not what you think. The glass was a little wet and slippery. That's all."

I exhale, though I'm not completely relieved. Dr. Gold said you never *think* symptoms are hitting you. It's everyone else who notices. I make a mental note to keep a closer eye on Cynthia. "Okay. Good."

195

She puts the broom back in the closet. "Have you told Ben?"

"No," I whisper. She says nothing, but I sense her surprise. "I'm waiting for the right time."

"Is there a right time?" she wonders softly.

"There's definitely one that's more right than tonight."

If I let myself, I'll say that every night until the end of the summer. This will be the first time I've actually had to reveal this to anyone, and it's *Ben*. I don't know if that makes it easier or much harder.

But as soon as I tell him, nothing between us will ever be the same.

That, I do know.

***

I wake up a few nights later, my sheets drenched.

Another nightmare I can barely remember. It's been happening more and more. Like the better my days are, the harder my nights.

Fragments of the dream swirl around in my brain— Brooke's face morphing with Dad's, his dimple becoming Cynthia's. My extremely broken family popping out at me like a demented jack-in-the-box.

But even after the images vanish, my uneasiness remains, unleashing a chorus of doubt in my brain that keeps me up for hours sometimes.

Hope is for suckers.

Your head is in the sand.

It's coming for you sooner than you think.

Some nights I feel like it's coming for me *right now.* Something big and shapeless and menacing, and I have to climb out the window to my spot and breathe.

Tonight, when I go out there, there's an amethyst waiting for me next to the hammock chair. My very own grounding stone.

I grasp it tight as I breathe in and out.

23

The subject of Ben's girlfriend came up again inadvertently around our next bonfire.

At some point, Lucy started a game of I Never. Most of the questions were more funny than anything else, but my body stiffened at a few of the ones Ben took a sip of beer for.

Like "I've never had sex in a car."

I mean, I knew he wasn't a virgin, but did I need the visual to match that?

Ben, sensing at some point that there was no place for this game to go but from bad to worse, finally suggested we make an exit and salvage the rest of the night alone.

Which is how we ended up on the deck of his dad's boat. The gentle rocking soothes me as I lie against him, a large Afghan blanket thrown over us. The night is clear, the stars stretching above us, and the only sound in the quiet cove is a moody indie song that softly plays from the small speaker.

I absently trail my hands up and down his legs.

"That feels nice," he mumbles.

"Hmm. Better than whoever you spent that night in the car with?" I try for a tone of casual, flirtatious nonchalance, and fail.

"Better," Ben half groans. "I knew that game was a bad idea."

I twist my body to face him and drop a kiss to the small hollow above his collarbone. "Really? How *much* better?"

Ben smiles into my neck. "So competitive."

"It's a flaw. I'm aware. But don't pretend Audra wasn't gorgeous. I have a full mental picture of her."

He shakes his head. "Everything was hollow with Audra. And she never knew me. Not really. Not the way you do."

"Because I know the version of you here?"

It's something Ben and I have talked about before. The Catalina version of Ben being his most pure self. The way we're so removed, it strips away the bullshit we'd normally be worried about every day.

Ben leans back on his elbows. "With Audra it was about her, the issues she was having, all the ways I needed to help her."

"Mr. Fixer to the rescue," I deadpan.

I expect him to laugh, but he pauses for a moment, his

eyes darkening. "You threw me for a loop that night. I don't think you realized how right you were." When he speaks again, it's quietly. "You actually made me realize something way beyond what you said."

"I did?"

His gaze is a million miles from me, and I stay quiet, knowing he'll talk when he's ready, rearranging my body in his lap so I can keep facing him.

"Remember when I said that if I want to break the pattern, I have to get to the root of it?"

I nod and rest my chin on his chest.

"After I left you that night, I was on the deck right here, and it was so obvious. It's Olivia. She's the root."

His sister. Eight years older than him. He almost never talks about her. I thought it was because of the age difference that they weren't close.

"She's the one person I've been trying to save practically my whole life."

"What do you mean?" My stomach fills with dread, imagining a host of scenarios in my brain, each worse than the next. "Is she sick?"

"In a way, yeah." He flicks his eyes to mine. "She has a heroin addiction. She's had addiction issues since she was fourteen. In and out of rehabs. Sober houses. Hospitals."

His voice is detached, like he's talking about some random story he heard on a podcast instead of his actual life, his actual sister.

To say I'm stunned is an understatement. "I'm sorry."

He shrugs, like *It is what it is,* before lying back on the deck, his arms folded under his neck. I slide next to him, both of us looking back up at the stars. Eventually, he starts talking again, his voice low as he tells me about the years of her living at home, disappearing for days and then coming back and crashing so hard he'd sneak into her room to check her pulse. How his parents' marriage, which was already in critical condition, collapsed entirely. How, one time, he found a small box of used syringes that she'd left in the bathroom downstairs. He'd shown his mom, and Olivia screamed he was a narc and left. They didn't see her for ten days, and Ben was sure they'd find her dead and he'd be the one responsible.

How even now, Olivia would come home every once in a while with promises to get clean and then steal from them and disappear.

As I listen, certain things suddenly slide into place with a click. Why he always makes sure to call his mom back right away. Why this college decision was weighing on him so heavily. The darkness I've caught in his eyes sometimes.

"That's why you wanted to do that documentary." I lay my head back against his chest.

"Not the only reason, but yeah, that's an extra incentive. And it's part of the reason my film teacher hooked me up with the crew to begin with. He knew about Olivia." He drapes his arms over me, suctioning me closer to his body and the steady rhythm of his heartbeat.

"Where is she now?"

"Somewhere in Oakland. We had a scare at the beginning of the summer when no one could find her for a few weeks. My dad was about to fly up there, but she finally showed up at a friend's."

My jaw drops and I turn to face him. Knowing Ben the way I do, part of me is shocked he's not dragging her into a rehab center as we speak.

"I can tell what you're thinking. Believe me, I've done all that before. I would do anything to get back my *sister,* the old Olivia." His voice is raw with emotion, and a lump burns in my own throat. "When I was sixteen and got my license, I used to just cruise the streets with a bag of In-N-Out Burgers, trying to see if I could find her, just to make sure she was okay, had something to eat. And when I didn't, I'd give the food away to someone else on the street. Because you always hope that some other stranger might be doing the same for your sister."

My heart breaks for sixteen-year-old Ben. My heart breaks for today Ben. Chip is right. *Everyone has their shit. Everyone has their own darkness.*

"But at some point it was like everything I heard for years at these Nar-Anon meetings finally sunk in. That, basically, there's nothing we can do. No one can get her sober. Olivia has to want it. And that's a fucking brutal realization."

He's quiet for a second. "So, yeah. I must have been unconsciously finding girls to save because I can't save my sister."

Oof. That one hits straight to the gut. "Um, can I just say that I feel like a total asshole now?" I cringe. "I'm so sorry, Ben."

He finally looks her in the eye. "That's the opposite of what I'm saying. My point is that from day one you saw this part of me that no one else ever has."

"Well . . . maybe not from day *one.*"

A smile dangles at the corner of his lips. "True. Once I broke you down with my charm, I had to know more about this person who saw me that clearly." His voice drops. "Even if I could never get a clear read on her myself."

Ben watches me carefully in the moonlight, and I sense that it's suddenly my turn.

I tamp down my sudden nervousness by keeping my voice light. "You look like you're trying to come up with a question for me."

His arm curls around my waist. "Nope. I give up. I don't think I'll ever figure out your story until you decide you want me to."

In volleyball we'd call this "a perfect set." He's lobbed the conversational ball into the absolute best spot for me to spike it into submission. If I was ever looking for the so-called right time, this is it.

But how would I even start?

The beginning.

"Okay . . ." I flush, still gathering the courage. *Am I really doing this? Is this the right time?*

"What is it?" His full focus is on me now.

I won't get another moment this perfect again. I know that. And as hard as my heart is beating right now, I can admit there's a small allure to finally telling him. To erasing this secret between us.

Here goes nothing.

"Well . . . I told you my parents were divorced, too. But I never really told you what happened."

My breath catches, and he squeezes my hand, like *Go on. . . .*

"My dad actually left when I was five. And I haven't seen him since."

I can sense him mentally cataloguing this piece into the larger database of information he has about me, the same way I just did to him. "Wow. You haven't heard from him at *all?*"

This is it. I'll start with the letter and go straight through the next six months.

But before any words escape, I flash-forward to that second right after, imagining his reaction. Of course he'll be kind. It's Ben. Product of therapy and a mother who makes him talk out his feelings, and also a generally empathetic, good person. He won't know exactly what to say—who would?—so I have a feeling he'll go with some sympathetic clichés. He'll latch on to this medical drug study and tell me I should feel so hopeful. And yes, I *do* feel hopeful.

But he'll never look at me the same way. Like a normal

person. Like a *better*-than-normal person. Like before the envelope was opened. It will color the way he sees me forever.

And I know how valuable the *before* is now. Maybe I'm selfish, but I just can't do it.

The words creak out of my throat like they're coated with rust. "I never heard from him again."

Half-truths masquerading as full truths. That's been my game all summer. But this time it's a bald-faced lie, and it lands with a thud in my stomach, the arm he puts around me suddenly feeling as heavy as armor.

Long after Ben shuttles me back to the dock, acting like I've shared a big secret with him when I know I haven't; after we walk up to Cynthia's house; after our last kiss of the night, I toss restlessly in my bed.

Was it wrong to lie to Ben tonight?

And before Dr. Gold can horn his way into this mental conversation, yes, I know there's no right or wrong. I have the moral imperative to keep this part of myself to myself for as long as I want.

But there's a catch-22 that's suddenly dawning on me. If you tell someone about this gene before they even really know you, when you're just someone they like to kiss, what's to stop them from walking away? But if you wait until it becomes *real* to tell them, you know exactly how much you'll lose if they leave.

The air in the room is deathly still. I creep out of my bed and out the window, clutching my amethyst in search of a breeze.

I inhale and exhale slowly, trying to see if I can grasp at something that feels like truth.

Ben and I exist in the *right now* in this summer, on this island. HD or not, anyone watching us from afar can probably see our expiration date approaching at the end of summer as clearly as if it was tattooed on our foreheads. Even if we made all the promises to each other in the world about staying together off the island, it wouldn't change the fact in three weeks I'll be knee-deep in volleyball in Colorado and he'll either be off shooting a documentary or settling into film school in LA. As much as the thought crushes me, as much as we'd make promises to try, it would never work between us long term. So then why ruin these last three weeks we *do* have together by telling him? I might as well enjoy the last few moments of the joyride, of Ben's total attention, of being this version of myself, before the inevitable crash.

This comforts my conscience enough that I get back into bed. But I don't fall asleep for hours.

24

Before

In ten hours we'd find out if Brooke was gene-positive. Twenty-four hours later it would be my turn.

Another testing rule. We weren't allowed to get our results on the same day. Dr. Gold said it was because we each deserved our own time to hear them, independent from each other. Two positives were too bleak to deal with all at once. But also finding out one person was negative, while the other was positive wasn't easy either.

Brooke and I had come up with what we thought was a solid distraction tactic for these nights before we got our results. We made a list of the funniest movies we could think of to watch one after another until we fell asleep. If we fell asleep.

But by the time we got to the fourth one, neither of us had laughed out loud once, and the butter on the untouched popcorn had congealed into soggy clumps.

For the past two days, only one thing had been on my mind. There wasn't a movie in the world that could distract me from it. And I was running out of time to tell Brooke.

"I have to talk to you about something," I said quietly, kind of hoping she didn't hear me.

She immediately swiveled her body around to face me. Her shoulders hunched so deeply, she resembled a small child. "I do, too. You first."

I focused on an empty space of air between us and let everything else blur. "I've been thinking that we shouldn't do this. Get the results, I mean."

"What? Why?"

"Because it's not something we really *need* to find out tomorrow. Maybe we should wait until we *have* to find out."

Every part of her face scrunched together. "We do *have* to find out because we *need* to have a set plan for our futures. Do you know how much goes into figuring out the financials of something like this? We can't plan anything unless we know what we're up against."

"But look what this has been doing to you!" I took a breath to get the wobble out of my voice. "What if finding out makes it even worse? You can't take this decision back. I just think maybe we should take a little more time to think about it."

"Time to think about it? Isn't that what we've been doing for the past six months?"

"That doesn't mean we can't change our minds."

208

Brooke inhaled and exhaled, and some color returned to her face. "Where is this coming from all of a sudden?"

I clasped my fingers together so tightly my knuckles turned white. "I'm scared."

"I'm scared too." She squeezed our hands together tightly. "But I'm still ready to find out tomorrow and move on either way."

She waited for me to answer. The Pit swished in my stomach like ocean waves. "Okay."

She threw her arms around me. We were both trembling and pretending that we weren't.

"Your turn." I forced a weak smile. "What did you want to talk about?"

Her eyes were dry and gritty when they latched on to mine.

"I found Dad."

25

"*H*ow about this one?" Lucy holds up a tiny gold tank. Clothes are scattered around us in her bedroom, blowing in different directions because of the giant fan we positioned in the middle of the room. Catalina in late July is sweltering hot. Yesterday we asked Man-Bun Marcus for a pitcher of ice cubes, then dumped them on our heads.

But the heat won't stop us from going all-out for Lucy's eighteenth birthday. Like she's trying to suck out the most juice from our last two weeks here, she's planned a two-day celebration starting tonight with karaoke in Avalon, continuing into tomorrow with an all-day boat adventure.

Unfortunately, my three-minute packing job for the summer did not include a single clothing item that works for a night out.

I eye the gold top skeptically. Lucy is far more partial to crop tops than I am. "Ummm."

She keeps digging through her closet. "Aha! Here we go." A gauzy white camisole with spaghetti straps. By far the best option I've seen yet.

"I'll take it!"

I burst into Cynthia's a few minutes later and hear her voice, wafting out from her room, talking to someone on the phone.

"I'm not sure if she's ready for that yet. . . ."

I look up to see Shanti check me out from her perch in the living room. Since she saved my life, I've grown to semi-appreciate her. "Hey, Shanti."

She looks right at me with her two little bird eyes and, in a voice that sounds exactly like Cynthia's, replies, "Oh, hey, Brooke."

For a second my stomach free-falls, then I turn back toward Cynthia's closed door. She's talking to Brooke. Are they talking about me? *Ready for what?*

I retreat to my room and take a stupidly long shower to block it out, knowing that if Chip comes home soon, I'm going to hear it from him about wasting water.

When I get out I break open the makeup bag that's remained untouched since I got here. It's not just to distract myself from whatever Brooke and Cynthia were talking about. Something about a night out in Avalon, where there are so many people and restaurants, makes me feel like I need to step it up. I slip into the delicate tank and pull on my one pair of nondistressed jeans before I attempt to mildly contour my cheeks. Not bad.

I check my phone, and I still have a few minutes before I need to leave. I scroll through a few messages from Nina about how her alias Nikki is doing. Just as I zip off a quick reply to her, a new email from Coach Jacobson pops up.

Hi, Abby,

Your paperwork is all set. Just need you to sign these medical release forms. Please send back by tomorrow.

Coach J

I open up my laptop and breeze through the first page—name, address, basic info—then scroll to the first question on the next page.

Do you have any ongoing medical conditions or illnesses you're aware of?

I stare at the question, unblinking. Months ago this was an easy answer. A no-brainer.

Today it's more complicated, a quick but stinging reminder that *nope,* I'm not the same person who was recruited to this team, even if nothing has changed on the outside.

It's one small question. A blip in the middle of these forms. But it feels like so much more.

I stare at the form until it blurs.

Do I check the "no" box, shut my computer, and move on? I doubt Coach Jacobson would ever find out it's a lie. Dr. Gold told us that our test results are completely confidential.

But I've been lying by omission for the past two months, and it's like acid slowly peeling away layers of my skin. Am I really planning to just lie about this for the next four years? To continue not telling anyone? Not even my teammates, who I'll be spending hours of time with?

I can't bring myself to check the "yes" box either, though.

Frustrated, I click over to the tab I have open to the article about the drug study. The one I've read a hundred times since Nina sent it, its words calming me whenever I need a little pop of sanity.

I scan through the article quickly, letting it wash over me. *Shattered expectations. Game changer. Real possibility.*

But this time I keep scrolling past the article, and my eyes snag on the comments that have multiplied since I last checked.

Every five years there's some supposed breakthrough like this. And then nothing.

Doctors have been saying "we're close" for three decades. Sorry if I can't get my hopes up this time.

Even if this works, it's not some magic pill. You'd have to get injected in your spine every month.

If you can even afford it. It'll probably cost hundreds of thousands of dollars. A drug for the rich. What about the rest of us?

We've been hearing about studies like this for years. Call me when there's something that will actually help my mom. My aunt. My brothers.

The words blend together until I can't read them anymore. I need to get out of here.

———

Ben grips my hand as we weave our way through the crowded karaoke restaurant to a table near the stage. "Everything okay?"

I've been sporting a Joker-esque perma-smile since I greeted Lucy on the Cyclone, desperately faking the level of excitement she's expecting. It's unnerving Ben's still able to sniff out my darkness. But I don't want to think about any of it, let alone talk about it, especially here with everyone. "What? I'm fine."

His brow creases. "You seem off."

Since my other "everything is awesome" tactics aren't working, I clasp my arms around his neck and kiss him. As always the world falls away a little.

By the time we slip into our seats across from Curtis and Lucy, Ben seems convinced that everything is okay.

"Birthday shots!" Alex and Aron, our zipline tour guides, who Lucy and Curtis invited to meet us, bring over a tray of shots.

I try to match everyone else's enthusiasm as we cheers to Lucy and take the shots.

It burns every inch of my throat the whole way down.

Alex and Aron leave with promises to come back with another tray.

"By the way, you guys all have to sing before we leave tonight," Lucy tells us, motioning to the stage where a woman belts out a heartfelt rendition of "I Will Always Love You."

Curtis snorts. "Yeah, right."

"Not even for my birthday?" Lucy makes puppy dog eyes at him.

Curtis doesn't budge.

"Come on," Lucy pleads. "You're the one always saying 'you only live once . . . '"

Curtis stares her down. "I'm fine dying without ever doing karaoke."

I shudder. It was only a split second, but of course Ben noticed.

His eyebrows raise. "You sure you're okay?"

"Just a tequila flashback," I joke. It's all so bleak I almost manage a real laugh.

As we wait for our food, I work hard to appear like normal Abby, or at least normal-adjacent Abby, employing white lies like Band-Aids. I've been waiting for that light, weightless sensation from the wine fest to rescue me. Instead, the shots have only made me feel darker, more helpless. More hopeless.

It's a relief when the waitress sets my dinner in front of me and I have something else to focus on.

"Right, Abby?"

I glance up from my burger, and Ben is waiting for an answer to a question I didn't hear. I nod with an ambiguous smile that can hopefully be interpreted as sincere or sarcastic, depending on what I'm agreeing to. His eyes linger on me a beat too long, like he's determined to figure out what I'm thinking.

Good luck with that, buddy.

I return to my half-eaten burger, but it now looks repulsive. Mangled and ravaged, like someone chewed it up and spit it out.

I push my chair away from me. "I'm going to run to the bathroom."

I whirl around before Lucy can hop up to join me. I only get two steps away from the table, though, before my path is suddenly blocked.

There's a middle-aged woman maneuvering a man in a wheelchair through the crowd. As the pair moves closer toward me, the man's painfully scrawny arms and his fiercely trembling hands come into view. Parkinson's, I'm guessing.

Everyone glances at the man kindly as they hurry to make room for him. Deep down, though, I bet they're all thinking the same thing: *Thank god it's not me.*

Or maybe: *I hope that's not me one day.*

But I'm staring down what I *know* is my future, the question being *when,* not *if.*

And I cannot fucking look away.

The man in the wheelchair attempts to lift his glasses off his lap, but he can't quite bring them to his face. He grunts in frustration as they drop from his shaky fingers to the floor.

Ben grabs them before they get crushed, handing them back. He must have been watching this whole thing too.

Immediately my mouth fills with saliva, and I'm seconds away from puking.

This is my fate. And it's coming for me way too soon.

It's suddenly obvious I've been fooling myself this entire summer. Shielding my eyes with a cheery optimistic blindfold, like it would somehow make everything okay. Thinking I could throw my fatal disease on the back burner, putting my faith in a single drug study. Convincing myself I was somehow dealing with this when all I've done is run from it the second I got here.

Ben casually wraps his arm around my waist. "My grandpa had Parkinson's. It's brutal."

A cold sweat breaks out on my forehead. "I know."

"You know someone with it too?"

I untangle myself from him and mumble something about the bathroom. Instead, I bypass it and barrel out the front door.

It feels like it's only a matter of seconds before I'm going to finally break down in tears, the ones I've been holding back for months, and when I do, it'll be a flood. My fingers scramble to whip out a text to the group that I'm not feeling well, then I race to get in line for the Cyclone.

I don't exhale until the engine rumbles and we're halfway to Two Harbors. It's not until I've staggered up the path to Cynthia's that I try to give my tears permission to explode.

Instead, I double over in front of the house and vomit my insides out. Apparently, I'm too dysfunctional to even cry.

I muster up enough energy to make it into my bedroom where my laptop sits, still open to Coach Jacobson's email. Quickly, I fire off a reply, press send, and collapse on the bed.

My eyelids flutter open. I try to swallow, but a small furry animal must have crawled down my throat last night.

Last night . . .

The Pit of Doom travels up from my stomach, crawls into my fingers, and reaches for my phone. I ignore the too-many-to-count messages from Ben and Lucy and pull up my email.

Coach Jacobson replied three minutes after I sent her the message to take me off the roster. It feels like one of the bad dreams I wake up in a cold sweat from, but her reply convinces me that yes, I actually did that.

Hello, Abby. As you requested, I've let the administration know that you will not be attending

Colorado in the fall. There will be no exceptions
beyond this point. Good luck to you.

I should feel something—regret, satisfaction, relief—but
it's just emptiness. I'm on an airplane that's going down, and
there's nothing I can do to stop it.

Dazed, I wander out of my bedroom for water and caf-
feine. Cynthia's voice softly carries out to the hall.

I push my greasy hair out of my face and pop my head
into the kitchen.

But Cynthia isn't alone at the table.

Perched across from her, sipping turmeric tea from my
favorite Two Harbors mug, is Brooke.

26

"What are you doing here?" My heart pounds in my ears. I whip my head over to Cynthia. "Did you know she was coming?"

Before Cynthia can answer, Brooke jumps up from her seat. "I'm sorry to surprise you like this, Abby."

My nostrils flare. "Then why did you?"

Cynthia rises from her chair. "Let's all take a breath—"

"Okay," Brooke breaks in a hoarse voice. "I know you're upset. I thought that—"

"That what?!" I explode. "If you came here, everything would go back to normal? That we can be *okay* again?"

"No," she whispers. She doesn't cry, but she wants to. "I tried to come out here the day after you left. Mom wouldn't let me. She said to give you time. And I did. But when I talked to Cynthia, she said you were doing really well—"

"I *am* doing really well!"

"So I thought it might be enough time." She bows her head to her chest.

"And you figured you'd just barge in?"

I brace myself for a rebuttal, but her eyes drop to the floor. This might be the first time she hasn't presented a solid defense.

We all jump when three quick knocks on the door interrupt our showdown.

My eyes widen. "Do *not* tell me that you brought Dad here."

Cynthia and Brooke meet eyes.

"You did!" I accuse.

"Abby, no. I swear," Brooke replies. "I didn't bring anyone."

Cynthia treads lightly toward the door and opens it, with Brooke and me a few steps behind her.

"Hey!" Lucy greets us, clueless she just dove into a deep pool of drama. She takes a few steps toward me, her eyebrows slanting with concern. "Are you feeling better? I've been texting you all morning."

I rub the nape of my neck, sinking my fingers into the muscles. I blocked out the fact that I bolted last night without saying goodbye to anyone. My brain feels like someone dug a giant hole inside and forgot to fill it.

"Much better." I search for a lie that doesn't require too many details. "I wanted to say goodbye, but I had this . . .

migraine, and I didn't want to miss the early Cyclone back. I'm sorry I bailed."

She gives a dismissive wave. "I'm just glad you're better. You weren't answering your phone so I wasn't sure if you'd be up for today. . . ."

Part two of Lucy's birthday celebration: snorkeling and cliff jumping. I completely forgot.

Her eyes drift from me to Brooke. "Hi."

Brooke moves in closer to me, wisely staying an arm's length away.

"Hi, I'm Brooke." She offers up a cute half smile that only I know is fake. "Abby's sister."

"I didn't know you had a sister, Abby."

I don't have to see Brooke's face to know those words stung. *Good.* She deserves it for showing up unannounced when I've given her every possible indication that it's the last thing I want.

I turn to Lucy with renewed energy. "I'm in for today."

Lucy's face brightens. "You sure?"

"I'll shower and meet you at the dock."

She glances between me and Brooke. I can see in her furrowed brow that she's struggling to unravel our relationship. She has the same expression when she's untangling her layers of necklaces. *Please don't do what I think you're about to do, Lucy.*

"You're welcome to come, too, Brooke."

"Really? Um . . ." Brooke shoots me an uncertain look. "Only if it's okay with Abby."

Well-played. She's backed me into a corner. If I say no, not only will I look like a bitch, but Lucy will definitely have follow-up questions about it later.

I give her my matching cute, but equally as false, smile. "Sure."

I take the longest strides possible down the hill so Brooke can't keep up. My arms swing like chicken wings, and I must look like the youngest person ever to compete in the power-walking championships.

"Are you okay?"

I cringe at Brooke's voice. I'm surprised she caught up to me with those stubby legs of hers.

"My friends don't know anything about . . . anything," I hiss. "So keep your mouth shut."

"Abby, I wouldn't do that—"

"Really? Because it seems *exactly* like something you would do."

I charge down the weathered wood planks of the pier with Brooke at my heels when I suddenly skid to a halt. Ben is crouched next to the powerboat, untying the bowline. He looks up, and for one fucked-up second, even as my life falls apart, I want to kiss him. I want to be back on his dad's houseboat. Or out on the kayak. Or doing anything where I can pretend that envelope stayed sealed.

But that's been my mistake from the start. Pretending. I manipulated both of us into believing I'm not a girl with an early death sentence hanging over my head.

"This is Abby's sister, Brooke." Lucy volunteers the information when I make no move to introduce Brooke to Ben and Curtis.

Ben shakes her hand, his eyes flashing toward mine. I can hear exactly what he's thinking; it's as if he's whispering it directly into my ear.

Why didn't you tell me you have a sister?

I turn to face the mountains with a sudden urge to drink in the beautiful coastline.

Lucy claps her hands together. "Everybody ready?"

She and Curtis hop on the boat, and Brooke carefully steps on behind them. I try to slink past Ben, but he's in front of me so quickly he must've anticipated my dodge.

"Can we talk for a second?" His eyes search mine.

I become enthralled with a hangnail dangling off my thumb. "I'm sorry I left like that last night. I had a migraine, and I was starting to get really dizzy—"

"Abby, talk to me." His voice is tense with impatience. "What's going on?"

"Nothing. I'm fine."

He edges closer to me. "You're clearly not fine. That's pretty much the only thing I can figure out about you right now."

He's seconds away from reaching out. He's dying to wrap

his arms around me and save me. But there's nothing he can ever do—that anyone can do—to save me from this. I have a bomb permanently strapped to my body and no idea when it's going to detonate.

I just want everyone to back off so I can blow up alone.

I latch my eyes onto his, my voice so low and harsh, I barely recognize it as my own. "I'm not your sister, Ben. Let it go."

His body stiffens like a soldier at attention. I move past him and on to the boat. When I plop down across from Lucy, she mouths, "Are you okay?" and gives a subtle glance toward Ben. I nod and produce a constipated smile. I won't let my impending doom pollute birthday celebration number two.

Curtis revs the engine, and I set my gaze on the glassy water to avoid scorching my eyeballs with a glance at Ben or Brooke. Ben is the wound. And Brooke is viciously twisting the knife.

"How long are you visiting, Brooke?" I hear Lucy ask.

I whip my head in Brooke's direction and make sure she catches the storm brewing in my eyes.

"Not long. I just really wanted to see my sister," Brooke replies.

Ben's face is stone, his voice flat. "Abby talks about you all the time."

I only glance at him for a millisecond, but it's enough for the anger in his eyes to burn through mine. I've never seen this side of him.

Good. Maybe I pissed him off enough that he'll leave me alone.

"There it is!" Lucy shouts. She points ahead of us to a sheer cliff wall that drops straight into the ocean.

As we get close Curtis idles the boat to a stop so we can swim to the base. We're about to dive into the water when Brooke's small, panicky voice stops us. "I'll just stay here in the boat and watch you guys. It's a little too high for me up there."

I want to scream, *THEN WHY THE FUCK DID YOU COME?* But I'm thankful for her fear of heights and any amount of physical distance I can put between us.

One by one the rest of us splash into the ocean. My arms and legs tingle from the frosty water, but it's a short swim to the cliff's base. We pull ourselves out of the ocean and onto a giant rock, shivering until the sun dries the cool water off us.

Deep ridges wind through the mountain, like veins, and Curtis leads us on a short climb up and across the small boulders. The take-off area for jumping is completely flat, and I'm guessing from the trampled plants that it's a popular spot for this.

"It's about a twenty-foot jump," Curtis says, breaking it down for us, "and you're going to need a running start to clear the rocks."

I peer over the edge to the aquamarine ocean that will cushion our fall. It doesn't look that far down. I'm a little disappointed.

Brooke waves from the boat, and a steady flow of anger returns, piping hot, like it's just been rewarmed in the microwave.

"Birthday girl first." Ben struggles to sound enthusiastic as he clears a path for Lucy.

She takes off at a sprint. I hear her excited squeal, followed by the splash of her body hitting the cool water. Ben and Curtis cheer for her, but I suddenly can't tear my eyes away from the ledge thirty feet above us. *That's* the one I want to jump off.

Ben takes the next turn, probably ecstatic to get as far away from me as possible. I don't think he's looked at me once since we docked.

As soon as Curtis takes off for his running jump, I start climbing. The ledge I spotted above glistens in the sun like it's the ultimate prize. All I want to do is get there. The path isn't quite as clear-cut as the one we just took, but there's enough of an obvious formation for me to follow.

It's like an out-of-body force, lifting me up the rocks, higher and higher. Whirls of pent-up anger and hostility buzz inside me.

I reach my hands up to grip the ridge, then push through my quivering biceps, until I'm all the way up. There's not much of a take-off spot. The ledge is small and jagged, with barely any room for more than one person to stand. I'm breathless but exhilarated when I lift my body from the ground.

I can almost hear my name echoing across the mountain

peaks, as if they too are celebrating my victorious climb. Actually, it's less of an echo and more like a thundering of my name. And it keeps getting louder.

I peer down below at Brooke on the boat, wildly waving her arms in the air like windshield wipers. "Abby! Don't! It's too high!"

The boat seems so far away, so far removed from where I am, that her words barely register. The craggy rock juts out ominously over the ocean, but I inch forward.

The rest of the group must've swam back to the boat because now there's a chorus of voices that ricochet right off me.

"You can't jump from there, Abby!"

"You're going to get hurt!"

"Come down!"

The screams continue, but they're easy to block out. This jump doesn't carry the same weight for them that it does for me.

I close my eyes and sway with the light breeze. My sweaty skin responds with fresh layers of goose bumps, despite the blazing sun overhead.

Pre-testing Abby would've never climbed up to this ledge. But pre-testing Abby had more to lose. I'm not leaping off this cliff to kill myself. But at the end of the day, if I jumped and didn't make it, doesn't that mean I'd escape a much worse fate than the one I'm already destined to?

I bend my knees, swing my arms back . . . and scream when a hand grabs hold of my foot.

"Curtis," I gasp. He pulls himself up, barely out of breath, and squeezes himself next to me on the narrow ridge. He's the only one who could climb the mountain fast enough to "save" me.

We study each other like we're strangers with a language barrier.

"Should I help you back down?" he asks. A new expression flashes across his face—like he just now recognizes me. Like someone told him we're related and he's trying to figure out all the ways we resemble each other.

I drop my head toward the ocean. It's like a sloshy hammock luring me to jump.

I don't want to back down from this.

I drag my feet on everything. And each time I do, it bites me in the ass.

Something flickers in Curtis's eyes. "Is this something you need to do, Abby?"

He may not say a lot, but he doesn't miss a thing. I nod.

He eyes the ocean, then assesses the cliff. "Okay. I've done this ledge once. Since you can't get a running start, you have to jump out as far as you possibly can. Try to keep your body straight. It's a long way down."

He steps back.

I take a deep breath, then leap off the rock with my heart in my throat. The cold air immediately mummifies me in a wind tunnel. The sensory overload of the free fall is so intense that my brain can't keep up with what's happening. Like my body jumped and left my brain on the cliff by accident.

I slam into the water with too much momentum, and the ocean gobbles me up. My body rolls into underwater somersaults I can't control. Disorientated, I claw my way to the surface. I just need air. I fill my lungs a second too soon and choke on a mouthful of water instead. I manically cough and struggle against the choppy waves that slam into my chest. I want to scream for help, but my breath is too shallow.

I don't want to die.

The notion stabs me with a giant injection of adrenaline and panic. I can't die like this.

An inexplicable burst of energy lifts me out of the water.

Or so my oxygen-deprived mind thought. Brooke has somehow harnessed superhero strength to pull me into our boat. She's drenched, Lucy is crying, and Ben is breathing like he just ran back-to-back marathons.

Sprawled out on my back, my panting turns into coughing, and as soon as I sit up, water evacuates my stomach and pours out of my mouth. I pull my knees up to my heaving chest and wrap my arms around them. I hid my diagnosis all summer to avoid being the girl everyone felt sorry for. This is ten times worse. I lower my gaze, too weak to handle the jumble of pain and shock on their faces.

"I'm sorry," I sputter.

"What the hell was that?" Ben's voice is full of controlled rage.

"You can't do that, Abby!" Brooke interjects, hysterical. "I know I don't have the right to say anything, but how can

I not? It's not bad enough already? You think jumping off a cliff is better than—"

Living with Huntington's disease. My eyes drill into her, silently begging her not to finish that sentence.

"Better than what Dad is dealing with?" she recovers.

Ben's questioning eyes sear me like a brand. The lie I told him about Dad the other night reverberates through my head. *I never heard from him again.*

Ben turns to Curtis with a look, as if his veins have been shot up with ice. "Let's get out of here."

Curtis starts the engine, and we ride back to the pier in complete silence.

27

rooke remains silent during the entire walk back to Cynthia's.

"My girls," Cynthia greets us brightly as we slog in, wiping her hands off on a dishrag from the counter. "Wasn't expecting you back yet . . ." She trails off at the sight of us. We must look like we've been through war. She hurries over to us in the living room. "What happened? Is everyone okay?"

Brooke jumps in with a dramatic rundown of the cliff dive before she turns to me, her eyes crinkling with frustration.

"Just tell me this, Abby," she says, her voice battered. "Are you *trying* to kill yourself? Is that what I just saw?"

"No." I shake my head furiously. "I swear."

"I don't care if you hate me forever, but if you are a danger to yourself, I will call Dr. Gold and get a psychiatric hold on you, so help me, Abby. This isn't something to mess around with."

"I wasn't, Brooke. Curtis has jumped that cliff before. People take off from there all the time." I look to Cynthia. "Blue Cavern Point."

"It's dangerous, but not unheard of over there," Cynthia concludes. I take a step closer to her, my new star witness.

"But why do it at all?" Brooke prods, more distraught. "What were you thinking?"

How can I explain this to her?

"Um, I mean, it's like . . . I've never wanted to go sky-diving before because it always seemed too extreme, way too scary. But now . . . I'd consider it."

Brooke tries to process this, but since it's not entirely logical, I can practically see her brain bump against it.

"If I may . . . ," Cynthia interjects, and Brooke and I mutter our permission. God knows what's about to happen next. If she suggests a healing circle, I'm out. *Out.* "Frankly, sometimes a diagnosis like this makes you want to take life by the balls a little more."

Comprehension finally slides across Brooke's face.

"Exactly," I agree.

"Or, shall I say, take life by the ovaries? Why should balls be the only thing exalted?" Cynthia quickly gets the message that neither of us are in the mood to debate the patriarchal leanings of the English language. "I'm going to finish getting my bone broth going. I'm right here if you need me, girls."

She sails back to the kitchen counter like she's the last lifeboat leaving the *Titanic*.

"I thought you were going to die up there!" Tears prick Brooke's sunken eyes. "I thought I was going to watch it right in front of my eyes." Another sob shudders out of her. "And I know I don't have a right to be angry or have bad days, like ever again, but how could that not scare the living shit out of me?"

Probably because I've been avoiding anything more than a two-second glance at her since she arrived, I finally notice how different she looks. Her dull, frayed hair. Her clothes sagging off her shrunken body.

She looks as broken as I feel.

"I said I'm sorry." I sound like an eight-year-old who's being forced to apologize. But just because I feel bad for putting Brooke through an emotional ringer today doesn't mean I forgive her for everything else.

She waits in silence for a long moment. "I guess that's it, then." She grabs her roller suitcase from its spot in the corner, quickly unzips it, and repacks the toiletry bag she took out this morning.

I edge a few inches toward her. "What are you doing?"

"Leaving."

It's exactly what I wanted, yes. But watching her attempt to zip the suitcase shut, her hands still shaking, I feel a pang of guilt. A *pang.* I slink down to the couch, suddenly drained. "Oh."

"If you don't want to hear what I have to say, there's nothing I can do. I'm not going to force my opinion on you."

A burst of bitter laughter escapes me. "That's a first."

"What's that supposed to mean?"

"Seriously?" I gape at her standing there, clueless, like her memory has been wiped.

She juts her chin out, and a hint of the controlling Brooke I'm used to breaks through. "What are you talking about?" I'm stunned silent by her rewriting of history, but she plows on. "I'm sorry I came, Abby. And even if you're not saying it, I understand why you don't want to see me." Her voice breaks for a second. "Trust me, I hate myself more than you ever could for not having this gene."

Wait. What did she just say? I practically leap off the couch in indignation. "Are you kidding me? You think *that's* what's happening? That I'm upset because I have the gene and you don't?"

Her eyes widen, like she can't believe how dense I am. "Yes."

I can *feel* heat steaming off my palms. If Cynthia can actually see my aura as she claims, I have no doubt it's fire engine red.

Even in my worst moments, I've never wished this on Brooke. I would never throw her into the flames to save myself.

"What is it, then?" she presses. "We were a united front when we walked in to get your results."

My blood boils at the words "united front." It's bad enough she used that phrase for six straight months. But to hear her casually reference it again, after everything, triggers my gag reflex.

"And then you stop speaking to me, you run off to Catalina, tell Mom you don't want to hear from me. If that's not it, then tell me what it is! Why are you so mad at me?"

"Because it's your fault!" All summer these words have been festering inside my head and now they burst out of me.

She recoils, as if I've punched her. "My fault?"

"I never would've gotten tested if it wasn't for you! And I wish I hadn't. My life will never be the same! Do you understand that? I will never be the same."

It's my darkest secret. Exposed. I take a few steps back, feeling like a feral animal that's suddenly trapped in a house—heart beating wildly, eyes darting, nowhere to hide.

Cynthia moves out from behind the counter. "Oh, Abby," she gasps softly, in a voice like she's never been sadder for me. She's the one with the right idea. Never getting tested. What a genius.

Brooke's mouth hangs open in total surprise. "The results were always going to be what they were going to be."

"But I could've waited! I could've had more time to believe everything was going to be okay. I know you wouldn't have been able to do that, but I could have! And now there's nothing I can do to take it back!"

This is the first time I've said it out loud. My chest heaves from the effort. It's a relief to finally unleash those words on her after they've been trapped in my mind for so long.

Brooke's voice is quiet. "You said you wanted the results too."

"Because you said that families who don't all test together fall apart and we had to be a united front in this!"

She winces. "Abbs, I didn't mean—"

"You thought it would be easier for us to plan our lives if we knew what we were both up against."

"I mean, I did think that, but—"

"It wasn't enough for you to have all the facts about your own life. You needed all the facts about mine, too!"

Brooke squints, as if the sun is directly in her eyes. "I thought this was something we decided *together*. Not that I decided for us."

"No. You did what you always do. Build up a case and bulldoze everyone until they do what you say."

"I don't do that—"

"You forced your way here when you knew I didn't want to see you. You forced us to read the letter from Dad when I said I didn't want to. You decided to find Dad without even asking me! Why the hell do you think I left? What was next? Forcing a visit with him?"

She digests this for a minute. "Okay, I hear you. But, Abby, this test . . . We talked about it for six months. Why would you just go along with it if you really didn't want to?"

The question hits me like a poison-tipped dart.

Why did I go against my gut? I could've changed my mind that morning. Brooke already knew she was negative. I could've backed out at the last second. Thrust my hand out to stop Dr. Gold before he tore open the seal. Told him

237

to forget it. I'll wait. See you in five years. Brooke might've been disappointed, but in that moment, right there, it was my call.

And I stayed silent.

I stare at the rug, but I can feel the weight of Brooke's gaze. I wait for her to plead her case. To call me out on the fact that I've taken no responsibility in this.

To say that the *real problem* is I've just followed Brooke blindly my whole life, thinking she has all the answers, instead of coming up with them on my own.

When I raise my eyes from the floor, though, her expression is one of blind pity. "I should've listened harder to what you were saying." Her voice is strangled, her cheeks red. "You're right. It is my fault."

I doubt she believes that, but she's willing to let my mistake live as hers if it makes me feel better. And with that, my heart tears open a little bit for her.

Brooke might have been the one who swayed me to the decision. But the bigger question is *why did I let her?*

She jiggles her suitcase handle. "I'll leave. Let you have more time. I get it if you don't want to be around me right now." She bites her lip, and my heart tears open a little bit more. "Call me when you're ready, Abby."

I shift my gaze away from her.

She hesitates for a second. "Can I hug you goodbye?"

Her voice cracks. And when I look back to her, about to walk out the door, my heart rips open wide.

"Don't go," I whisper.

Her lower lip quivers. "Are you sure? It's—"

"Don't go," I tell her more firmly.

She holds my gaze steady. "Okay. I won't."

"Also, you can't." Cynthia sniffles from the kitchen.

"True." A small smile finds its way to my lips. "The last ferry of the day already left."

Brooke chokes out a laugh. "I guess you're stuck with me, then."

We all fall asleep that night at what would be a reasonable bedtime for a toddler. When I shuffle into the kitchen the next day, I've slept through most of the morning. It's practically lunchtime. Cynthia is cutting vegetables from her garden and tossing them into a colorful salad.

Brooke is settled at the table, gripping her mug like it's sacred.

"Turmeric latte?" I gesture toward it, already knowing the answer. It's my favorite, too, and at this point I can smell turmeric a mile away.

"Yes! How have I survived without ever drinking this?"

"I've got yours started, Abbs," Cynthia calls out, puttering around the kitchen. "Coconut or oat milk?"

I slide into the chair next to Brooke. "Coconut, please. Thanks, Cynthia."

Brooke gives me the side-eye. "I didn't know oat milk existed before I got here."

"There's a lot I didn't know existed before I got here." I grin, but the corners of my mouth shrink back in as my own words echo in my ear.

After lunch Cynthia shoos us out of the house with the directive for me to show Brooke the island.

"I can't believe you've been living here for this long." Brooke marvels as we head toward my favorite hiking trail. "It's so . . ."

"Remote?"

"Tiny. Like miniscule. And what is the deal with the Wi-Fi?"

I laugh. "Don't ask."

We hike uphill beneath a row of palm trees. I'm not fooling myself. Things are not anywhere close to back to normal between us. It's not because I'm angry anymore, though. Most of that melted away last night. It's more like I feel lost in my own house. Our lives are now severed into two chunks. Brooke and Abby before HD. And Brooke and Abby after. I don't know what the second chunk looks like or how to navigate it. It feels awkward and fragile. As we wind our way higher up the rugged hills, Brooke already a little out of breath, we default to small talk.

She fills me in on bits and pieces about her friends back home, but stops midsentence when we reach a summit a half-mile uphill. It's one of those perfect Catalina vistas. Sparkling blue water, cactus-studded hilltops, boats bobbing in the coves, the sun softly drenching it all while the breeze from the ocean glides past us in a whisper. It's pure "vida Catalina magic," as Curtis likes to call it.

Brooke digs her eyes into the view, and I see the exact moment she gets it.

"This place is kind of incredible," she murmurs in awe.

"It is." I hear the ownership in my voice. For the rest of my life, Catalina will always be a version of home. "It's been good for me to be here."

Brooke gazes quietly out to the water, and for the first time, I wonder what her summer has looked like. Cooped up in our house in Colorado, her life shattered by my results too. That envelope Dr. Gold opened with my name on it didn't just tell me my future—it told Brooke hers, too. One in which she has a sister who's probably going to become a stranger to her at some point. Who will, most likely, say some pretty terrible things to her. Who will start off needing a little care, and then a lot. And if it's too stressful for Mom, or if, years from now, she's not around anymore, it will land squarely on Brooke to pick up all our pieces. The last woman left standing.

I flash back to those antianxiety pills Dr. Gold pre-scribed her.

"You probably could have used this too." I motion to the

ocean view, not quite looking at her. "I feel bad I was the only one who got the escape hatch. . . ."

"It makes me *happy* you had it." She takes a deep breath. "And I'm fine. I've been fine."

I'm reminded of something she said in the middle of our argument at Cynthia's. *I don't get to have bad days anymore.*

"You're still allowed to talk about your bad days, Brooke."

"No, I'm not," she dictates in her matter-of-fact attorney voice. "Think about it: How can I tell *you* I've had a bad day? A shitty summer? What a slap in the face that would be, right?" An incredulous laugh escapes her. "I can't."

"Brooke—"

"How can I *complain* to you ever again? How selfish would that be?" Her voice is shaking now. "Because let's just be honest—if there's anything that's not fair here, we all know what it is."

"Stop!" The word bursts out of me more forcefully than I intended. She's starting to scare me.

But she can't stop. Brooke has had her own words festering all summer too. "Why you and not me?" A guttural sob escapes her. "You think that doesn't torture me too? You don't think I stay up all night wondering why I'm the lucky one?"

Looking at her—shriveled, tired, splotched with tears—it's hard to reconcile her as the "lucky" one.

"It's DNA," I remind her. "It's nothing either of us had anything to do with."

"But I wish it was me!" Tears bathe her face with sorrow. "I would take a bullet for you. Any day of the week. I need you to know that." Our eyes meet. "I would take HD for you. I wish I could."

The words alone harden my blood with grief. It would *destroy* me if Brooke had this. To watch her go through this. To know there's nothing I could do to ultimately make it better.

And there it is. Exactly how she feels. Brooke's not the lucky one. HD leaves no family member unscathed one way or another. I know that now.

Raw instinct takes over, and I clobber her elfin body like I'm a linebacker. "It's not your fault this happened." My words seem to dissolve whatever last bits of anger I was holding on to, and I wrap my arms around her even tighter. Like I used to when I was a little girl, begging her not to leave the house for playdates or activities when I couldn't tag along.

Brooke exhales, and when she speaks again, it's barely audible. "I guess my point is, I know you said you don't, but I wouldn't blame you for hating me."

"I don't," I implore. I'm determined to make her feel better. "It makes more sense for it to be me, anyway. You've got it all together. The world needs your brilliant legal arguments. What are they missing out on with me? Someone who basically lives in the 'Deal with Later' pile? I'm not even going to college."

She snaps her head toward me. "What are you talking about?"

"Uh, yeah, I kind of messed that all up." I explain the

243

medical records email, but the airtight logic of my reaction a few nights ago seems a lot shakier as I hear myself recount the details.

Brooke works through it, mentally checking off boxes so she can best advocate for her new client. "Have you reached out to Coach Jacobson? I'm sure she can convince admissions to make an exception."

I'm still not sure I'd want her to. Not that it matters, anyway.

"She specifically said 'no exceptions,' and believe me, I used up all my free passes with her." I dig my sneakers into the dirt. "I'm sure it wasn't hard to replace me. She probably already has."

"Are you kidding me? It's like you can't see who you are sometimes, Abbs." For a moment she gazes at me like I'm the big sister.

"When do you go back to school?"

Her body sags. "Whenever I can get my shit together."

"When have you ever had a problem getting your shit together?"

"It's not a big deal," she says quickly, but a dark cloud sweeps across her face. I stare her down. "Fine. I've just been having trouble sleeping. And I get these stomachaches all the time that are, like, impossible to get rid of. But Dr. Gold is adjusting my prescription so I think it'll get better soon."

I link my arm in hers, unable to shove down the excruciating pain at seeing my type-A sister so completely adrift.

"I *did* schedule a meeting with my mentor before classes

start next semester," she adds, her words pumped up with a bit more positivity. "I'm hoping by then I'll have adjusted my life plan spreadsheet so I can review it with her."

The wave of familiarity is comforting. "A new life plan spreadsheet? Lay it on me."

"I'm going to end HD."

I search her face for signs that she's suddenly cracked, but her eyes pop with resolve.

"Seriously, that's my new life plan. Whoever I need to fundraise for, whatever medications I need to lobby for, for better insurance policies—I'm going to be part of getting this drug or this cure for you one way or another."

"No pressure," I crack, though I'm touched by her fierce dedication.

She smiles, and the tension of the moment releases, as if a drain has been pulled loose.

She leans her pint-sized head on my arm. "I've missed you, Abbs."

"Me, too. Do me a favor, though."

"I want to say 'anything.' But that scares me."

I grin. "I want real Brooke. Not the sugarcoated version. No censoring your bad days."

"I have plenty of people to complain to. If anyone deserves to *not* hear me complain ever again, it's you."

"What if that makes it worse? Like Brooke's life is so perfect, she *literally* never has a bad day and it makes me feel way more depressed about my own life?"

"Okay. You may have a point there," she concedes. "But if you ever want to hurl at the sound of my voice complaining about my annoying roommate or my curling wand dying, please tell me to shut the eff up."

"Noted."

A giddy energy overtakes us as we make our way back. We mess around taking photos of the two of us at every summit, judging and eliminating until we finally find one we both like. I text it to Mom, who replies with fifteen heart emojis. Clearly this sister reunion has been stressing her out from afar.

"So, there's one more thing we need to discuss," Brooke says carefully as a lizard darts by us. I know exactly what she's referring to just from the tone of her voice. *Dad.*

"Brooke, I can't."

"We have to, Abbs. I know you think you have a sense of everything going on with him, but there are things I need to tell you."

"Please. Not now. I am tapped out."

I wait for her to argue with me, but she looks drained. Or maybe she's remembering everything I said last night and she's actually listening to me.

"Fair enough. For now."

For now. The words echo in my head like I've shouted them into a canyon. I wonder how long "for now" can last.

Right before sunset, we reach the final leg of the hike, the one that circles back over the front beach. I spot Curtis in the distance whipping through waves on his kiteboard. I causally check if Ben is nearby filming, but I don't see him.

Brooke slows down to watch Curtis. "He's something else."

I think back to the moment between me and him on the ledge. "He's pretty great."

"All your friends seemed really nice, by the way."

"If they still are my friends," I mumble. "I ruined Lucy's whole birthday."

"She was worried about you, not upset. I think she just wants to know you're okay."

I quickly text an apology to Lucy.

Lucy: All good. I hope you're feeling better.

Me: Can we do a birthday redo?

Lucy: Only if you promise to sing.

The fact that she's at least joking around makes me feel slightly better.

"And Ben's really great too," Brooke adds pointedly.

My face tightens with regret. "I've pretty much ruined that."

"Not possible. Not the way he was looking at you yesterday, Abby."

"Like he should've let me drown?"

Her face gets dead serious. "Let me tell you, I've waited my whole life for a guy to look at me like that."

I ignore the butterflies that burst in my stomach, because they're suddenly weighted down with lead. "But will he still look at me like that once I've told him everything?"

Brooke presses her lips together, not answering right away.

"What do I do?" I plead.

"I can't tell you that, Abbs."

"Why? Because if it doesn't work out, I'll blame you and not talk to you for another three months?"

"Partially, yes. Have we already moved on to the joking phase about that?"

"Apparently."

Two bikers approach, and we press ourselves against the side of the mountain to make room for them to pass.

Once we start walking again, I turn back to Brooke and chuck my pride. "Please. I am longing for some Brooke logic on the matter."

She contemplates it for a moment. "At some point you'll probably feel like you need to tell him the truth. I don't know if it's now or not. Only you know what that breaking point is. But I can say that at the very least you owe him an apology right now."

"I know."

"I have no clue what happened between you guys yesterday, but he was still as worried as I was when you were up there."

We reach a fork in the road—one path cuts across to Cynthia's, the other leads to the beach. Where I'll probably find Ben.

"Should we head home?" I veer toward the Cynthia path.

Unfortunately, Brooke's onto me. "You jumped off a cliff yesterday no problem, but *this* scares you? I thought you were suddenly all about grabbing life by the ovaries."

"Jumping off a cliff is way easier than this."

"Than what? Facing Ben?"

"He'll be the first person I've ever told." Fear chills me to the bone.

"Which is huge," Brooke agrees. "It's your decision. No judgment here, no matter what."

I look out to the ocean and see his dad's boat bobbing in its usual spot. I think of my last night there with Ben, what he told me about his sister. That at a certain point he had to learn to walk away.

How long can I feed him half-truths and push him away before he decides the same about me?

I understand what Brooke is saying about a breaking point.

I might lose him if I tell him the truth.

But I'll definitely lose him if I don't.

28

I reach the sand in time to see Ben dragging a kayak up from the water. I guess he went alone today.

The beach is desolate, and the jackhammer rate of my heart rings in my ears as I march toward him. When he spots me, there's no smile. Not even a frown. There's *nothing.* Like I'm a stranger. Worse than a stranger since Ben usually treats them like long-lost friends, too. If only Brooke could see the way he's looking at me now. Maybe she'd change her assessment.

"Hey," I try awkwardly. My cheeks burn, and I want the sand to swallow me whole.

He gives me a curt nod that feels like cold water being dumped on my head.

This is the other side of the coin with Ben. When his attention is on you, it's so all-consuming. Like you're the star his planet revolves around. It makes the opposite feel that much worse. Like you've been abandoned in a distant corner of the galaxy, dark and cold and lonely.

I shift uncomfortably in the sand. "I'm sorry. About before."

There's a flicker of interest in his eyes. "Which part?"

"Um . . . all of it?" His face goes blank again. Apologies have never been my forte. I take a deep breath. "I shouldn't have said that about your sister."

He finishes shoring the kayak, arranging it in line with the others. "What was that up there? Some kind of death wish?"

How can I explain to him, I have the opposite. I have a *life* wish. "It was something I wanted to try. I didn't mean to scare everybody."

"Right. Well, Curtis was a fucking idiot for letting you do it." His eyes snap darkly to Curtis all the way across the beach, bringing his kiteboard in, and I wonder if this is another mess I've left in my wake.

"Was there something else?" he asks. His sharp, needlelike look is a good indication that this is the last shot I'm getting, so I better make it count.

"Ask me anything," I blurt out.

He bristles. "So you can not tell me the truth? I think we've played that game enough this summer, Abby."

"Please. I want to be honest with you. Give me a chance."

Ben gives me a look, like *Then go ahead*.

"I don't know how to start. But I'll answer whatever you want."

He doesn't say anything, but he doesn't walk away, either. It's the first opening I've gotten from him, and I pounce.

"Isn't that what you're supposed to be good at? Asking the right questions. Getting the story."

His lip quirks slightly. "Okay, Abby. You got me there. Let's sit."

"Why?"

"Because I have a lot of questions."

We end up in one of the palapas as dusk settles over the empty beach, sitting side by side in two lounge chairs. It would be a lot easier in the kayak, where he can't see my face and I don't have to see his.

After a moment he says, "Your dad . . . Is he sick?" This is what he's guessed after Brooke's comment on the boat yesterday.

"Yeah."

"Why couldn't you have told me that?" From the frustration in his voice, this is a sore point. That I didn't trust him.

There're a lot of reasons I never told him about it, obviously, but I settle for the biggest. "It felt better to pretend it wasn't happening." His eyebrows raise a millimeter, and I can tell it's not what he was expecting to hear.

"Was that the truth the other night? When you told me you haven't seen him since you were five?"

"Yes." I turn my head to face him. "But you asked if he'd ever reached out again . . . Six months ago he sent me and Brooke a letter out of the blue. That's how we found out he's sick."

"From a letter? That must have been crazy." His eyes warm, my truth seeming to absolve me from my earlier lie, though he doesn't yet realize how much more truth there still is to tell.

Our fingers dangle closely together, and he squeezes my hand. "I'm sorry about your dad."

I think he's the first person to tell me that. "Thank you."

"What does he have?"

I ignore the voice inside my head telling me to run, to lie, to hide.

"Huntington's disease." I can hear the quaver in my voice.

His brow creases. "What's that?"

"It's a fatal disorder that causes the breakdown of nerve cells in the brain." I watch him try to decipher the answer I've memorized. "It's basically like Alzheimer's, Parkinson's, and ALS combined into one megadisease."

"Shit." He exhales deeply, then pushes himself up on his elbows. His gears are turning. He doesn't know it yet, but I have officially reached the point of no return. "What are the symptoms?"

I recite them like a grocery list—depression, memory loss, impaired movements, losing control of your ability to think. He nods along, but I sense it's not fully landing. My instinct is

253

to stop myself at this point. But I'm halfway there, and if I'm really doing this, he needs to hear the ugliest parts. "In the last stage, you can't walk or communicate, and have dementia on top of that. It's brutal, Ben. Symptoms started later in life for my dad, but they usually start earlier. Like when someone's in their late thirties or forties."

"And there's no c—"

"Cure. No."

His face falls. "Is there some kind of treatment that at least helps?"

I curl my knees into my chest, wishing I could make myself small enough to disappear. "A few medications can help with the depression and the chorea. Those are the jerky movements. But, no . . . there's no treatment. A new drug that's being tested looks like it might actually help. But that's years down the line. If it pans out at all."

"And you said it's fatal?"

Pressure squeezes my throat. He looks so sad for me. That this is happening to my dad. "Yes. People usually die from the symptoms."

"What do you mean?"

Anyone but Ben would be okay with a glossed-over version of this conversation. They'd nod along and say how sorry they are, eager to move on from their own discomfort. But not Ben. He won't carelessly throw out a few sympathetic phrases or ide-ologies before he's collected as much information as possible.

"Like . . . choking to death. Because they lose the ability to control their tongues. That's the most common way people die with Huntington's disease."

That shakes him, and he leans back in the lounge chair again. Processing. I turn my gaze toward the ocean, only partially lit now by a sliver of sun. I can't watch Ben's face as he absorbs my answers, building on them brick by brick until all he needs is that last one. The final brick to construct the full narrative.

"Do they know what causes it?"

There it is. I can hear the sound of fear pumping through me. "Yes. It's genetic."

He shifts his body in the chair uneasily. "What does that mean?"

Tremors ripple across my body. "If a parent has the gene, their children have a fifty-fifty shot of having it too. There's a blood test you can take to find out."

His jaw tenses. Our palapa is suddenly pin-drop quiet.

He knows.

He probably knew as soon as I said "genetic," but now he's certain.

This is like diving into a plate-glass window, then stabbing myself with the shards. But I have to say it out loud.

"Brooke and I debated taking the test. We had to go through counseling first because . . . uh, it's really hard for people to deal with the results. But we decided to do it."

Silence. He doesn't move a muscle. "And we got the results a few days after I graduated. Before I came here. Brooke's test was negative."

I close my eyes when I say it.

"And mine was positive."

I open my eyes and wait for his reply. Three seconds. Five seconds.

He doesn't look at me.

He doesn't reach out for me.

He keeps his eyes fixed on the sky, an impenetrable expression on his face. "That . . . sucks."

That sucks? I wait a beat to see if there's more, but he remains silent and avoids eye contact. I mean, sure, it's hard to know what to say. I wasn't expecting a beautifully composed sonnet. But it's *Ben*. He's had something enlightening to say on every topic I've hurled his way all summer. I was hoping he'd be the one to get it right.

Or, if not right, to give me something resembling human emotion.

I tuck my chin between my knees, determined not to show him how badly he's just hurt me. I've already laid myself bare enough. "You have to admit the whole thing is hilarious. The irony."

He *finally* looks at me. "What do you mean?"

"Mr. Fixer. I was on your radar from the beginning, and you didn't even know it. And here you thought you broke the cycle." I laugh and suddenly can't stop. "I'm *incapable* of being saved. It's like I had a target on my back."

"Abby." He sits up fully, twisting around and swinging his legs toward me. "Don't do this." He rests a hand on my shoulder and tries to pull me closer. "I didn't . . . I'm just . . . This is not what I expected you to say. Give me a second."

I wriggle out of his embrace. "It's okay. I don't need pity. I don't need some big speech. You have your answers now."

"I shouldn't have pushed so hard for this. I didn't realize . . . ," he mumbles, looking down at his feet burrowed in the sand.

He wishes he didn't know.

That alone carves out such a huge chunk of my heart, I'm surprised I can still hear it thumping. I wish I didn't know this about me either.

"It's fine," I cut him off. I need this conversation to be over. It was ridiculous to think I could spring this on him and he'd somehow understand. I gave him too much credit, blinded by my attraction to him, seeing a depth that clearly was just a figment of my imagination. "It's actually good you know. Because now you can see why we can't be together."

I spring from the lounge chair, but he anticipates the move and is already up. He grabs my hand, and we stand there like that for the briefest moment, our eyes locked. A glimmer of the Ben from this summer flashes behind his eyes. The Ben I thought he was.

"Abby, stop. Come on. This doesn't have to change any-thing."

He's so cavalier it kills me.

"But it does, Ben. For me it changes everything."

Before I know it I yank my hand away and am running through the sand. I don't stop until I get all the way to Cynthia's house, breathless and broken.

29

I hover on the porch, tucked into the swing listening to the ocean until it's completely dark. I don't have it in me to face Brooke and Cynthia. To relive the moment with Ben all over again, only this time accompanied by their raw sympathies, the reality sinking in for Brooke that this is my life now. This is what it looks like when I reveal the truth to someone.

That's what I didn't understand about this disease. That each time you get a semblance of a regular life—college, Ben—it snatches it away. And every damn time, it's like opening that envelope all over again.

I knew free will was bullshit. My fate was sealed the day I was born.

By the time I go inside, the cottage is quiet. I tiptoe into my room to find Brooke already sound asleep in my bed. She produces a series of little sighs and delicate snores, the ones

259

Mom and I long ago coined "the snorechestra," and it sounds like home.

Her iPad is next to her, like she fell asleep reading it, and when I move it to the nightstand, the screen pops to life, to the home page of the HD Denver fundraiser. She undersold herself earlier. Apparently, she's become a cochair for the entire event. Emotion catches in my throat as I see the other tabs she has open. One about fundraising ideas from bake sales to mud runs to viral video challenges. Another tab open to a petition she's signed, demanding that Congress passes a bill against insurance discrimination for HD patients. Even with everything she's going through, she's still taken this by the ovaries.

A sudden surge of gratitude sweeps through me. Almost every pillar in my life has collapsed, but here's my big sister, in Catalina, no less. The one person not letting me down no matter how far I tried to push her away.

Maybe the only person who will be here for me from beginning to end of this mess.

It's depressing. But it's the truth. I know enough from the HD boards that the brunt of care goes to the siblings at some point.

It makes me think about Cynthia and Dad. Is there a point where she'll become his caretaker? Brooke said there are things she needs to tell me about him. At some point I won't be able to run from it, from him, I know that.

Quietly, I put down the iPad and shuffle into the living

room. There's a bookshelf where Cynthia stores all her pre-historic photo albums. I haven't flipped through any of them, knowing who's waiting for me behind those weathered plastic sleeves. But right now, I have this undeniable compulsion to see him.

I don't have to look far. On the very first page is a photo of Cynthia and Dad.

I let myself truly look at his face, something I've avoided for more than a decade. I examine it carefully, searching for the ways his face is different and the same as the one in my memory, to wonder about him in a way I haven't in years. To wonder what Brooke wants to tell me about him.

I keep flipping through the album until I reach a photo near the end that stops me cold.

It's a family photo from Disneyland. Cynthia holds a petite seven-year-old Brooke. I have an accusatory finger pointed in Cinderella's face. Mom has her hand over her mouth, stifling laughter, and Dad is grinning at me like I'd just won the Nobel Prize for Peace.

I never knew there was photographic evidence, or that Cynthia was there, but I've heard the Cinderella interrogation story dozens of times. Apparently, I asked Cinderella why she wanted to marry the prince when all they did was dance for an hour.

My eyes again drift to Dad's face, his expression fiercely proud, his hand reaching out to me, like maybe a few seconds later, he scooped me up and gave me a kiss.

We were a family.

The back of my throat burns as I look at all of us, bursting at the seams, so happy, so unaware of how good we had it in that moment.

How could he have just walked away? Even if he was depressed, how could he do this to us? But maybe it's pointless to wonder. I should know by now how quickly things can be taken away from you for no reason at all.

I head back to my room with the photo in hand, despondent. I didn't think I could feel worse after Ben, but somehow I've managed to make room for a whole new cycle of grief. Just when I think I've hit rock bottom, I keep finding new lows.

I gently nudge Brooke to the side, tucking myself in next to her, like we've done countless nights over the years. Out the window, the moon lights up the sea of the back bay.

It's like my first day in Two Harbors all over again. Me, alone with my thoughts, staring at the ocean. But seeing inside my soul isn't as scary as it was two months ago.

I already know it's heartbroken.

I hear a faint rustling, probably a fox scurrying across the hillside.

But a moment later a dark shadow falls across the window. Someone is right outside. A quick flash of fear bolts me upright.

I look to Brooke, like she'll have an answer as to what to do, when I hear his voice. "Abby, it's me."

Ben.

The fact that it's him outside my window and not a stranger does nothing to decelerate my pulse.

I slip out of bed and step out quietly, the sultry evening air warming my bare arms, like a shawl.

"What are you doing here?" I studiously avoid looking him in the eye. I won't let him see how much he's hurt me.

"Abby, I'm sorry. I messed up. I said the wrong thing." Something in his voice makes me bring my gaze up to him. He's disheveled, his eyes red-rimmed and bloodshot. "It's not an excuse, but I . . . was floored. I was upset. I *am* upset." He shakes his head, then adds under his breath. "Like, that word isn't grossly inadequate."

I shake my head in frustration. "Yeah. I was *upset* too, Ben. I thought—" I cut myself off. I can't tell him I think so much of him that I thought he'd be the one person who actually knew the right thing to say. How much it broke my heart when he didn't.

"I get it now. I'm sorry. I get it. I just read every article about HD I could find online. Watched the videos. Jesus." He cringes, and I wonder what he's imagining right now—the chorea, limbs wildly out of control, or maybe a heartbreaking, slurring testimony from someone in their thirties.

When I look back to him, he's watching me carefully. "I don't know how you got out of bed every day this summer." He takes a step toward me. "I'm in awe of you."

"Stop." I want to be the strong disease hero about as much

as I want to be the fragile sick person. And in any case, I don't know that I've been the pinnacle of dealing with things well.

"Some of the things I've said this summer . . . You must have . . ." He falters and rubs a hand through his messy hair. He's thinking of our kayak conversations. Free will and fate. "I feel like an idiot. I'm sorry."

"You didn't know. I never faulted you then." What I've left unsaid hangs between us. *Not like now.* I feel myself instinctively backing up toward the window.

"I fucked up before. I know that. I was shocked, and I'm not always good on the spot." He senses my hesitation. "Really. I hate opening gifts with an audience. I suck at games with timers. I don't always have the right response when it counts. I've always been better with an editing room." He takes another step toward me. "I wish I could go back in time, pop in take two of my response, so you could understand how I really feel."

Curiosity stops me in my tracks. "What would that look like?"

He lowers his eyes to mine. The intensity warms the skin under my thin tank top. "I will be here for you whenever, however, forever." He takes a third step toward me, his voice softer. "That's what I should have said. That's the truth. And not because I want to fix you. I don't think you're broken. Never have."

I'm not sure I can accept this as real—it feels too good to

be true, like he still doesn't understand what he's agreeing to. "But . . ."

"I get that it changes everything. I do. But it doesn't change the way I feel about you."

Suddenly I'm the one at a loss for words. I don't have a reply that could hold a candle to that.

"Um, I guess I'm not so great on the spot either," I admit. "It's probably better we know this about us now."

"Know what?" There's an edge to his voice.

"That we'd be a really shitty charades team."

A smile hits his eyes, the air shifting to the charged energy that's existed between us all summer.

"I don't know where we go from here." I can barely catch my breath with the way he's staring at me right now.

His eyes darken, his voice raw and low. "Yes, you do." He moves closer until our bodies are nearly touching, his hands wrapping around me.

"It's not that simple," I say, trying to hold on to some control, though my body is telling me to shut up, to just say yes, to give in right this second.

"I played by your rules," he murmurs into my ear. "I spent half the summer trying to not want to be with you, Abby. Trying not to scare you away."

I should've known he was that perceptive.

"I can't keep doing that." He ropes me into him with one hand and cradles the side of my face with the other, lifting my eyes toward him. "It's not enough. I want to be with you, Abby."

My pulse nearly stops when I catch a glimpse of his vulnerable stare.

"Tell me you want this too," he whispers.

"I don't know, Ben . . . ," I mumble into his shoulder. Of course I want it. That's not the problem. But *can* I want it?

He kisses a trail up my neck until our faces are inches apart, our eyes looking into each other's. "I do. Abby, I love you."

I suck in a breath. *I love you.*

Those three words undo me. I close my eyes and let myself believe we can do this forever.

We slip back to his room on the houseboat.

His arms wrap around me, and his eyes burn with a question.

There's only one way for me to answer. I pull him close and bring my lips back to his, telling him with each kiss, *Yes, I want this. Yes, I want all of you. Yes, yes, yes* until we're falling, sinking into the bed, into each other, and everything contracts into a string of sensations.

The flimsy fabric of my camisole slipping off me.

My palms canvassing his skin, sliding over muscle, wanting to feel every part of him.

His voice low in my ear, whispering, promising.

His hands softly everywhere his lips aren't.

We're a tangle of limbs and lips, hot skin and warm breath.

The sudden coldness as he peels his body off mine, rustling for a condom.

And then he's back, the moonlight dancing over our bodies. His gaze rakes over every part of me, stretching this moment, his hand gently brushing my hair off my face.

"Ben," I whisper. I reach for him, grasping until we find each other, until we're one.

I'm falling through the air only to realize I can fly.

I'm invincible.

His stare burns through me—our eyes, our bodies, our souls, fused together—and I swear, I will never forget this moment. Long after my memory has been ravaged by this disease, I will find a way to hold on to this shred, and it will sustain me.

30

An explosion of bright color jostles me awake. My first Catalina sunrise. I groggily pick my head up from Ben's shoulder, looking through the small porthole at the swirls of amber and peach stretching across the mountains.

I love you.

His words still tingle through me.

I rub a hand across his chest, not wanting to wake him yet, a wave of warmth overcoming me as I watch him. It's beyond affection, beyond desire, beyond friendship.

He's the best person I know.

And with that thought, my stomach free-falls like I'm cliff diving again, and the Pit of Doom makes its delayed entrance this morning.

He's the best person I know. *And I will ruin him.*

I look at him again, and suddenly it's so obvious.

How did I not see that last night?

Those three little words that set me free last night will shackle him forever.

He said he didn't care, that it changes nothing for him. But those words sound like tinny half promises to my ears now. I'm sure he believes that, but there's no way he's let himself think this all the way through.

At some point the reality of what he's just signed up for will dawn on him. But knowing Ben, he won't let me go. Even when he should. Even when he *wants* to. He'll hold on out of loyalty or pity or a hope that he can somehow *fix* it.

Without a sound I slide out of the bed, quickly dressing, throwing on a sweatshirt of his I find hanging on the door.

When I glimpse back to him, his eyes are open, watching me. He blinks a few times. "You're freaking out," he says.

"I'm not." It sounds false, even to me. He sits up, reaching out to me, but I inch away delicately.

"You were seriously just going to walk out of here?"

"I'm giving you a chance to reconsider. I'm not holding you to anything you said last night." He's about to protest, but I keep going. "Reading a few articles about Huntington's disease doesn't mean you're ready to say"—I swallow down the rock in my throat—"what you said last night."

His eyes fire up. "I knew it before last night, Abby. I love you."

The words no longer thrill me. They scare the shit out of me. They should scare the shit out of him, too, if he was thinking straight. "That's the problem."

His brow furrows, before clarity overcomes him. "Abby, no. Don't go there."

"I can't do this to you."

He's up and standing now, bringing his hands to my shoulders, forcing me to meet his stare. "I told you last night. I don't care."

"You will, at some point." That's how much I care about Ben. That I could never let him go through this. I'll sacrifice myself before I let him do it for me.

"So, people who are gene-positive can't allow themselves to be in relationships? Come on, Abby. I read enough on the HD sites and message boards last night to know that's not true."

The thought of Ben reading through those sites suddenly nauseates me, like he's seen me exposed, naked under the harshest fluorescent light. I break free from him, even though the hollow absence of his skin on mine is physically painful. "I don't want to do this to you. It will make me feel like a monster."

His voice is soft and patient. "But you don't know what could happen. None of us do. I mean, I could get cancer before you ever get a symptom." The thought of Ben with cancer renders my throat dry. My face must be chilled-to-the-core stricken because he takes my hand and says, "I'm just saying that a lot could happen while you're waiting around for symptoms to hit. It's not a reason not to try."

Dr. Gold said the same thing. That I should be living my life—college, career, love—and not just counting down until the inevitable, especially when I don't know when that day will come. What if he's right?

What if I'm throwing all of this away for nothing?

Ben seems to sense my uncertainty and digs in harder. "Maybe this drug will be approved and be even better than everyone thinks."

"Maybe." The golden carrot of HD. Dangling just close enough that you're not a total fool to believe in it, but not close enough to give you anything real to grasp on to. "Or maybe miracle drugs and cures are just things I tell myself so I can get through the day without a panic attack."

Ben's eyes widen. "Abby . . ."

"I need air." I push the door open, heading up the stairs.

Ben catches up to me seconds later on the deck, still pulling a T-shirt over his head. "Abby, stop."

I shake him off. "No, you're right. I *don't* know how many good years I have." He looks at me, like he's not sure he should agree with me, even though it's what he just said. "That's the shitty part of HD. It tells you your ending, but leaves out the important parts, like the how and the when. Trust me, you want no part of that."

"Everything isn't decided already, Abby." His tone is sharp. "And you can't even see it when you have a choice staring you in the face."

"You can't see that no matter what choice I make, it all ends the same way! With you getting hurt because of me!"

Ben exhales a deep breath. When he speaks again, his voice is calmer, reasonable. "Okay. Let's back up." He licks his lips. "We can keep talking about this. Figuring it out."

This is the problem. He thinks he can still convince me.

"I'm trying to do the right thing here. For both of us."

"Abby . . . do you hear what I'm saying? Nothing has to be decided right now."

He moves closer, and I'm worried if I let him get too close, I'll give in.

He lowers his face to mine. "We can . . . take a step back from what happened last night. We can slow things down. But I *will* be here for you." I immediately drop my gaze to my feet. I feel my resolve slipping. I need to get away from him. That's all I know.

"I have to get back to Brooke." The quickest excuse I can come up with. "Please take me home."

He nods, reluctant. He doesn't love pausing this right now, but he's not going to stop me, to give me a reason to call it off altogether right here, right now.

We motor across the quiet back harbor in the dinghy, until we reach the pier.

"We'll talk more later," he says definitively as I step off the boat. "We'll figure this out. Okay?"

I nod. I can see his brain already working, the arguments he's building to convince me. He's already seeing all the ways he can fix this.

But I already know it's done.

31

I slip back into Cynthia's house and silently pad down the hall, hoping to crawl back into bed unnoticed. But when I enter my room, no stealth maneuvers are necessary. Brooke is fully dressed and hurriedly packing her suitcase. The fact that she's tossing clothes in and not carefully rolling each item tells me something is amiss.

She stops for a second when she sees me. "Where have you been?"

"Uh . . . with Ben." I brace myself for a flurry of questions, but her expression barely changes. Something is *really* wrong. "What's going on?"

"It's Dad."

I'm seized by the usual nausea at hearing his name, but the scared look on Brooke's face unnerves me further. "What happened?"

"He had a fall in the middle of the night."

My chest tightens. Is walking already becoming difficult for him?

"I don't know exactly what happened, but it's bad."

I sink down to the bed. "How bad?"

"Fractured leg, possible brain hemorrhaging. They rushed him to the ER."

"Is he going to be okay?"

Brooke pauses, and a weird expression crosses her face. "I'm not sure. I just know I want to be there. The ferry to Dana Point leaves in fifteen minutes, and it's not too far to the hospital in San Diego from there."

"San Diego?"

"That's where he lives. Mom is on the way too. She already hopped on a flight." She's pelting me with so much new information, I can barely absorb one thing before the next one comes hurtling my way. Like I'm behind a ball machine set to diabolical.

Brooke looks at the clock: 8:45 a.m. "Crap. I'm going to be late." She stops packing for a second and straightens. "I think you should come too."

I suddenly realize the clothes she's throwing into the bag are *mine*.

"Your choice," she's quick to add.

"Then why are you packing half my closet?"

"I don't want you to lose the option. We have to leave in two minutes."

She watches me, expecting a decision *right now.*

"Okay." I surprise myself almost as much as I do Brooke with my quick answer.

"Okay, as in yes, you'll come?"

"Yes. I'm coming."

If she'd asked me why I decided to come along with her, what made me say *okay,* I'm not sure how I would answer.

Is it because curiosity has finally won out? Because after looking at those photos last night, I *am* curious. At seeing Dad in person after so long, but also to see for myself how he's handling HD, as if that might give me some kind of clue about my own future. Or maybe it's that I'm scared he'll die, and this might be my last chance to see him, and even though part of me is chanting *Who cares,* the other part is quietly whispering that the regret would always haunt me.

Or maybe because even if he ends up okay, I'm sick of delaying the inevitable until *later.* This disease has tied Dad and me to the same train track, and I might as well accept it and see him, instead of putting it off any longer.

It's probably all of the above. But in any case, I'm doing this for me, not him. I know that. I'm new Abby. Dealing with things head-on. Being proactive.

And so I ignore the little voice in my head telling me this is the oldest Abby story of them all. That Catalina has become so messy and hard that escaping to a hospital room across the ocean from Ben suddenly sounds like a very welcome break.

        ———

Cynthia sees us off at the door with care packages of warm coffee and homemade orange-cranberry muffins.

She gives me an extra-long hug, pressing her soft cheek against mine. "I'm happy you're going."

"Are you sure you don't want to come?" I ask as we pull apart. If things are seriously wrong, doesn't she want to see him, too? Even with a rocky relationship, he's still her only brother.

"I will. But I want to give you all some space. You haven't seen him in thirteen years. I saw him last week."

I look up at her in surprise. "You did?"

"When I went to the mainland to get Shanti's food."

Brooke calls out to me from the top of the trail that winds its way to town.

Cynthia scooches me out the door. "I can always hop on a ferry later. You need this."

"What if he doesn't recognize me?"

Cynthia gives me an odd look. "What do you mean?"

"They said his brain might be hemorrhaging."

Her expression clears. "Right. Whatever it is, you can handle it, Abby. I know you can."

Chip appears in the doorway behind Cynthia. "You forgot something, Abbs." He presses the amethyst into my hands. "Just in case."

"Thanks, Chip."

Brooke calls out to me again, and Cynthia gives my hand one last squeeze. "We all make choices we regret. That's how we learn how to make the good ones."

32

"I think I—" Brooke interrupts herself by dry heaving in the trash can again. The choppy waters have done a number on her stomach.

"I can see Dana Point. Only a few more minutes," I assure her, rubbing her back.

A nice man brings over a ginger ale. A little more color pops into Brooke's cheeks after she sips it, but her overall complexion is still one shade lighter than army green.

She practically sprints off the ferry when we dock, her legs shaky and trembling, and I follow behind her, toting our luggage. If stepping off the ferry in Avalon was culture shock, this is culture electrocution. I watch everything whiz by from the outskirts of my vision because seeing it head-on is too overwhelming. Giant buildings, cluttered streets, *stoplights*.

The combination of the deafening noises is like listening to your least favorite band at full volume.

It isn't until we're in the cab on the way to the hospital that Brooke is recovered enough to speak. She finger-combs her hair, takes a sip of water, and pops a breath mint. "Abby, we have to talk about Dad."

"I know." There's no more avoiding and sidestepping. "Have you . . . *seen* him?"

"A few days after you took off, I flew to San Diego to see him."

I'm already confused. "Why did he make you come to him?"

She eyes me like I'm fragile. I hate it. "Abbs, there's no way Dad could travel anywhere. That's why Mom and I went to him."

"Wait, Mom went too?" My voice cracks, evidence of the fragility I just balked at.

She hesitates. "Dad lives in an assisted living facility. He's just entered the final stage of HD."

My jaw goes slack. "That's impossible."

The final stages are when you can't perform daily functions and have to rely on professional care. He was diagnosed a little more than six months ago. How did the disease progress that quickly? Or did it take that long for the doctors to realize it was HD and not something else?

"Can you, um, turn the air up, please," I mumble to the taxi driver.

"It's a lot to take in. Just try to breathe." Brooke squeezes my clammy hands. I guzzle a mouthful of air, but it makes me queasier. "That's why I was stalking you this summer, Abbs. I thought you should at least have the choice if you wanted to see him before . . ."

Bleary-eyed, I squeeze her hand back, hoping she understands that's me saying "thank you."

"There's one more thing you need to know before we get there." I bob my head up and down. "There's a woman who's going to be at the hospital. Dad's . . . I don't know what to call her."

"A woman?" My brain dials back into the conversation. Not at full capacity, but enough to formulate coherent sentences. "Is that why he left us? For this woman?"

"No, no. He met Ellen much later in an HD support group. She has HD too, but only mild symptoms so far. Very early stages."

If he met her in an HD support group, that had to have been less than a year ago. "He and this woman are like a couple?"

"I don't know exactly how it works. They love each other."

I shift uncomfortably, and the ripped leather seat crackles underneath me.

Brooke squeezes my arm. "It'll make more sense when you meet her."

The hospital is one of those massive sprawling developments, with a million entrances and wings and pavilions. But I'm grateful for each extra second it takes as we ask for directions, track back to elevators we missed, because that's one more second I get to put off all of this becoming unavoidably real. *Why did I think this was a good idea?* By the time we reach the waiting room, I'm low-key hyperventilating. I hold on to the doorframe, trying to steady myself, and when I lift my eyes, I see her.

Mom lights up, instantly rising out of her seat and opening her arms for me. Her eyes are swollen from crying, her cheeks visibly sunken, and I wonder if she's eaten at all since I left.

I practically dive-bomb into her.

She holds me tight and doesn't loosen up, even after a few long seconds. It's okay. I'm here for it. I inhale her scent—her usual floral conditioner, mixed with airplane—and I just want to hold on tighter too; some primal part of my brain lighting up with one single word over and over again: "Mommy Mommy Mommy."

At some point Brooke joins our embrace, and the two of them drench my face with their tears. When we finally pull apart, I notice the woman in the chair next to Mom's, watching us avidly. She's in her mid-fifties, with a chic bob haircut and a tailored dress.

"Abby, this is Ellen," Mom introduces.

"I've heard a lot about you," she says graciously through

282

tired eyes. I press pause on my impulse to reply along the lines of *So funny, I'd never heard of you till five minutes ago.*

"It's nice to meet you," I say instead.

Her right arm makes a series of small, jerky movements. Witnessing her abrupt and unpredictable chorea makes my fingers go numb. She's the first person I've seen in real life with HD, and it suddenly feels like I'm looking into a crystal ball.

"How's Dad?" Brooke asks, and that light-headed feeling returns.

Ellen and Mom both go to open their mouths, and there's this awkward *You go ahead, no you go ahead* moment. Clearly Ellen is the one who's more involved with his day-to-day care and doctors, while Mom is, in some ways, a stranger who's swooped in out of nowhere.

But she's also the one he created us with. I guess that wins because Ellen sits back and defers to her.

"The good news is that the CT scan confirmed there's no hemorrhaging," Mom answers. "They're going to keep monitoring him for another twenty-four hours. We'll be able to see him in a little bit."

My body sways like I'm still on the deck of the ferry. I want to understand what Mom is saying, but dizziness pounds me, my mouth suddenly dry as parchment. Water. I need some water.

I must make a wrong turn somewhere in my search for

the vending machine, because instead of reaching the elevator banks, I end up farther down the maze of halls. The last names of the patients are jotted down on dry-erase boards on the doors, each room containing a different family's suffering. *Jones, Hernandez, Lubbitsch.* The weight of it grips my throat, and I'm one minute from sending Brooke a *Please find me* text when I see the name written on the next door.

Freeman.

Also known as "Dad" in a different era of my life.

The door is barely ajar, the opening simultaneously tantalizing and terrifying.

After all these years of being apart, of having no clue where he was, alive or dead, he's *here,* just feet away from me.

My brain is buzzing, and before I can change my mind, I've quietly pushed the door open.

There's no fewer than five machines on either side of Dad's bed, blocking my view. It's not until I take a step forward that I'm able to see him, eyes closed, chest rising and falling rhythmically. He's asleep.

I exhale in relief. A few moments to see him before he sees me. The leg that's not fractured peeks out from underneath the blanket, irrefutably skinny, skin pulled tight over bones. His hair, dark and thick in the photos from Cynthia's album, is now peppered gray and thinned out in a short haircut.

Emboldened, I take one more step forward, let myself study him closer. His mouth hangs open, and his head is drooped. His arms are dotted with tubes, and his other leg is wrapped in a cast. But underneath it all, it's still *him,* and I'm instantly brought back to the last moment I ever saw him.

A regular school night, I was already in bed, my hair combed into two braids that dampened my pillow. Dad was handling the bedtime-story portion of the evening, which was always a bonus, because he would do all the voices. High, silly ones and deep, scary ones and funny made-up accents.

That night, just before he got up from my bed, he told me he'd read me one extra story. I remember wondering how I got so lucky. He opened up *The Giving Tree,* and by the end, his eyes were glassy. I was worried that he was upset, and he told me it was just the book. That it was a good book, but a sad book. Because the tree had tried to give the boy everything, but he didn't understand that until it was too late, and yet the tree still loved him.

"I'm like the tree, Daddy," I told him. "I love you when you're not here." Were those my last words to him?

He hugged me, no tighter than usual, and gave me a kiss on the forehead. I never saw him again.

As I got older I heard the rest of what happened that night. After a similar good night to Brooke, he hauled his suitcase down to the kitchen, where he told Mom he couldn't do it anymore and he was leaving. I'm sure there was more said than just that—a fight, a time when Mom was convinced he'd be back in a few days—but by the time she told me about it, years later, she couldn't remember it as anything but a big blur.

Why did he do it?

For years I've told myself that I'm done being hurt by it. But seeing him here, getting socked in the face by everything we could've had if he hadn't left, I'm not over it at all. Not even close.

Suddenly his arm jerks up, nearly banging into his chin.

Is he waking up, or is it just part of his chorea?

I don't want to wait around to find out.

I can't do this right now. Not yet. Not alone.

I whirl around, skidding out of the room as fast as I can and shutting the door behind me. I make it down the hall before I stop, breathless, one arm propped against a wall for balance, and I slide down to the cold linoleum floor.

And then it happens.

It's so sudden there's no time to stop it.

Tears explode down my face. Buckets of them, as if my body has stored each suppressed tear over the years, only to release them all now in a tsunami down my cheeks. One messy, ragged sob after another racks my body, until I'm scared I can't breathe. And just when it feels like I'm going to suffocate, I'm able to gulp in one deep, shaky inhale, before another sob hits.

I'm crying so hard it's making me dizzy. I feel like Alice in Wonderland. I could swim in this amount of tears.

"Are you okay?" The words come from above me.

It's Ellen. *Great.*

The sobs slow down, but the tears keep coming out in a long, languid stream.

"I'm fine." Dazed, I wipe the tears off my face with my sweatshirt, even as more replace them.

She plants herself on the floor next to me, tucking her dress under her, and hands me a pack of stiff hospital tissues. "I can see that."

Normally, I might appreciate this kind of light-hearted sarcasm in a dark moment, but not when I'm on the verge of another anxiety attack or emotional breakdown or whatever it is that's happening right now. I hug my knees into my chest to stop my body from shaking, the same question still going through my head. The one question I've apparently never stopped asking, whether I knew it or not. "Why did he do this to us?"

She looks at me in surprise. "It's a gene, Abby. He had no control over it."

"No, I mean, why did he leave us?"

That one renders her silent. It makes me cry harder, soaking tissue after tissue with tears and mucus. Whoever said crying is cathartic is an idiot.

"I shouldn't have come." I say it more to myself than to her, but she scoots closer.

"You would've regretted it if you didn't," she replies way too firmly, considering we met five minutes ago. I wonder if this is HD showing itself, the way it scrambles the brain's understanding of social cues.

But something in her eyes tells me that maybe she has all the answers.

Just then, we hear the clanging of the metal doors opening at the end of the hallway. Brooke and Mom light up in relief when they see me.

"Abby, there you are!"

They take in my splotchy tearstained face with surprise and look between me and Ellen.

"Are you okay, sweetie?" Mom asks, helping me up from the floor with an extended arm. "Thanks for finding her, Ellen."

"Of course. I'll see you in a bit. The coffee cart is calling me." She tactfully slips away, the metal doors announcing her departure, and leaves the three of us in the empty hall.

"The doctor came out while you were gone," Mom says gently. "We can go see him now." A shudder rolls through me, fresh tears prickling.

Brooke places a hand on my shoulder. "Abbs?"

"It's just a lot," I reply truthfully, dotting my eyelids with tissues. "I'm trying the best I can, but it's a lot."

"I know." She rubs my back, and I'm appreciative of this new Brooke. The one who is refraining from giving me a lecture on "dealing with things" and is content to let the moment sit.

"Visiting hours are going to end soon," Mom says eventually. "If you want to see him today, it has to be now, sweetie."

Watching Dad for those few seconds while he was sleeping reduced me to a pile of emotional rubble.

What makes me think I can handle this?

Then again, how much more upset can I get?

We reach his room together, and his voice carries through the door. A garbled, angry slew of words, of which I can make out a few: "don't," "stop," "alone."

We step inside and huddle by the door, partly obscured by a privacy curtain.

"Time for your medication, Mr. Freeman," the nurse directs, unfazed by his outburst.

From where I'm standing, I watch him trying to sit up, disoriented, his left elbow jerking against the bed railing, his back sliding down the angled mattress.

"He's not always this angry," Brooke whispers to me, and for a second I wonder how the hell she knows that. Then I remember—of course, she's seen him already this summer. "He does better at the facility where they know him."

Once the nurse leaves, Mom and Brooke step toward the bed while I hide behind them like a shy toddler at a party.

"Hi, Dad," Brooke says calmly.

He gives her a jerky nod. "Brooke," he barks loudly, jarring me. He then mumbles something I can only half hear. I make out the word "terrible."

"This place *is* terrible," she agrees, giving his arm a reassuring pat.

I don't know how she can be so *okay* with him. Yes, she's had more time than me to acclimate to this. Yes, his fragility is disarming. But does that mean he can ditch us for our whole lives, only to have us swoop back, ready to help, right when he needs it most? I want to be a good person—I want to be the kind of person who can be instantly okay with that, to see his vulnerability and say all is forgiven—but it doesn't sit well with me. I can't snap my fingers and issue redemption so quickly.

"Jeff," Mom greets gently, and it takes a moment for his eyes to find her.

"Les . . . lie." His voice is shaky, the two syllables a labor. I know they already saw each other earlier this summer, but it's surreal to see them together like this. She gives him a tight smile, the kind where I can practically feel the lump in her throat.

"We brought Abby this time." She nods to me, and I step out from behind them, closer to Dad. His body instantly goes into overdrive, his shoulder jerking up again and again as his eyes dart around the room. He's confused, I can tell. Agitated.

My heart sinks. I knew coming into this room to not expect too much, but I guess I hoped for something more meaningful when he saw me.

"Hi, Dad," I whisper.

His eyes finally reach mine, flickering insistently. "Abby." He recognizes me.

He swings him arm wildly toward me, and I almost flinch before I realize he's *motioning* to me. To sit down next to him. I do, cautiously, on the side with his good leg, careful not to disturb the mess of tubes around him.

"Letter!" he barks, and I startle.

I look back to Mom and Brooke, who are suddenly holding their breaths. Mom doesn't meet my eyes as she pulls something from her bag.

I swallow as I take the envelope out of her hands. Even with all of Dad's fidgeting movements, like a person who just can't get comfortable, I can feel his eyes on me. I haven't opened it yet, but my whole body is shaking. Because I know whatever is in this envelope is about to change my life yet again.

I feel a hand on my shoulder—Brooke's, steady and re-assuring; she's standing behind me—and I unfold the paper along the creases that have clearly been opened and closed before.

It's typed up neatly, the date in the top left corner. But it's not from this summer.

It's dated from *three years ago.*

I look back to Brooke, and she gives me a nod. *Go ahead.*

And so I start:

For my Brooke and Abby,

I'm not sure when you'll read this letter, I hope you will one day. But I need to write it now, while my mind is still mine, so I can say this in my own words.

My mother was sick for years, and we all thought it was Alzheimer's and depression. But when the symptoms kept escalating, the doctors eventually tested for HD. The results came back positive, so I got tested privately and was also positive.

That was ten years ago.

My head rears up as my brain scrambles to do the math. He wrote this letter three years ago, got tested ten years before that. Not eight months ago at Christmas when Brooke and I first heard from him.

He found out he was positive *thirteen years ago.*

He's known all this time.

"You found out when I was five," I say breathlessly, clutching on to the hospital bed's guardrail to steady myself. I can't wrap my head around it. He found out he had the gene the same year he left us.

My brain is spinning, but I look back down to the letter, desperate to understand.

I need you to know this—I tried to stay.

But every hug, every smile, every "I love you"

sliced my heart open. It was impossible for me to look you both in the eyes, knowing I could've passed this fate on to you, my girls. My loves. And I knew it would only get worse. The two of you would have to watch me suffer through this disease, symptom by symptom, questioning whether this would be your future too.

For weeks I tried to figure out how to tell your mom, realizing it would force her into the same hell as me. Because once I told her, she would never stop wondering whether either of you had the gene. I couldn't do that to her. I wanted to give her more time without knowing. To wait until you were at least old enough to be able test yourselves, once Abby was eighteen. And I couldn't see a way around that if I stayed.

I take a gulp of air because I feel like I'm drowning. Brooke rises from her chair to sit on the other side of Dad. Mom migrates to the chair beside the bed and sits down next to me. I take another deep breath.

I'll never know if leaving was the best decision I ever made, or the worst. I was trying to do the right thing for our family. I wanted all of you to be free of this burden for as long as possible. But I also know that deep down, that's what I've been telling myself because I'm the one who couldn't handle it.

I've wanted to reach out a million times. I almost picked up the phone a thousand.

Every minute of every day you've been in my heart. You are my heart.

I love you,
Dad

A hand clamps down clumsily on mine. Dad's hand. Tears roll down both our cheeks.

"I wish . . ." Dad can't finish the rest. He doesn't need to.

"I wish too," I whisper.

Brooke puts her hand on top of Dad's, and Mom puts her hand on top of Brooke's. It's the first time the four of us have been in the same room since I was five. And that's how we stay until the nurse tells us visiting hours are over.

33

*E*llen's large traditional-style house rests on a hill that smells like freshly cut grass, even at night. Before we left the hospital, she insisted we all stay with her.

I'm so dazed I can barely see straight as we follow Ellen inside. This house could probably swallow three of ours back home. My eyes flick between the antique furniture and the high ceilings, an avalanche of formality after a summer in Cynthia's eclectic cottage.

Ellen shows Mom and Brooke where each of their rooms are, then leads me down the hallway. She stops at the door of a delicate floral guest room.

"Here we are. Fresh towels are in the bathroom. Whatever else you need, just let me know." She reaches out for my hands and sandwiches them in between her warm, velvety palms. "I'm glad you're here, Abby." I shove aside my awkwardness with random physical contact and return her gentle squeeze. I now realize she and Dad have been together a long time.

I clench my bottom lip in my teeth to stop it from quivering. "Is there anything we can do for my dad?" I'm suddenly desperate to help him. "Like getting him into of those trials? The ones for the new drug they're testing."

"He's too far beyond that." I appreciate Ellen not sugar-coating it, but her answer shovels out chunks of my heart. "But you've got more time with him. And some of those days, he'll be feeling good. You'll really be able to talk to him."

I rub my swollen eyes. "And the other days?"

"They won't be easy. But I can promise that you'll forget about those on the good days."

But will Mom and Brooke?

Ellen grips my hands tighter in hers. "Twenty-five years ago I opened my envelope. I've had a long time to try to figure out how to live with this disease hanging over my head. And I want you to know, it's not all bad. Good can come from this too." Her conviction tells me this isn't just a cliché feel-good message. She believes this. Will I ever? "I'm here for you whenever you need me."

Our glassy eyes meet, and I manage—barely—not to cry.

As soon as she closes the door behind her, I drop my bags and curl up in a disheveled heap on top of the bed. Tears tumble down to the wildflowers on the pale green duvet, as if they're watering them. Is it possible to become dehydrated from crying too much?

My whole life I've been asking why. Why did he leave us? Now I finally have my answer, but in all the scenarios I've come up with over the years, none have been as tear-out-my-insides devastating as this. The irony is so bitter I could choke on it.

He left *for* us. *Because* of his love for us. The ultimate sacrifice. And as much as this day has pummeled my heart like it's a punching bag, I believe that's what he thought he was doing.

But I also understand the other part of what he said. That maybe the sacrifice wasn't just for us. I know better than anyone how your world shatters after a positive result. There could've been a part of Dad who just wanted to escape it all. Wasn't that my first instinct too?

Now I've experienced both sides. Being the one who escapes and being the one left behind. At least I have an answer, though. An answer that releases the weight that's been living in me so long I almost forgot it was there.

I push my tear-streaked hair out of my face, and it feels like it's old gum stuck to the bottom of a desk. I need to shower. If not for me, then for everyone I come into contact with tomorrow.

I clutch the duvet with both hands and hoist my stiff body off the bed. My phone rolls out from underneath me, lit up with messages. Missed calls from Lucy. Texts from Lucy. A concerned text from Curtis: *Abby, are you okay? We're all really worried about you.* I have to count the words—ten words. That's like a novel from him. The swell of homesickness for Two Harbors is so fierce, I can smell the eucalyptus trees.

And there is a long chain of texts from Ben. He sent the first ones a few hours after I left.

> Ben: Why aren't you answering your phone? Where are you?

> Ben: Is this a signature Abby move? We need to talk and you just bail.

As much as I had an actual reason to get on the ferry, there's part of me who knows he's right.

> Ben: And now you're not even texting me back?

> Ben: So . . . I just talked to Cynthia. Whatever you're going through right now with your dad, I wish I was there. I want to be with you. No matter what. I love you.

My heart betrays me and melts at that. But nothing has changed since this morning. I'll still end up hurting him one way or another.

A painful throb travels up from my temples to my forehead. I sink back down on one of the ten throw pillows.

> Ben: If you're worried about destroying me—that's what's going to happen if I'm not with you.

There's one last text. He sent it just a few minutes ago.

Ben: Or maybe it's not me you're worried about?

My gut clenches.

Against all odds, he finally figured me out. And bonus points because he saw it before I did.

I'm scared I'll crush him, but I'm more terrified that he'll crush me.

Ben has a choice. Fixer or not, if at any point he decides it's too hard, too complicated, too soul crushing, he can leave—tomorrow, a year from now, ten years from now. He's not the one chained to this disease. He'll feel bad, but eventually, he'll find someone new, someone brilliant and perfect for him, with no messy genes. He'll move on. He'll fall in love again. And that's what will destroy me forever.

Because I never will. Not with the way I feel about him. I'll be left with my fate and a trove of painful, beautiful memories reminding me of just how much this disease has stolen from me. Until the disease takes that, too.

34

I dart down the hall to Brooke's room.

If my guest room is a garden, hers is a sunny day at sea. The walls are bathed in soft blue, with cheerful splashes of butter yellow on the bed linens and pillows. I bury myself underneath the pale honey comforter next to her. She's still wide-awake and lifts her stiff eyelids from the pillow.

"Best sleepover ever," she deadpans.

"Did I make it in time for the face masks?"

Brooke grins and snuggles in closer to me. "I'm glad you know now, Abbs."

My stomach twists and turns like it's braiding itself. "When I'm in the final phase, I want to be in a facility like Dad."

Brooke juts out her chin. "No."

"What do you mean 'no'?"

"I'll agree to long-term care. But *in-home* care," she lawyers me. "I want you to be in our home."

I spring up to a sitting position. "Our home?"

"My home. Our home. Who cares?"

"Your future husband and your future kids." I burn my eyes into hers, desperate for her to actually hear what she's saying. "You can't, Brooke. I was right next to you in that session about survivor's guilt. I get it. But you don't have to do this to release yourself from guilt you shouldn't have anyway."

Brooke rests her fingertips on her chest, unshakable. "That's not why, Abby. I want to do this."

"You don't understand what it's going to be like—"

"Jesus, Abby!" she cries. "You don't think I've done the research to understand exactly what it's going to be like? I have fourteen spreadsheets on this!"

A surge of love and gratitude for my sister knocks the wind out of me.

"Okay." I interlace my fingers with hers. "But only if this can be an ongoing discussion. I need time to wrap my head around it."

"Deal. And if at any point it's safer or better for you to live somewhere else, I'll facilitate that. I promise."

"Is that code for you're planning to commit me?"

Brooke cracks up, and the sound smooths out some of the wrinkles in my broken insides.

We pull apart when we hear two light raps on the door.

Mom pushes it open, and the three of us share a *Can you believe this shit is actually happening to us?* look. Mom wraps herself inside the warm, cozy sheets and nestles between us, and I melt my head into her chest. She strokes my forehead and scalp, the calming ritual we've had since I was little.

I look up at her. "Knowing everything you do now, do you wish Dad had told you the truth? Instead of leaving?"

Brooke and I watch her face intently as she stares off at an empty space in front of her.

"Yes. I wish he'd told me the truth."

I prop myself up on my elbows. "You don't think it would've been worse to watch us grow up, knowing we might have the gene?"

"It would've been hard," she concedes. "But when your dad left that night, he told me nothing. He said he was sorry, and then he vanished. Every night, I'd lie in bed, willing him to walk through the door so the nightmare would end."

"Me too," Brooke whispers.

Mom squeezes her hand. "Eventually, I realized he was never coming back, and he must've had some kind of major mental breakdown to keep him away from the two of you. But for me, nothing was worse than not knowing. Not being able to help you girls make sense of it."

I stare up at her in awe. "Mom, you're superhuman."

"I don't know about that," she says with a chuckle. "There were plenty of times I cracked under the pressure." She pulls the blankets around us even tighter. "At least I finally understand why he made his decision. He didn't want us to suffer."

"But we suffered, anyway," I counter.

"You're right." Mom gently kisses my forehead. "I wish he hadn't decided for all of us, which suffering was better or worse."

The three of us lean against one another, quiet in our agreement.

"Actually . . ." Mom breaks the silence. "I think, in general, running from a problem doesn't usually save anyone."

I whip my head to Brooke, suspicious. "You told Mom about Ben, didn't you?"

Brooke gives me a deer-in-headlights stare, which is all the confirmation I need.

Mom chimes in, "Cynthia told me too."

"Great," I groan, falling back on the pillow. She's obviously not wrong, though. I ran from HD. I ran from Brooke. I ran from Ben.

Mom takes my face in her hands. "Abbs, this may not affect you when or how you think it will. Then where will you be? Alone and hurting because you were scared of being alone and hurting?"

I stare at the comforter. "It's complicated."

A few tears spill down her cheeks. "You're right. But every time you fall in love—with or without HD—you run the risk of getting hurt. Fear is never a reason to miss out on something you want."

Brooke and I simultaneously lean our bodies against our indestructible mom.

She kisses the top of my head. "HD is just a part of your life, Abbs. Not all of it. Not even close."

I close my eyes, holding her tightly. She resumes our mutually soothing ritual until I drift off to sleep.

I wake with a start, Mom beside me and Brooke snorchestrating on her other side. A quick glance to the clock on the nightstand tells me I've only been out for an hour. It's barely past ten.

I tiptoe out of Brooke's room and into the dark hallway. The house is so quiet a sneeze would sound like a foghorn. I feel my way across the hall for my room and don't bother turning on the lights when I find it. I toss the decorative pillows aside and crawl into bed where my phone lies waiting for me. The reason I came back in here.

My palms are sweaty with uncertainty as I pull up the texts he's sent in the last half hour.

Ben: I love you.

Ben: I need you.

Ben: But just in case you never talk to me again, you should see this.

There's a video attachment.

My thumb hovers over the play button.

All summer I've been convinced it's my secret, my genes, holding me back with him.

The bigger question is, if I had met Ben without knowing anything about HD, would I still have run scared?

Ben said at the beginning of the summer that once you figure out the reason behind a pattern of behavior, you can break the cycle.

I was so busy diagnosing him, I never looked at my own battle scars. The way I've *always* held back, *always* been quick to run. I don't need Dr. Gold to explain there's a five-year-old still living inside me, petrified that Ben will kiss me good night and walk out the door one day, without reason, without warning. That I'm so scared of being blindsided again, I'd rather do it first.

I can already hear the excuses I would've given him, even if HD had never entered my orbit. *We're going to different colleges; it won't work. Long distance is too hard. Let's not ruin the friendship.*

I've spent a whole lifetime making choices based on missing facts and misinterpretations about why Dad left. And ever since he walked out of our lives, it's like I've been swimming with a life vest. Floating along the path of least resistance so nothing else could crush me. And falling in love with Ben is like diving into the deepest waters with nothing but his hand to hold on to.

So now I know the reason.

All I have to do is break the cycle.

I press play.

Right away, I realize it's his five-minute short film assignment for USC. The story of his summer.

The opening is a wide shot of Two Harbors, with a dreamy, sultry song in the background. I wait for the camera to settle on Curtis kiteboarding, but instead, it lands on *me*. Ben caught me in a private moment, eyes faraway, mind elsewhere. It's from the beginning of the summer, those first few days of total numbness.

The video seamlessly transitions into me at the center of it all, instead of on the edges. There are moments I knew I was being filmed, but as I watch shot after shot, the most incredible ones are when I had no idea the camera was on me. It could feel weird or voyeuristic, but it doesn't. It feels like I'm getting to see myself through his eyes. The song grows softer as the camera captures that moment of me dancing on the beach at sunset with Lucy and Curtis. Then Ben enters the frame, a hand wrapping around my waist before he kisses me.

The story of his summer is *us*.

The coloring gradually swirls darker, and I'm suddenly in the outer frame. Then the camera pans down to a single pair of feet in the sand. Ben's. Alone.

My heart jumps in my throat when I see the text that appears along the bottom of the screen: *For the record, I hate this ending. Looking into doing some reshoots if my lead is up for it.*

The screen goes to black, and I blink a few times. It was

306

like nothing I've seen before, hyperreal like a documentary, but also beautiful like an old silent film. I knew he had to be talented, but I didn't realize he's *this* talented. It's stunning and honest and also a heaping serving of vulnerability slammed right to my side of the court, as if he's saying, *Your turn now.*

35

'm alone in the back of the ferry, seats away from the trash can that became Brooke's best friend on our way to the mainland, and feeling queasy myself due to the bundle of nerves duking it out in my stomach.

But my heart explodes as I see the first signs of the rugged, rocky Catalina peaks. Last time I was on this ferry to Two Harbors I was running away. Now I'm running toward something, *someone.*

The beach is still quiet and fogged over this early in the morning, with only a few dozen tourists trickling off the boat with me. I debark, waving quick hellos to the few waiters who have days off and are waiting in line to take the ferry to the mainland.

A quick cursory check tells me he's not at the hut, though

I see Lucy and Curtis busily opening up. Lucy must feel my stare, because she suddenly looks up, her eyes widening at the sight of me. She scampers across the twenty yards between us and squeezes me tight. "Abby . . . how's your dad? I heard he had a fall."

"He's okay," I answer. "In his own way." I'm sick of secrets. I want to tell her everything. But that will have to wait for now. "Do you know where Ben is?"

"No. He texted me and Curtis last night that he wasn't going to come in today. He didn't say why."

I give her a squeeze goodbye and then hike to the quiet cove on the back side of the island, where the houseboat is docked. It's cool and gray—no hikers on the trail—just a single dinghy cruising in the mist.

I practically sprint down the path to the dock, but then stop in my tracks. I have no idea how I'm actually going to get to the houseboat, moored five hundred yards out. Breathless, I scan the area for something I can use—a kayak, a paddleboard. I'll take a piece of driftwood at this point. If worse comes to worse, I'll just swim.

That's when I see him. Ben emerges from the small dinghy, hopping up to the edge of the pier, a duffel bag in tow.

Where is he going?

He ties the boat to a post, then rises, and his back suddenly straightens sharply. He sees me. But he's squinting like he's not sure I'm real.

I rush toward him. "Ben!" I want to throw my arms around him, but he hasn't moved a muscle since he saw me. Maybe hurt can't be avoided, but humiliation definitely can.

"What are you doing here?" He doesn't sound mad. Just confused.

"I was going to text back, but . . ." I nod toward the duffel bag. "Where are you going?"

He rubs a hand over his hair. "I was rushing to get to the ferry." He says it like I should understand.

"The ferry?"

"To get to San Diego."

"For me?"

"No. For SeaWorld. I've never been."

I don't laugh because part of me is scared he's serious.

"Abby, yes. I was coming to see you."

"I knew you were joking." I can feel the embarrassing shade of red spread across my cheeks.

"But why are *you* here?" He edges closer to me, finally seeming to believe that it's *me,* in the flesh.

"Um, I watched your movie." I take a breath. "I thought some reshoots were in order."

He tilts his head. "Really . . ."

It feels like my organs are battling for space.

Come on, Abby. Don't choke now. You're so close.

Then, what once seemed impossible to say, bursts out of me. "Because I love you."

I feel his smile against my mouth, just before I kiss him,

and the rest of the world falls away around us in the cool morning.

The alarm on his phone breaks the moment. "The ferry is leaving in ten minutes." He presses a kiss to my neck before he looks back at me like he still can't believe I'm here. "Do you need to go back?"

As much as I hate to leave this island, our cocoon, I want to get back to my family. To Dad.

I don't have to say a word for him to get it. "Do you want me to come with you?"

"Yes." It's messy and scary, and he's going to see Dad at some point, and I don't know if I'm ready for any of that. But I still want him there with me.

We make it back to the ferry just in time. While Ben takes his suitcase to the bottom deck, I climb to the top to find seats. I settle into the last row, inhaling the quiet, the Catalina magic that makes my blood hum, and I close my eyes.

I let myself drift back to that envelope moment. To the split second before Dr. Gold tore it open.

But this time I picture myself stopping him, imagining what my life would look like after that.

Leaving it sealed would mean no Catalina. No Cynthia and Chip. No Ben. No realizing what's important, no reason to actually focus on what I want. A giant question mark still hangs over my future. I know that. But there's a giant question mark over everyone's future, whether or not we realize it.

Thinking about my death forced me to think about my life. And it jump-started it.

When I open my eyes, Ben is sliding into the seat next to me. I lean into him, our bodies tangling together, my head nested in the crook of his shoulder. He pulls out his phone, sticks his arm out, and films us, just like that, as Catalina recedes in the background, until it's no more than a dot, a memory.

Eight Months Later . . .

I sit cross-legged in my pajamas on the floral bed in Ellen's guest room and stare at the journal in my lap. The one Cynthia gave me my first day in Two Harbors. The one I've carted around with me for the last year, the pages still blank. It doesn't feel quite as toxic as it did last summer, though. After Dad's funeral yesterday, there's part of me that actually *wants* to crack it open. Thoughts are swirling around in my head, bubbling up to the surface like they need to be released.

"Usually people write in those things," Ben muses from where he's walked in the room.

"So I've heard." I twirl the pen in my fingers uselessly.

He tilts his head at me with that smile that's just mine, and right on cue, my stomach flutters. You'd think its effect on me would've worn off by now, considering I've seen him almost every day since last August, but nope. It's that good.

Ben ended up deferring for a year—not to work on the documentary, but to take our version of a gap year together, to appreciate this time *right here, right now.* For real this time.

We went to San Francisco and Denver; we met up with Lucy in the Florida Keys during her spring break to watch Curtis crush his record in a kiteboarding competition. And we spent the time in between with Dad, in San Diego.

I swallow down a few tears and stare back at the empty page, willing myself to fill it. It's been in this last month that Dad stopped having good days, and it was just about caring for him however we could; about Mom, Brooke, and I showing him the same love that we knew he'd always carried for us all those years we were apart.

We've always been our own little unit, but now we feel destructible, more tightly bound than ever, even as we've made room for Ben, Ellen, Will, and of course, Cynthia and Chip. Our family expanding, even as we lost the person who brought us all together.

Ben climbs into bed, and I lay my head against his chest, losing myself in his spicy scent.

"You know I was in this room when I realized how crazy in love I am with you," I murmur, skimming my fingers across his chest.

"So this room makes you smart. . . ." He pulls me closer and I loosen my grip on the journal.

Before our year off comes to an end, we're spending the summer in Two Harbors, the only place I want to be after losing Dad. It also feels like the right place to prepare myself for freshman year in the fall. The second I strolled onto the beachside UC Santa Barbara campus, its landscape looking just like Catalina, I knew I'd found the one. It didn't hurt that it's only an hour and a half from Ben at USC. The one thing it doesn't have is Nina, who thankfully understood why I changed course. She's already booked two trips to visit and has begun referring to my dorm room as her "winter home."

Ben turns on his side to face me, a question already brewing in his eyes. "What's stopping you from writing in that journal?"

"I don't know where to start," I admit.

"That's the easy part." His heart thumps against mine. "Start from the beginning."

He lies back, handing me the pen that's fallen beside me, and suddenly it doesn't feel so hard.

I take Ben's advice and start from the beginning.

Obviously, it happened right before Christmas. Because don't all extremely shitty things happen right around the holidays?

Authors' Note

While Abby and Brooke are fictional characters, we strived to keep their journey through Huntington's disease as accurate as possible.

However, some details were streamlined or adjusted:

The drug trial that offers Abby hope is based on several drug studies currently in various stages, all aimed at stopping the HD mutation. In 2017, the results of one such study were hailed as a major breakthrough. That study has been expanded into a three-phase trial. Small but encouraging updates continue to be released.

Because news and science change so quickly with regard to these studies, for the purpose of Abby's story, we aimed to capture the essence of these drug trials. On the one hand, they are incredibly exciting and can offer genuine, scientifically backed hope that effective treatment may indeed be a possibility soon. But they can also be frustrating in that there are a lot of unknowns regarding the efficacy and the side effects of these drugs, as well as when they might be available.

The protocol Dr. Gold adheres to with Brooke and Abby follows the one dictated by the Huntington's Disease Society of America (HDSA). However, genetic counselors may handle situations within this protocol differently. Some genetic counselors choose to find out the results at the same time as the patient (as Dr. Gold does), while others choose to check the results prior to delivering them.

Finally, though we spoke to, listened to, and read stories and accounts of many people affected by HD, at risk for HD, or with HD in their family, all of our characters are 100 percent fictional, and any resemblance to anyone in real life is purely coincidental.

We encourage anyone who wants more information about Huntington's disease to check out the online resources provided by both the phenomenal HDSA (hdsa.org) and HDBuzz (hdbuzz.net), a site founded and run by Dr. Ed Wild and Dr. Jeff Carroll, scientists who disseminate news of the latest HD research in plain language with the aim of making it understandable for those facing HD and for their loved ones.

Thank you for taking this ride with us.

Alyssa & Jessica

Acknowledgments

It was the strength and love of the extended Mulligan, Johnson, and Color-Dark families that inspired us to write this book.

Kate, you were the first person we ever talked to about this book, and your guidance, knowledge, and support were invaluable to us, as they are now.

Jenne, thank you for so openly sharing your heart, thoughts, and experience with us and for helping to ensure that Abby and Brooke's journey was portrayed as authentically as possible.

In our research on HD, the following sources were essential in helping us shape Abby and Brooke's story: *Can You Help Me?* by Thomas Bird, *In-Between Years* by Steven Beatty, and *Life Interrupted,* edited by Sharon McClellan Thomason. The Help4HD podcast, HDBuzz, and the many testimonials and posts we read on the HDSA website also gave us a deeper and wider understanding of the complexities of this disease. Thank you also to Natalie Carpenter at HDSA for your help in our research and enthusiasm for this book.

We couldn't have written this without the amazing hospitality we received in Catalina, particularly from the helpful staff at the Banning House, from Elizabeth Gates at the Harbor Reef, and from Aron Martin and Alex Pugh, our zipline guides, who answered all of our random questions.

Speaking of random questions, thank you to Maria and Simon Hammerson for sharing their extensive knowledge about African grays with us.

To the team at Delacorte Press, we are thrilled to work with you on this.

Wendy Loggia, this book would've been a mess without you. Your thoughts, insight, and wisdom were our guiding light in stripping away the excess (and there was a lot!) so that Abby's story could shine on its own.

Alison Romig, thank you for all your thoughtful suggestions, which led us to evaluate parts of the book in a completely different way.

Audrey Ingerson, you were the first to find and champion this book, and we're so grateful for that. We miss you!

While on the topic of champions: Holly Root, our superhuman agent, thank you for helping this book find its home and for all the advice along the way.

Thank you to Adeline Colangelo and Katie Knight for

picking up the phone and dropping everything to be our readers at the exact moment we needed you.

To our friends and Mom Tribe for all your support during the writing of this book, especially Alexis White, Rama Fakheri, Lindsey Jacobson, Sarah Nussdorf, Catherine Hathaway, and Anna Thiam, for driving, feeding, and in general caring for our kids (and us) when we were on deadline.

From Jessica: To my family, thank you for accepting me as a hot mess while I wrote this book. To my parents, Gentille and Terry, thank you for your constant love and encouragement. Extra love and thanks to Linda and Gary—as well as Phil, Tamar, Mandy, Max, Brian, Addie (again), Dina, Spence, and the extended Nelson clan—for lots of babysitting and help. Finally, thank you to Josh for holding down the fort, talking me off ledges, bringing me popcorn and collecting my tea mugs, and to Oliver, Sawyer, and Archer, for being exactly who you are.

From Alyssa: Gemma and Theo, you are my heart and soul, and thank you for only barging into my office some of the time while I was writing this. Dan, thank you for cheering me on with a huge smile even though you never got a break. Mom, Dad, Honey, and Steve, thank you for your unconditional support and understanding when I disappeared into my writing cave during all of your visits.

And finally . . . to each other. There's no one else we'd rather laugh, cry, and write with. XO

ABOUT THE AUTHORS

Jessica Koosed Etting and Alyssa Embree Schwartz met the first day of freshman year of college and have essentially shared a brain ever since. They've co-authored the YA thriller *The Lost Causes* and the contemporary YA series Georgetown Academy. The duo also work as screenwriters in both film and television. They were prompted to write this book by a Huntington's disease diagnosis within Jessica's extended family.

jessicaandalyssa.com